BOOKS BY HELENA NEWBURY

Helena Newbury is the *New York Times* and *USA Today* bestselling author of sixteen romantic suspenses, all available where you bought this book. Find out more at helenanewbury.com.

Lying and Kissing

Punching and Kissing

Texas Kissing

Kissing My Killer

Bad For Me

Saving Liberty

Kissing the Enemy

Outlaw's Promise

Alaska Wild

Brothers

Captain Rourke

Royal Guard

Mount Mercy

The Double

Hold Me in the Dark

Deep Woods

KISSING THE ENEMY

HELENA NEWBURY

FOSTER & BLACK

For everyone who's ever loved someone they shouldn't

ISBN: 978-1-914526-13-8

1

IRINA

You can trace it back.

All of it. The fire and chaos, the tears and joy. The seismic shock that our love sent through our friends and families. Every glorious stolen kiss, every moment of danger. Every time he pulled me against his chest, every time we were torn apart.

It started before he climbed onto my balcony.

Before the kiss in the snow.

Before we met in Central Park.

It started before I ever saw Angelo Baroni.

It started when he saw me.

2

ANGELO

Peterson went pale as I burst into his office. He started to get up. "Mr. Baroni! I wasn't expecting—"

I put my foot on his chest and shoved. Peterson shot across the room on his wheeled office chair and slammed into the floor-to-ceiling window. Hairline cracks spread across the toughened glass, but the pane held. Peterson sat there bug-eyed and panting, staring down in terror at the tiny people twenty stories below.

I hooked my toe under the front of his chair and tugged him back towards me, castors squeaking. My voice was low and very, very cold. "I gave you a generous cut for getting my containers through customs," I reminded him. "I told you I didn't care who else you took bribes from. But I was very clear about one, simple thing. What did I tell you?"

Peterson shook his head, feigning ignorance. I shoved his chair at the window again. This time, there was a cracking sound as it hit. A spider web of lines fanned out across the glass. Peterson started to panic-breathe.

I'm a big guy. Six-three and most of it muscle. But when I'm really pissed off, my voice goes what people call *dangerously quiet*. I hauled Peterson back towards me. "*What did I tell you?*"

"I swear, Mr. Baroni, I don't know what—"

I shoved his chair again, putting every ounce of my anger into it, and it hit the glass with the force of a quarterback going into a tackle. The window finally broke, cascading down in a million glittering shards. Peterson's chair teetered on the brink, the outdoor air whipping around him. *"Women!"* he screamed. *"You said no women!"*

"Women," I confirmed. "You smuggled women. In my fucking city." I put my foot higher on Peterson's chest and pushed. The chair tipped. Peterson gripped the chair's arms, knuckles white, staring down at the street.

"Here's what's going to happen," I told him. "You're going to keep my containers moving. You lose your cut for the next six months. And if you ever, *ever* help someone traffic women again, I'll chain you to that fucking chair and toss you into the harbor myself."

Peterson nodded frantically. I lifted my foot and his chair crashed down onto its wheels. Peterson hurled himself out onto the carpet and scrambled on hands and knees away from the window. "Thank you, Mr. Baroni!" he dug in a pocket, hands shaking. "Here! Take these as a gift. My company's a sponsor. Tickets to the ballet."

"Do I look like I go to the fucking ballet?" I snatched the little strips of cardboard out of his hand and stuffed them into the pocket of my overcoat as I stalked out of his office.

In the hallway, workers shrank back as I passed. The women clutched their paperwork to their chests, eyes a little too wide, breathing a little too fast for fear alone. When I'd gone, they'd tell each other how terrified they'd been and how they hated men like me. And then, that night when they were all alone, their hands would creep down between their thighs....

That's what I am to them: a monster, a fantasy. I live outside their safe, happy little world and I'm fine with that. I don't want their fucking world. I have my own, one built on power, honor and respect. We are the *Cosa Nostra* and I am the youngest, hungriest boss in twenty years. I love New York. I love my piece of it, one of the most fiercely-contested territories there is. And I will never, ever let anyone take it away from me. Not the Irish, not the street gangs and *especially* not the Russians.

Outside, the sky had turned the color of the sidewalk. I fingered my phone: my driver, Tony, could be there in ten minutes. But I'd said he could have the afternoon off....

Fuck it, I'd walk. I wasn't going to make him miss his kid's baseball game.

But before I'd gone half a block, it started to rain. A freezing, slate-gray onslaught so hard it drowned out the traffic noise. My overcoat shielded me for a while, but I could feel the icy drops working their way under my collar and down my back. My pants were getting soaked, too, the expensive fabric clinging wetly to my legs. I'd be soaked to the skin in minutes.

I looked around for shelter..and frowned. I was outside a theater and the name on the poster was familiar: some ballet thing. I dug in my pocket and found the tickets Peterson had given me. Yep, it was starting right now.

Do I look like I go to the fucking ballet? But it would be dry inside. *What the hell...* I pushed open the door.

A smiling woman took my tickets and showed me to my seat. I had no idea what I was going to be watching. *Ballet* was something the New York elite went to see. These days, I had that kind of money —I even moved in those kinds of circles, though I scared the shit out of those people. But I didn't have time for art, not with an empire to run. Not with the Russian mob invading my territory.

Then the dancers came out on stage and I frowned and leaned forward in my seat.

It wasn't dancing—at least not like I'd ever seen. The women seemed to float as if they didn't weigh anything at all, making long, graceful leaps, coming down on one delicate foot and then powering back up into the air without apparent effort. I watched, still frowning but transfixed. Maybe those rich New Yorkers were onto something. In their tight white costumes and gauzy skirts, the dancers seemed otherworldly, like elves or pixies or whatever the fuck they have in those fantasy movies.

And then my life changed.

As the music swelled, *she* leapt onto the stage, long legs extended almost horizontally, doing the splits in midair. *How the fuck is she doing that?* I felt my jaw drop. *Wires. There must be wires....* But there weren't any. She could just move with a grace so far outside anything I'd known, it seemed like magic.

She seemed to hang there, the stage lights picking out every detail of her body: her perfectly-pointed toes, the exquisite smoothness of her thighs, the twin hillocks of her upthrust breasts. Her lips were pursed in concentration, satin-soft and pink, contrasting with the delicate tan of her skin. I've never wanted to kiss a pair of lips so much: her expression was just so *noble,* so richly fucking *unknowable.* If the others were elves, she was their queen, untouchable by mortal man. Her hair, tightly pinned into a bun, was platinum-blonde and that only enhanced the look: she was an ice queen, regal and perfect.

My hands tightened on the arms of my seat. I didn't care how *unknowable* she was. I had to know her. I didn't care how untouchable she was: I had to touch her. I needed to feel those lips under mine, *now.* I needed to run my hands along the length of those long legs, feeling the warm flesh through the thin fabric of her tights, and cup her *there,* right where she lived, and rub her until she moaned into my mouth. I had no idea who she was but I needed to find out. *Right now.*

She landed and spun on one leg, going faster and faster. Each time she'd whip around to face the audience, I caught a glimpse of her face: those pursed lips, that tightly-pinned hair. I was seeing her in freeze-frames, drinking in the image of her until the next one replaced it. Her eyes were so cold, so imperious, yet with just a hint of molten heat....

Jesus, I needed to do *bad things* to this girl.

She bounded across the stage and was gone. Immediately, the other dancers were forgotten: all I cared about was seeing her again. I was leaning so far forward in my seat, it creaked. The guy in front of me twisted around in irritation, but I just gave him a glare and he paled and faced front.

Then she reappeared, lifting herself right up onto the points of her toes and stepping so lightly across the stage that she could have danced on a soap bubble. How did she *do* that? Didn't it hurt?! I was noticing detail after detail, now, and every one of them was sweet fucking perfection: the soft skin of her neck, revealed by her pinned-up hair, ripe for kissing. The firm curves of her ass, when that gauzy skirt floated up, athletic and yet feminine. Her long, supple legs, one moment stretching out into the splits, the next scissoring together and propelling her skyward: I wanted them wrapped around my waist, wanted those ankles hooked behind my ass, urging me on.

I sat there for an hour, spellbound. I'd never sat in such rapt attention in my life, not even watching the Yankees take on the Mets with ten thousand on the table.

Then the dancers were taking bows, the lights were coming up and, too late, I realized it was over. And something I'd never felt before seemed to clutch at my chest and grip tight. *Shit!* I didn't even know her name!

I jumped to my feet, my heart suddenly thumping in my chest. *I'm never going to see her again!*

My hands tightened into fists. *Unacceptable.*

Backstage. That's where she'd be, right? I headed for the stage, fighting through the tide of people heading towards the exits. But when I tried to vault up onto the stage, someone grabbed my arm. "Um...sir? You can't go up there!"

I turned and glared...but it was just one of the ushers. She shrank back and the fear on her face made me stop. *What the fuck are you doing, Angelo? You're acting crazy!*

But I couldn't help it. Something had taken control of me.

I took a breath and tried to speak calmly. "The dancers. I gotta speak to one of them. Where are they?"

The usher blinked. "They'll be in their dressing rooms by now," she said uncertainly. "But the public's not—"

I nodded and turned away from the stage, heading for the nearest exit like a good boy. But as soon as I hit the hallway, I peeled off and headed straight for a door marked *No Admittance.*

I didn't get where I was by following the fucking rules.

I thundered down a flight of stairs and emerged into a hallway. I knew I was in the right place: there were women in stage make-up chatting and laughing, but most of them were already in their street clothes. *Shit! They're leaving!*

"Are you supposed to be back here?" asked a voice behind me.

I turned and found one of the dancers looking up at me. I hadn't figured on how small they'd be, up close. The top of her head was only up to my shoulder. She was pretty enough, with long chestnut-colored hair hanging in tresses down her back. But she wasn't *her.*

"I'm looking for one of the dancers," I told her. "The one with the platinum-blonde hair."

"Irina? She left already."

Shit! But at least I had a name. *Irina.* I gave the dancer my best smile. "Are you all in a ballet..."—shit, what was the word—"*team?*" Maybe I could find out where they were dancing next and get a ticket.

"Ballet *company,*" she said. "No, we're—Wait, how did you come to the ballet and you don't even know which company you're seeing?"

I ran my hand up the back of my still-soaking hair. "I kinda stumbled in."

She gave me a doubtful look. "Yeah. I can tell. We're students from Fenbrook Academy."

I'd vaguely heard of it. Some upscale performing arts place. That TV star, Jasmine Kane, went there. "So I can find her there? What's her last name?"

The dancer gave me a *what the fuck* look and stepped back, and I realized how stalkerish I sounded. It probably didn't help that I loomed over her, my shoulders almost brushing the sides of the narrow hallway. *You moron!* But I was out of my element, here. I couldn't remember the last time I'd gone after a woman: usually, I just showed up at a party and they'd start sidling up to me, all big-eyed and breathy, hot for the whole criminal thing. I'd take them to my apartment, ride them hard and then have trouble remembering their names the next morning.

This was different.

I took a deep breath and put out my hands in a show of peace. "I'd just really like to run into her again."

For a second, the dancer's face seemed to soften and I thought she was going to help me. Then she quickly shook her head.

Shit! I'd blown it. The dancer shifted from foot to foot: I was standing between her and the exit, blocking her. I thought about staying there, *making* her tell me...but I wasn't going to start scaring women just to get my way. With a sigh, I stepped out of her way and leaned back against the wall, rainwater trickling down my neck as it was squeezed out of my hair. What the fuck was wrong with me? I didn't even know this *Irina*, hadn't so much as spoken to her, but my heart was *pounding*.

The dancer walked past me. A few seconds later, I heard the door at the end of the hallway open and night air flood in. I waited for the door to close, but it didn't. Then, "Hey!"

I looked round at her.

"If you really want to meet her, she'll be dancing in Central Park tomorrow. Noon."

It felt like my whole chest lifted. "Thank you!" I wanted to shower the girl with flowers, or chocolate, or fucking Rolexes.

"Yeah, well...I'll be there too. So don't turn out to be an asshole," And she was gone, the door banging shut behind her.

In the sudden silence, reality started to set in. *What the hell am I doing?* I felt like I'd been temporarily possessed: why was I down in the basement of a theater, chasing after a ballet dancer? I didn't have time for this. I had territory to protect, deals to make.

So why did the thought of seeing her again make a grin tug at the corners of my mouth: the first time I remembered smiling in a long time?

Irina, I thought. *I'll see you tomorrow.*

3

IRINA

It was so cold that our breath hung in the air: a trail of tiny white clouds that marked where we'd danced before another dancer's outstretched arm or leg whipped them away. We were dancing to a section of *La Sylphide* that was fast and energetic - because *energetic* is what you need when you're in a leotard and the temperature's close to freezing.

Rachel, my roommate, was shivering. She gave me a *what the hell did you talk me into* look as she leapt past me and I gave her a sympathetic smile. But the truth was, the cold didn't bother me all that much. Maybe it's because even New York in February is nothing compared to Moscow.

Or maybe it's because I've started to welcome the cold. Instead of fighting and shivering and trying to keep it out, I want it to soak through my clothes and my skin and into my bones.

If I was entirely numb, I couldn't feel anything at all. The past—the bad stuff—disappeared. And dancing took so much concentration that it stopped me thinking about the horror of my future. Between the two, I could almost imagine I was free.

I leapt up onto a park bench, my shoes crunching in the frost. Then I stepped up onto the arm, balanced on one foot and began to tip forward towards fourth arabesque, my other leg rising into the air behind me. I was making the most of it because I knew we wouldn't be able to dance for long: I was going to lose feeling in my feet pretty soon. Plus, the string quartet who provided the music were freezing, too.

I extended my arms and let my upper body sink a little further into the freezing air. It almost hurt to breathe it in, the air was so icy. I reveled in it.

Dancing's always been my escape. When I was a kid, ballet classes let me pretend I was just like any of the other little girls, right up until the time I had to get back into the armor-plated limo. When things started to get dangerous, around the time I was twelve or thirteen, and I was first sent to stay at my uncle's house for a few days, I danced around the big, echoey hallways and kidded myself I was really in some famous dance school. And when the violence ripped my parents away from me and I had to go to live with my uncle permanently, dancing became my last-ditch plan to get to America.

I'd thought, that day I stepped off the plane, that I'd finally escaped. I was that naive.

I arched my back, pointed my toe...and that's when I saw him.

The crowd was big despite the cold, maybe a hundred people. The charity music and ballet performances had been running for a few years, now, and they'd become a *thing*—we were even in the tourist guides. But it wouldn't have mattered if there'd been a thousand people in the crowd. I would have noticed him immediately.

It wasn't just the immaculate black suit, which looked as though it cost six months' of my rent, or the equally classy overcoat or gleaming shoes. It wasn't his size, even though he was *big:* at least a head taller than me, his chest broad and solid. It was his sense of purpose. I've never, ever, seen anyone with such absolute focus: he looked like a sprinter coming off the blocks, eyes locked on the finish line.

Except...his eyes were on *me.*

And he was dangerously, sinfully gorgeous. Some Russian guys can be handsome in a rough-hewn, brutish way. They were tanks; this man was a Ferrari, sculpted by the devil himself to bring about a woman's downfall. High, elegant cheekbones were matched with dark brows, just the right blend of beauty and raw male power. Soft, sensuous lips were balanced by a solid jaw dusted with black stubble. But what hit me were his eyes: rich, dark brown with tiny flecks of amber and burning with that *purpose*...he wanted to—

I flushed and wobbled. I *never* wobble.

I came up out of the arabesque and jumped down off the bench, heart thumping in my chest. I flowed into a pirouette and then started a series of jetés that would take me all the way across the path because I needed the thinking time. I needed to process what I'd just seen in his eyes. It had leapt like a spark across the gap between us and now it was spreading through me, roaring and blazing like wildfire.

He wanted to kiss me. Fuck me. Possess me. All of those things and all at once. It wasn't the clumsy, ugly lust guys throw at you in the street. It was like a force of nature. I'd never felt anything like it in my life.

And as the crackling fire turned to throbbing heat, I felt something tugging, answering, from inside me.

I liked being cold. I *needed* to be cold. But right then, just for a second, I wanted to be warm again. I wanted that special sort of warmth you only get when you're pressed tight up against someone, their arms wrapped around you to warm your back. I wanted to be warmed by him and I wanted the hotter, darker heat I saw in his eyes. I wanted to let that melt through all the ice, burn me up and freakin' *destroy* me, vaporize my atoms until I was just a moan carried on a scorching wind.

I risked a glance at him as I turned. His eyes were still locked on me: Rachel and the quartet might as well not have existed. His gaze followed me as I bent my knees and sank down into a plié. The air didn't feel cold against my skin, anymore. His stare was wrapping me in heat, caressing every millimeter of my body from my extended foot to where my leotard stretched tight between my thighs. I'd never felt so *watched* in my entire life.

I rose and spun into a pirouette, glimpsing him in pieces as my head whipped past him—

Thickly-muscled legs under tailored pants—

A tight, toned waist above the shining leather belt—

Big hands, olive skin next to white shirt cuffs, hands that could easily pin you to the bed—

White shirt smooth over hard abs, broadening to a powerful chest—

God those shoulders, the guy was built like a bull, all intimidating power—

I broke out of the pirouette and danced on, trying to get an image out of my head. An image of me pressed against him, my white leotard soft against his dark suit, my arms over his shoulders, wrapping myself to him as he leaned down and owned my mouth.

I stumbled and cursed: *chyort!* What the hell was wrong with me?

And then I passed Rachel, coming the other way, and saw her give a quick glance towards the guy and then at me. My chest tightened. Did she know him? Had she invited him, or set this up?

At that moment, the music came to a close. As the crowd applauded, I saw the leader of the quartet, a tiny cellist named Karen, rise to her feet and hug her hands to her chest. "OK, enough," she said. "I need hot coffee *now*. I think my fingers are frozen to the bow."

I'd finished on one leg, arms upraised to the sky. I slowly lowered them and gave a quick glance towards the guy in the crowd. He was applauding along with the rest, but his eyes still hadn't left me. Just for a split-second, my gaze met his and I felt it again. This time, the feeling was even clearer: his burning need, rolling towards me in waves...and my matching response, a sudden, urgent *ache* that came from deep down inside. It was as if he'd awakened me, as if he'd struck exactly the right note to make me resonate.

I swallowed and looked away, then marched over to Rachel. Yep: she was glancing at him again and smirking. "Do you know him?" I whispered angrily. "Is this *you*?"

Rachel walked over to her bag and started pulling on a hooded top. "I might have mentioned you'd be here," she said innocently. She gave me a filthy smile. "He came looking for you after the show. *Quite the smitten kitten.* I would have told him where to go except…"—she glanced at him—"*cheekbones.*"

I thumped her in the arm. "*Vy idiotskaya—*"

"You're welcome." She smirked. "Have some fun for once. Drop the ice maiden routine." And she started to back away.

Too late, I looked up and saw the guy marching towards us. The crowd was parting ahead of him: people took one look at him and just stepped aside. "Wait!" I whispered to Rachel. "You're *not* an idiot!" I grabbed for her arm. "Don't leave me with him!"

But she was already out of reach. And then the man was just a few feet away and I had to turn to face him.

I could feel every defense slamming up. What Rachel calls my *ice maiden routine,* except it's not that at all. It's not an act: it's a survival mechanism.

In Russia, plenty of men wanted me…but not for *me.* They wanted me for who I was, for a way into our family. They were rich and powerful and, because they were all in the same business as my uncle, violence came easily to them. Violent, often drunk men who were used to being obeyed. The idea of marrying one of them made my stomach knot…but that's what I was expected to do. I was supposed to smile and date and choose one, marry him and start producing the next generation of the dynasty.

The only way to avoid it was to keep pushing them away until I could get to America. I learned a thousand different ways to say *no.* I was polite when I could be, savage when I couldn't. And all the time I was cold, cold, cold. It went on for years and it was hellishly, heartbreakingly lonely, but it was better than the alternative. If I gave in even once, if I let myself be drawn into their world, I knew I'd be trapped in it forever. And I was determined not to let that happen.

Except now here I was in America and I hadn't escaped my fate at all. And the coldness?

I didn't know how to turn that off, anymore.

The man reached me and *God,* I hadn't realized how tall he was. Up close, the top of my head only came up to the top of his chest. It didn't help that I was still in ballet slippers. I felt myself tensing up, eyes going everywhere except his face, partially because I was trying not to encourage him and partially....

Partially because, if I looked into his eyes again, I was scared I'd feel *that* again, that lick of pure fire that seared through all the ice I could possibly throw out and scorched me from the inside out.

"*What?*" I finally mumbled, my eyes on his shoes.

"Irina." He said it as if he was testing it out, matching the name to the person...and I realized he was still gazing at me, drinking in every little detail of me, even though I wasn't dancing anymore. I could feel his eyes on the loose strands of hair that had escaped my bun, on the little patch of skin revealed by the neck of my leotard, on my bare, freezing arms.

I'd known he wouldn't be Russian, of course. But his accent was still a surprise: it was everything I'd dreamed of, back in Moscow, the throaty rasp of every US movie hero. Plenty of times, I'd thrashed under the sheets, hand between my thighs, to a fantasy of an American guy who'd say my name just like that as he fucked me. But this was even better. That low rumble, like a V8 engine that throbbed through my whole body, had been tuned and given a musical note: it sang like a sports car instead of just bellowing like a truck. I couldn't place it but I wanted to hear more of it. *Now.*

And immediately, I clamped down on that feeling. So what if he had a sexy accent? It didn't change anything. I looked around for my bag. Found it. Started to walk over to it.

He followed. "You dance.... Shit, I don't even know how to describe it. It's amazing."

That made me frown. He didn't sound like the guys who normally come to ballet shows, or stop to watch it in the park. They'd wax lyrical about *graceful jetés* or how my pas de chat *was magnificent.* This guy sounded blue collar, not white collar, yet his clothes were expensive. *Literally* white collar clothes: a snow-white shirt that looked tailored, a black suit cut to fit his muscled body perfectly. And yet I could see something beneath the crisp whiteness, now that he was closer: big, black shadows on his pecs that could only be tattoos. What sort of man dressed in a thousand dollar suit but had a tattooed chest? I was momentarily fascinated.

No, you idiot! Get out of there! "Thank you," I muttered, as gruffly as I could. I picked up my bag.

"I'm Angelo."

I sneaked a glance at him and finally figured it out: the name, the olive skin and jet-black hair, the subtle, musical note in the New York accent. *Italian-American.* And then the glance slid and changed into a gaze and then I couldn't stop it: we were staring at each other. The air was so cold and he was so close that I could feel the warmth radiating from his body and his breath toying with the loose strands of hair which fell against my cheek. I needed to look away but I just...*couldn't.* And the thing that really shocked me was that he had the exact same expression on his face. This big, gorgeous man looked as out of control as I was.

And then a freezing gust of wind cut between us, numbing my bare arms and stinging my cheeks. And I remembered who I was...*what* I was. I had to end this now, before it ever began.

"The collection bucket's behind you," I said, nodding to it. "If you want to make a donation."

I waited until he turned away from me and pulled out a roll of bills.

And then I ran.

4

ANGELO

That accent.

I hadn't expected it. Delicate but savage, like frozen shards of the finest wine. *Holy shit.* She spoke and about a million images filled my mind: every Russian stereotype I'd watched in a movie or seen drawn in a comic book. *Da, comrade* and red stars and hammer and sickle flags, Cold War spies seducing our agents and ruthless, pouting, blonde women in fur hats. *Jesus Christ.* It took my breath away. But it made sense: where else was a beauty like her going to come from but Russia?

She went, in that second, from being the most gorgeous woman I'd ever seen to being simply *off the chart.* She couldn't be number one: numbers were now fucking irrelevant. Other women were fucking irrelevant. And her frostiness...I was used to women giggling and flirting, grabbing my arm and whispering in my ear. She was the opposite and it made her all the more enticing. Especially because of what I'd seen in her eyes, when I could actually get her to look at me: a spark of fire, hot enough to glow even under all that ice. She liked me, even if she didn't want to.

And then, suddenly, she was gone. I stood there blinking like a moron for fully three seconds.

Oh, no. No you don't.

I sprinted after her. Her friend from the night before gave me a panicked look—shit, now I really *did* look like a crazy stalker. But I didn't care: I wasn't going to lose her again.

She moved fast, even in those weird ballet shoes she wore. As she ran, she pulled a black hooded top out of her bag and tried to pull it on over her head, but then she nearly collided with a jogger and thought better of it, stuffing it under her arm instead. *She must be freezing!* "Stop!" I yelled, and saw her tense, but she didn't slow down.

I pushed myself harder, shoes pounding the icy path, feeling like a rhino chasing after a gazelle. She slipped between the passers-by; I just battered them aside. *"Stop!"*

If anything, she sped up. I threw myself forward and managed to grab one wrist, then hauled her to a halt. She cried out in frustration and shock and looked down at my hand. My big fingers completely encircled her slender wrist.

"Just...*stop,*" I panted. "I just want to talk."

She was panting, too, and the way her breasts rose and fell under the tight leotard had my cock swelling against my thigh.

"I'm going to let you go, now. Don't fucking run away again."

She just glared at me, as if ready to go for my throat.

I took a deep, slow breath. *"Please."*

Her expression relaxed just a fraction. I slowly released her wrist, both of us looking down at my hand as I broke contact. Immediately, I missed the touch of that soft skin. And she followed my hand with her eyes as if she missed my touch a little, too.

"Why did you chase me?" she asked, lifting her eyes to my face.

"Why did you run?" I gazed down at her. God, she was beautiful. And that accent was making me fucking delirious, every syllable carved from ice, razor-sharp but with that throaty, sensuous rasp. "I just want to talk. I think that—" I stared at her, suddenly tongue-tied. Why was this so difficult? I'd whispered in plenty of women's ears that they were *so fucking gorgeous* while I was pounding them. But that didn't do Irina justice. "I think that...*sei bellissima,*" I said at last.

Maybe she knew it meant *beautiful* or maybe she could tell I meant it, but I swear, just for an instant, I saw a flare of color in her cheeks. But then she shook her head, almost as if to clear it, and glanced left and right, ready to run again. *Shit!* I couldn't let her slip through my fingers again,

Then she shivered. Immediately, she glared down at her bare arms as if furious she'd shown weakness. But it was too late: I was already whipping off my overcoat and settling it around her shoulders. "Here," I said. "Take this. You're freezing."

She squirmed as I put it on her, as if she really didn't want to accept it...but I knew just how much difference the thick cashmere made because I could feel the wind knifing through me as soon as I took it off. And the coat was warm from my body...I saw her resistance melt and she relaxed just a little, letting the coat fall over her, the fabric drowning her small body. She really *was* freezing: the back of my hand brushed her bare shoulder as I pulled my hands back and she was like ice. Just that tiny contact, skin-to-skin, was enough to make her head whip round and stare at my hand uncertainly but she didn't pull away.

Her friend skidded to a stop behind her, but Irina didn't even notice. And when she saw how we were looking at each other, her friend slowly backed away.

I lowered my voice, making it as gentle as I could. But I couldn't stop the hard edge of lust that crept into it: I needed her too much. "Irina," I started—God, I loved saying her name. "Why did you run? Why do you *keep* trying to run?" I blinked. Glanced down at myself. Had I gotten so used to intimidating people that.... "Are you scared of me?" The idea sickened me.

She shook her head. And the weird thing was, I believed her. She had every excuse to be scared of me, but she wasn't.

I took a deep breath. "You dance like a fucking angel," I said. "You're the most beautiful woman I've ever seen. I just want to get to know you."

She stared up into my eyes and it was like all those layers of ice were slowly melting away. I could see deeper and deeper into her, down into her scalding, molten depths—

And then she shook her head quickly and looked away. "I can't."

The frustration boiled up inside me. "*Why?*" I'd studied every inch of her so intently, I would have noticed a ring but I checked her finger anyway. *Nope.* "Do you have a boyfriend?"

She closed her eyes for a split second as if she'd given a silent, bitter little laugh. "No."

"Then let's go for coffee!" I held out my hand towards her.

She pressed her lips hard together and shook her head again. And then she started to slip the overcoat from her shoulders. I felt a sickening lurch of fear—that *panic* again, like I'd felt in the theater. What the fuck was going on? I'd never felt anything like this before. "Give me your number, at least!" I said. "Tell me your last name!"

Another shake of her head, and now she was tossing the overcoat to me and turning to go. My eyes locked on her wrist. I could grab her again...but then what? Take her prisoner? "What the hell is the matter? Tell me!"

She gave a sad little smile—just a tiny twitch of her lips. *God,* it was heartbreaking. I wanted to find whatever was causing her this much pain and batter it into submission against the frozen path. "I just can't," she said.

She turned and walked away, not even stopping to pull her hooded top over her head, even though the wind was like breathtakingly cold. I stood there helpless for a second and then called after her, "*Cafe Auben.* I get dinner there at eight, every Thursday. I'll be there tonight."

She faltered, long enough that I knew she'd heard me. But then she walked resolutely on and I stood there watching her until she was out of sight, my chest tight with the thought that that might be the last time I ever saw her.

5

IRINA

I didn't get into my street clothes right away. I wanted to put as much distance between Angelo and me as I could because I was having to fight the urge to turn around and....

Throw myself into his arms and let him devour me with those lips. Press my body so hard against that hard chest that my breasts flattened against him and every inch of us was in warm, close contact, from my chin to my ankles—

What the hell is wrong with me? I'd never reacted this way to a man before. And I'd never had a man pursue me like this, charging straight through every layer of ice I threw out like a crazed bull. *Doesn't he know when to quit?*

I remembered that focus in his eyes, that drive. No, he really *didn't* know when to quit. He never would.

And part of me really liked that. I started to feel a pull in my shoulder, an *ache*. I wanted so much to turn around and look at him.

No! Starting something with him would be beyond crazy. My uncle would never allow me to date an American—a *civilian*. And as soon as Angelo found out who I was, he'd be scared off anyway—and with good reason. Either way, we'd be broken apart and I couldn't take that pain. Better to be numb and not feel at all.

I drew in a big lungful of freezing air. The warmth from dancing had long since faded and, in only a leotard and tights, I was getting seriously cold. It should have felt good. It *always* felt good. But now....

Now I just wanted to be warm again. I wanted to be wrapped up snug in his huge overcoat, the faint scent of his cologne and the heat of his body enveloping me. I wanted to wrap it around both of us and press myself tight to him, let his blood and fire melt me into liquid.

My chest tightened. I didn't want to be alone anymore.

I shook my head and cursed myself. *Slabovol'nyy chelovek! Weakling!*

I stopped and pulled on my jeans, then my *Fenbrook Academy* hooded top. I'd be *just fine.* But when my clothes were on, I didn't feel any better.

I was on one leg, swapping my ballet slippers for sneakers, when Rachel slammed into me like an enthusiastic puppy. I yelped, flailed and managed to keep us both upright.

"*So?*" Rachel asked. "Who is he?!"

I groaned and shook my head. "It's not going to happen. And please, don't send any more men my way. You know I can't."

Rachel knows that my uncle won't let me date Americans. She just doesn't know *why*. She has no idea my whole family are *bratva*— Russian Mafia. And if I have my way, she never will. She's my best friend and I couldn't take it if she was scared away.

"You could see him in secret," said Rachel. "Your uncle would never have to know." A slow grin spread across her face. "That would be *so romantic!* He could send you love letters!"

For a second, I imagined Angelo writing love letters. He *did* come across as romantic: the old school, hot-blooded, sweep-you-off-your-feet kind. I'd never known a guy like that. Then I sighed and shook my head. "Leave it."

"But he's a total—" Rachel's phone bleeped, thankfully cutting the conversation short. She dug frantically in her purse for it and almost dropped it twice getting it up to her face. Then she read the email and punched the air. "*Yes!*"

I felt my eyes go wide. "Is it—"

"*Yes!* Check your phone, see if they—"

At that second, my own phone bleeped. I grabbed it and checked the screen. I'd gotten the same email Rachel had: a callback from the audition for a TV commercial we'd both attended the day before. "*Yes!*" And the best part was, we were auditioning for different parts so we weren't competing.

Rachel put her arm around my waist and tugged me forward, leading me out of Central Park and into the street. "This is going to be awesome," she said. "And have you any idea how much they *pay* for those things?"

I grinned back at her. She was right: if we got the parts, neither of us would have to worry about rent for months. Then I noticed something in the email and my grin disintegrated.

"What?" asked Rachel.

"It's tomorrow," I said quietly. "At two."

Both of us work in the same electronics store. I wasn't due to work tomorrow—my shift started in a few hours—but Rachel was.

"Oh shit," said Rachel softly. Both of us stopped walking. "No. No, no, no…" Her shoulders slumped under her leather jacket. I felt my chest constrict. "These things are like getting hit by lightning. You remember Natasha Liss? She got her big break doing that commercial for washing powder."

"There'll be others."

"Not like *this!* God, I could have danced the *shit* out of this one!" She bit her lip. "I could just quit the store."

"You need the money. What if you *don't* get it?"

She bent almost double and let out a long, strangled groan of frustration, drawing stares from passers-by. "*Argh!* Why do you have to be so damn *Russian* and logical all the time? You're like a Russian Mr. Spock!"

I nodded sadly and rubbed her back. It wasn't fair. She deserved to get this part….

I closed my eyes. "I'll work your shift tomorrow," I said. "You go to the callback."

Rachel spun around and gaped at me. "What? *No!*"

I swallowed down the lump in my throat. "You worked really hard for this. I heard you practicing in your room, doing the allegro over and over." I shrugged. "I probably wouldn't have got my part anyway. You have a better chance, so you should go."

"That's bullshit! You're a way better dancer than me!" She shook her head. "No. I won't let you do this!"

I put my arms around her and drew her close. My own disappointment was swelling up inside me, but I crushed it back down. "You're going to go to that callback," I told her firmly, "and you're going to ace it." I bent her forward and kissed the top of her head, then ruffled her hair. "*Da?*"

"*Da,*" she said reluctantly. It sounded funny in her soft, American accent. Then she threw her arms around me and crushed my ribs. "Thank you, Irina."

By the time I made it across town to our house, I only just had enough time for a quick shower and change before I had to head out to my shift. I hurried up the path and ducked under sparkling icicles that hung two feet long from the roof of the porch. Rachel and I had a bet going on how long they'd get before the end of winter.

Our place isn't much. The clapboard is stained and broken in places, it's freezing in winter and hot in summer and it's not really convenient for Fenbrook or anywhere else. But it's cheap and lovably quirky: my room even has an old, wrought-iron balcony I can stand on when I'm having my coffee in the morning.

I raced inside, already peeling off my clothes. Naked, I climbed into the shower and was just about to turn on the water when the doorbell rang. *Chyort!*

I wrapped a towel around me, padded back to the door and checked the door viewer. My heart sank as I saw six-foot-plus of imperious suited muscle, topped with hair as silver as a bullet.

Vasiliy. My uncle.

I opened the door. "You didn't think to call, first?"

He waved away my protests. "I was in the neighborhood." He looked around and sighed, shaking his head as he always did when he visited. "Why do you live in this place?" He sounded genuinely confused.

"I *like* this place." And we both knew what I meant by that. I liked it because I could afford it without help from him. We glowered at each other for a second and then kissed each other on the cheeks.

I love Vasiliy. He helped raise me when I was young and then, after my parents died, he took care of me. Without him, I wouldn't be alive today.

But without him, I wouldn't have been in danger in the first place. Vasiliy is the embodiment of everything my family is famous for, everything I ran away from. He isn't *in* the Russian Mafia; he *is* the Russian Mafia.

"You'll have to make yourself tea," I said as I closed the door. "I really need to take a shower—"

The door was pushed open again from outside. *Chyort!* Vasiliy hadn't come alone.

"You look fine as you are," said Mikhail, grinning as he stepped inside.

Mikhail is the epitome of everything I hate about Russian men. He doesn't have an ounce of Vasiliy's class or intellect, just lots of money. And while Vasiliy, even in his sixties, is still a tough, good looking guy, Mikhail is running to fat even though he's only forty. His face is always pink and shiny, as if he just ran up a flight of stairs, and when he looks at me a chill goes the entire length of my spine. It would be bad enough if he was just Vasiliy's business partner, but he's more than that.

As far as Vasiliy is concerned, Mikhail's going to be my husband.

Mikhail's eyes crawled over me. I pulled the towel tighter around myself and wished I'd put my clothes back on before I answered the door.

"I'll make tea," said Vasiliy. "You have your shower. Then we can talk."

I hurried off to the bathroom, feeling Mikhail's gaze on my ass the entire way.

It's not a forced marriage, as such. Vasiliy won't *make* me marry Mikhail. He's happy for me to choose a man....as long as that man is Russian and a member of the Russian mob. I know he's doing it out of love: he thinks only a gangster can protect me from our family's enemies. But that doesn't stop my future feeling like a prison cell being built brick by brick around me.

Back in Moscow, I'd been surrounded by gangsters—suitors, in Vasiliy's mind. That's when I'd learned to be cold, to keep pushing them away. I'd thought that I'd escape my fate by moving to New York, but I'd only made things worse.

I'd been in America only a few days when Vasiliy arrived and told me about his new partnership with Mikhail, a local bratva boss who needed Vasiliy's money to expand. By then, I'd enrolled at Fenbrook and it was too late to change my plans. Now Vasiliy spent almost all of his time in New York and visited me almost daily. Escape? I saw more of him than ever. And here, instead of a procession of suitors, there was just one: Mikhail. No way was I going to marry that creep...but that left us at an impasse, because no way was Vasiliy going to let me be with an American. I was going to be unhappy...or very, very lonely.

I closed the bathroom door, dropped the towel and climbed back into the shower. The steaming water slowly thawed me...and reminded me of a different kind of heat.

Angelo...I silently mouthed his name. Just thinking about him, remembering those brown eyes, made me gently sway my hips in a circle as if being touched. The whole thing was impossible, of course. I'd done the right thing—the *only* thing—by pushing him away.

But there was something about him...he had a passion that I'd never seen in a Russian man. Angelo was dark, smoky lust and scalding anger. He was chaos to their logic, impulse to their cold rationality. Angelo was red wine and thorny roses and hot, hot blood. He was the opposite of everything I'd known, everything I was. That should have made us completely incompatible...so why was I so drawn to him?

I caught my breath as I remembered the looks he'd given me, like he'd been ready to throw his coat down on the frozen path, tear off my clothes and take me right there on the ground....

I realized I'd spent longer soaping my inner thighs than I really needed to, the edge of my hand rubbing, my hips grinding in slow circles. I forced myself to stop, rinsed off and grabbed a towel. But however hard I tried, my thoughts kept going back to Angelo and, every time they did, I felt myself flush from the inside out, just the memory of him lighting me up.

Then I turned off the water and the sudden chill brought me back to reality. *Idiot.* My future was out there, lounging on the couch.

I hurried into my room and pulled on the pants and polo shirt I wore for the store. Then I opened the door so that I could call down to Vasiliy and Mikhail. "I have to run to work," I told them as I sat down at my dressing table to do my make-up. "I'm sorry—you should have called."

Vasiliy's heavy footsteps came up the stairs. In the mirror, I saw him lean against the door frame. "Why do you insist on working?" he asked.

"You know why."

Another sigh. He thought I was stubborn, refusing to take an allowance or gifts. But I didn't want his blood money. I was determined to support myself, even though it meant working two jobs.

"You are as stubborn as your mother was," Vasiliy grunted. He moved a few steps closer and lowered his voice. "You should get to know Mikhail. He could look after you."

"I can look after myself," I said tersely, combing my hair.

"If you don't like Mikhail then come back to Moscow: there are more men there."

I met his eyes in the mirror. "I have a life *here!*"

He walked over and looked down at me sadly. "Irina...what do you think you'll do when you graduate? Become a dancer? Marry some American and get a little dog and a house with a white picket fence?"

I said nothing, just stared resolutely at his reflection.

He squatted down behind me until his face was next to mine. "You are a Malakov," he said, squeezing my shoulders. "This is your life."

"I don't want it."

"It's not something you choose, Irina! The family needs you. Even if we didn't, you can't have this...*civilian* life you dream of. Even if you turn away from us, other people will never forget who you are. My enemies are your enemies. You need a man like Mikhail to protect you." He glanced over his shoulder towards the living room, then lowered his voice. "Marry him and you could stay here in New York."

I stared helplessly up at him. What could I say? That the thought of sharing my life, my *bed* with Mikhail made me want to throw up? That I just didn't see anything approaching warmth or love when I looked into his eyes, only ugly lust and a hunger for power? That whenever Vasiliy's back was turned, Mikhail tried to grope me?

There are some things you can't say to your uncle. I settled for: "I don't love him."

Vasiliy just looked at me sadly, as if I was a child who didn't understand how the world worked. The worst part was, he hadn't used to be like this. Back in Moscow, he'd been tough but fair...he'd used to smile and joke. Then I announced I was moving to the US and he became...*cold*. Something had changed and I couldn't figure out what.

The frustration rose inside me, hot and jagged: it wasn't *fair*. I crossed my arms and glared at myself in the mirror. If I kept looking at Vasiliy, I was going to start crying and a Malakov never shows weakness.

Vasiliy's hands relaxed on my shoulders and he let out a long sigh, then leaned sideways until his head rested against mine. "*Chyort,*" he cursed. "I wish your mother was here to talk to you."

I closed my eyes and felt my anger slowly slip away. He was the closest thing to a father I had and he thought he was doing the right thing. "I really *do* need to get to work," I told him, my eyes still closed.

I felt his kiss on the top of my head and then he was moving away. I heard frustrated muttering from Mikhail in the living room as

Vasiliy collected him: he wouldn't get to "accidentally" brush my breast or fondle my ass tonight.

When I heard the front door close behind them, I finally opened my eyes and stared at myself, and that made it real. *This is my life.* Go back to Moscow? That wasn't an option. I came to America to make a life here, so that one day my kid sister, Lizaveta, could join me. If I went back to Moscow, we'd both be trapped there forever and, when she finished boarding school and was old enough, she'd be expected to marry a gangster, too.

Which left Mikhail. A life with a man I hated.

I felt the heat begin to build behind my eyes. *No.* I clamped down hard on it before the tears could start. Angelo? A real life, a happy life with someone I liked? That was a fantasy, a fairy tale. *Grow up!*

This is your life.

I quickly stood, grabbed my purse and ran out before I could think anymore. And for the next four hours I smiled sweetly and explained ultra-high-def TVs and asked people if they wanted extended repair plans and I crushed all thoughts of freedom down into the depths.

The busy store, glowing screens and noise made for a different kind of numbness. Cut off from emotion, the coldly logical part of me started to think, *maybe Mikhail won't be so bad. Maybe I can grow to love him....*

By the time I'd finished my shift and taken the subway home, I'd almost convinced myself. You can convince yourself of *anything,* if you try hard enough.

And then, as I reached my house, I saw the icicles. I'd been in too much of a hurry when I left to notice, but now I stopped and stared. Every single one of the long, gleaming spikes was now lying in the yard, shattered into a million glittering pieces. Someone had snapped them off at the root and hurled them down on the frozen ground.

I closed my eyes. I could see it unfolding in my mind: Mikhail following Vasiliy out of my house. He'd been bitter and resentful because he wouldn't get to slide a hand up my skirt that night. And so the first beautiful thing he'd seen, he'd destroyed.

This is your life.

I stared and stared at the glittering fragments of ice. And something cracked, deep in my soul. A tiny drop of everything I'd been trying to contain seeped out and, when it hit the surface, it ignited like gasoline.

I ran into the house and grabbed a dress. Angelo had said he'd be there at eight. If I ran, I could just make it in time.

6

———————

ANGELO

I nursed a Scotch and waited. Mario, the bar's aging owner, had said the Russians would be in any time now. Normally, the frustration would have gotten to me. I'm not good at waiting: life's too short.

But tonight, I didn't mind so much. It meant I had time to think about her.

My overcoat had been around her shoulders for only a few seconds, but I could still smell her scent on the collar and it filled my mind with the cornflower blue of her eyes and the silken sheen of that platinum-blonde hair. I felt my fingers unpinning it, letting it slide down her back in a shining wave. I wanted to feel it against me. I wanted to part it like a curtain to kiss my way down her naked back.

It was just dark enough, at my table, that if she'd been there I could have pulled her out of her seat and onto my lap. Dark enough that, if she'd been wearing a skirt, I could have hauled it up her thighs and stroked her pussy through her panties, my actions hidden by the table and her thrashing cloaked by the shadows. I could have brought her to silent, panting climax right there, feeling the pleasure roll through her as she trembled against me. And the whole time, I'd whisper in her ear exactly what I'd do to her when I got her back to my place.

I was itching, *aching* for this girl. Had been ever since I'd seen her on stage and it had only gotten worse since Central Park. I couldn't remember ever being this desperate to get a girl into bed. But there was something else, something that worried me. Wrapped around that hot, primal desire to bed her was something else, something lighter and harder to pin down. It slipped away every time I tried to focus on it, but it was there. Whenever I thought about seeing her again, just *seeing her,* not even spreading her thighs and fucking her or slipping my cock between her lips, I felt...*impatient.* Tense. Like I couldn't draw a full, deep breath until I was with her again. What the fuck was that?

Maybe I was tired. God knows I had enough on my plate.

Just as I thought it, the Russians arrived. Two big guys, probably ex-military, their bratva tattoos just visible above their shirt collars. They swaggered in like they owned the place.

I hate Russians...with one recent, platinum-blonde exception. I've never understood them: from what I've seen, they're power-crazed and ruthless, without any of the honor of my people.

And in particular, I hated these two Russians because they were sent by Mikhail Stasevich, the local Russian mob boss. A nasty SOB, but until recently not too much of a problem. Vicious if you backed him into a corner, but he hadn't had enough money to expand. Then he'd teamed up with Vasiliy Malakov, an old-school bratva boss from Moscow who wanted a New York base through which to move guns. With Vasiliy's money, Mikhail was trying to take over my turf.

I'd be damned if I was going to let it happen. My dad fought hard for every foot of this territory and it'll be Baroni forever. I'd sworn that the day he and my mom died.

That brought me to the main reason I hated Russians. The one that hit me every single morning, making me tumble out of bed and hit the ground doing push-ups so that I would be ready when I needed to be. The one that made me finger my gun every time I thought about it....

The one that demanded I kill every last one of them.

The two Russians hustled Mario into a back room. I silently followed, the rage building in my chest. I reached the back room just in time to see them pressing Mario up against the wall, a knife blade gleaming against his throat.

"Ten percent," said the one with the knife in fractured English. "Is good deal. You take it."

"No," I said firmly, announcing my presence. "He won't."

Both of the Russians spun to face me and I saw in their eyes that they recognized me. "Tell Mikhail it ends *here*," I said. "This is the start of *my* territory." I started walking towards them. "One street over, you shake down whoever the fuck you want. But this? This is Baroni turf. Always has been. Always will be."

The two Russians glanced at each other. The one with the knife held it ready, weighing it in his hand. I was a tempting target: two against one, and he'd get to be the big guy who took out a mob boss....

But that's not how the game is played. No one—at least, no one smart—wants all-out war and that's exactly what killing me would bring. So it came down to intimidation. It came down to who had the biggest balls.

I walked right up to him, until the point of the knife was nicking my suit jacket, and stared him right in the eye. The room was so quiet I could hear his breathing. *Show no fear.* My father's voice in my head. *Show no weakness.* I could hear his hand clenching and unclenching around the handle of the knife and feel the point twisting and scraping against the fabric of my suit. He was as big as me and he probably had fancy military training I didn't, plus he had his buddy beside him.

But he didn't have what I had. He didn't have the will my dad bred in me, the will to do *whatever it takes* to maintain control. I'd die to defend my turf and that meant he didn't scare me. But I scared the shit out of him.

His eyes flickered and I knew I had him. "Get the fuck out of here," I told him, my voice barely more than a whisper.

The guy stepped past me. "This isn't over," he muttered. "Mikhail wants this territory. We'll be back."

From behind me, there was the metal *click-clack* of a shotgun being pumped. "No you won't," said a calm, deep voice. Everyone looked up as the man stepped into the room.

Rico. My *sotto capo,* my second-in-command and my best friend since high school. He was in his usual long leather coat, his favorite shotgun cradled in his arms and pointing right at the Russians. He'd been outside in the car, with orders to follow the Russians inside once he'd made sure there were only two of them. Just in case I needed backup.

The Russians looked at each other again and scowled, but they knew when they were beaten. They slunk past me, the knife disappearing into a pocket. The tension drained out of the room. Mario gave a loud sigh.

I turned and grinned at Rico. "Thanks."

Rico lowered the shotgun. "You would have been fine without me," he said graciously.

Maybe. Maybe not. It worried me how cocky and aggressive the Russians were getting. The thought of Rico and that shotgun might just keep them from coming back for a while. And it had felt good to have him watching my back. It always did.

I embraced Mario and told him not to worry and to call me if the Russians were dumb enough to shake him down again. Then I strolled out to the car with Rico.

Rico knows as much about the business as I do and he handles a ton of the day-to-day shit I don't have time for. My guys respect him like no one else. If we weren't such good friends, I'd be watching my back, expecting a coup.

"You want me to drop you at Cafe Auben?" Rico asked. He knows my routine.

I nodded.

"I'll join you."

I hesitated. Normally I loved spending time with my buddy, but I was hoping—*praying*—that Irina would show up.

I didn't even need to say anything—that's how well Rico knows me. He glanced across at me, saw my expression and his jaw dropped. "Wait. Are you meeting someone? Do you have a *date?!*"

I shrugged, embarrassed. But I couldn't stop a smile tugging at the corners of my mouth.

He started driving, staring out through the windshield in silence.

"What?" I asked at last.

"I'm just trying to figure out when you last went on a date. I'm back three....no, four years."

I elbowed him in the guts. But he was probably right. I didn't go on dates: I met a woman, fucked her once or twice and moved on. I didn't have time for fucking romance.

But Irina? I had time for her.

I still couldn't get my head around her being Russian. She had zero in common with the Russian thugs I battled every day—it was difficult to accept they were from the same country. Although I'd be lying if I said there wasn't a little part of me that loved the thought of seducing one of their countrywomen. *Da, comrade,* see how you like that.

"So who is she?" asked Rico. "Hot?" He was grinning, now, practically bouncing in his seat in excitement. Which was kind of funny because Rico's as big as I am, solid muscle, and the car was creaking on its springs.

"Of course she's hot," I told him. "What the fuck do you think?" Again, I couldn't help grinning. Which was crazy: I didn't want people —even Rico—thinking their boss was turning soft. But something about her made me feel...I don't know, *lighter.*

Lighter....and hotter than I'd ever been for any woman. I really hoped she showed up because, if she didn't, I was going to have to track her down all over again. I wasn't giving up on her any more than I'd give up on my dad's territory.

7

——————

IRINA

I walked slowly up to the cafe, heels crunching in the snow. Warm light spilled out through the big plate glass windows, making the sidewalk gleam gold. I stayed back in the shadows. I wanted to see if he was there before I—

There. I caught my breath as I saw him. God, the man had *presence.* He sat right in the middle of the cafe, completely unfazed at sitting alone. He didn't read the menu or tap at his phone in an attempt to look busy. He just gazed around, utterly relaxed.

He hadn't ordered anything yet. *He's waiting for me.* I felt my heart start to race.

Every eye in the place was drawn to him, especially the women. I could see women on dates surreptitiously glancing at him over their dates' shoulders and two waitresses giggling and blushing in the corner as they sneaked looks at him. I hated them immediately. *He's mine!* And then flushed because that was nuts: I'd barely met him. He wasn't *mine.*

Then he turned and saw me through the glass. Our eyes locked.

And I realized I was *his.*

It was freezing, out on the street, but I lit up from within with a violent heat that made me audibly gasp. It was as if I was an ice sculpture and someone had poured lava into the center of me, making me glow red, yellow and white even as it melted me completely. The warmth radiated out, hit my skin and made me flush, then contracted back in and twisted down to my groin.

I was his. His gaze felt like it was going to pull me right through the window. Like no one else in the world mattered or even existed. Like he'd fight through a thousand men to get to me.

And he wanted me *right now*. He wanted me on the table in front of him, my ass thumping down on the table as he hauled my dress up my thighs, my legs kicking either side of him as he tore off my panties and rammed himself inside me.

I didn't think I looked special. I'd had to get ready in a hurry, quickly adding a touch more make-up and scrambling into the little black dress. I'd left my hair loose, hanging straight down my back. And most of me was covered by the thick black coat that reached down to my thighs. But I'd never seen desire as strong as I saw in his eyes. *I. Was. His.*

This is nuts! He's an American! I should walk away.... But I knew I was kidding myself. The lust in Angelo's eyes was so strong it was almost frightening...but it was nothing compared to the deep, hot ache that was my body's response. I took a deep breath and stepped inside.

He got up out of his seat. I caught my breath as I neared him and he reached for me. I wasn't sure what he was going to do: embrace me, kiss my cheek...a full-on kiss on the lips?

His hands landed on my upper arms and he traced down them to my hands as he drew me closer. I could feel the heat of him throbbing into me—I hadn't realized how cold I'd gotten, standing outside on the street. "You're freezing again," he told me. His big hands closed around my smaller ones, engulfing them, and the warmth crept up my arms, soaking into my chest.

I swallowed and the room seemed to tilt and spin. I could feel the layers of ice fracturing and splitting, devastated by his heat. He drew me even closer, our bodies less than an inch apart. I had to tilt my head back to look at him and, as soon as I looked up into those brown eyes, I was lost. God, he was gorgeous. I wanted to brush my fingers through that gleaming black hair, slide my palms over his curving pecs. With his overcoat off, his suit jacket could open a little more and I had a better view of those mysterious tattoos beneath his shirt. I couldn't make out any detail but they were *big,* covering the whole top part of his chest.

He squeezed my hands, his thumbs slowly caressing my knuckles as if to show me what he wanted to do with every inch of my body, later on.

"I'm very glad you came," he said at last. That rich purr of a voice resonated through my body but there was a stress behind it, too, and he squeezed my hands just a little on the *very* and the *glad* while staring deep into my eyes. *Those words don't describe it,* his eyes said. *They're just the best I can do.*

When he finally released me, it was with great reluctance. I could feel the tension in his body—as if he was barely managing to restrain himself from just grabbing me and kissing the hell out of me.

I stripped off my coat and sat down. He pulled my chair back for me. *That* was a first, too. Did all Italian-American men go to manners school? As he helped me slide my chair under the table I could feel the strength in him, the way he made me and the chair just *float.* He put his hands on my shoulders for a second, thumbs brushing the back of my neck, and everything seemed to stop. I could feel the pent-up tension in him again, all the more palpable because I couldn't see him. He was hovering on the very brink of control. He wanted to throw me forward so I was bent over the table, pull up my dress and—

I heard him take a long, slow breath and then his hands lifted and he came around the table. When he sat, his eyes were blazing, almost *angry* with lust, as if he cursed me for having this effect on him. *But I'm not doing anything!*

I had to look at the menu just to break the tension. As soon as we were ready to order, he summoned a waitress. Not *called. Summoned.* He only had to lift his head an inch and glance in her direction and she scurried over, ignoring everyone else. She'd either been eying him up since he walked in or it was just something about him that commanded attention—maybe both. She was my age, pretty with long, dark hair and a white fitted blouse that showed off a lot of cleavage. I braced myself for his inevitable flirting.

But he barely glanced at her as we ordered, his eyes fixed on me. And when she did a flirty little giggle and asked if there'd be anything else, he just dismissed her, politely but with great finality, and leaned in to me as if to say, *I'm with this woman. Don't bother us again.*

I'd never experienced that before. Russian men—at least the ones I'd met—never considered themselves *taken* or *off-limits* until they were married. And the other women knew it: make the mistake of leaving your date for a few minutes and you'd come back to find another woman perched on his knee. You had to fight viciously to keep him—literally, with some women handing out brutal beatings in nightclub toilets if they thought you were competing for "their" man. The aim of the game was to keep your man interested for long enough to coax him up the aisle, at which point he was yours...except for the mistress in some discreet apartment somewhere, plus the hookers he'd fuck while away on business.

Angelo had only just met me, but he looked at me like I was the only woman in the world.

"Tell me about dancing," he said as soon as the waitress was gone. "How do you *do* that?"

"What?"

"*Float.* And spin around on your toes and shi—stuff."

He was trying not to curse in front of me. In his eyes, I was innocent and he didn't want to corrupt me. It was almost funny: *innocent? Me?* Imagine his reaction if he knew some of the things I'd seen, thanks to the family business.

What kept me from laughing was how good it felt. No one had ever cared about trying to shield me from things before—even Vasiliy just accepted that violence was part of my world. I'd grown up around tattooed men who'd spent most of their lives in prison: I could probably out-curse Angelo, given the chance...but the fact that he thought of me as innocent made me light up inside in a way I wasn't expecting. It was almost like glimpsing myself as I would have been if I'd been born into a normal family. I *wanted* to be innocent. And I wanted him to corrupt me.

I told him about Fenbrook Academy and early-morning practice, about dancing the same piece a couple of hundred times, about calluses and stone bruises and climbing stairs on your ass because your feet hurt so much. I told him about transferring from the ballet school in Moscow, skimming over why I'd left. I focused on the good stuff: how I'd always loved America and wanted to come here.

The food arrived and we savored every bite. Talking with him was so...*easy*. I could feel myself relaxing, the layers of ice gradually thinning and cracking. With other men, I had to weigh every word, worried in case it sounded dumb...or sounded too intelligent. With most of the guys Vasiliy introduced me to, *talking* really meant polishing their egos.

Not with Angelo. I got the feeling he hated bullshit more than anything else. And he didn't talk like a rich person, with all their little games and attempts to score points. He talked about simple pleasures like eating hot dogs at Coney Island and swimming off Sandy Hook Beach. I told him about watching my cousin Luka play ice hockey when the government froze all the paths in Gorky Park, and buying *blinchiki* filled with butter and jam from street stands.

I suddenly caught myself. *This is crazy. I shouldn't be here.* This whole happy date was an illusion, a soap bubble that would be destroyed as soon as Vasiliy found out about it. But....

I liked him.

It was more than just lust. That was still there: the conversation would slow down every few minutes and we'd just gaze at each other. My eyes slid down the lines of his hard pecs under his white shirt; his eyes skimmed over my bare shoulder and then all the way down the side of my dress, following the shape of my body as if he longed to do the same thing with his palm. But I *liked* him. I liked his confidence and his warmth and his refreshing lack of games.

He's too good to be true. There were distant alarm bells in my head:

something familiar about him. But that made no sense: he was so different to the Russian guys I knew.

He told me about growing up right there in New York, with scarcely enough money to eat. How things had slowly improved as his dad worked his way up the business and how Angelo had followed in his footsteps, eventually taking over his dad's position when he died.

"What is it you do?" I asked.

He opened his mouth to speak, pride in his eyes. As if he knew I'd be impressed. I suddenly knew what it was going to be: he was in banking, and it was going to be some place I'd heard of, some place that would make my jaw drop. *I'm a vice-president at Goldman Sachs.* That would explain the money and the confidence. It was weird, because he didn't *sound* like some Harvard-educated guy from a rich family. He sounded blue-collar and proud of it.

But at the last minute, he seemed to change his mind. The pride faded from his eyes. "Y'know. Just business. Loans. Insurance."

I frowned. I could tell he was downplaying it. Why?

No matter. I realized I'd dodged a bullet—if we got onto the subject of jobs, he might ask what my folks did, and then we'd get onto my family. I didn't want to go there.

He poured the last of the wine and, as the final heavy red drop fell into my glass, I felt it begin. He didn't say anything, but the question started to form in the air between us. The end of the meal was here: *what now?*

This is where I'd normally say something, like, "Wow, I'm really tired," or "I have an early rehearsal tomorrow," just to start clueing the guy in to the fact that *no*, I wasn't going home with him. Even if I liked the guy, I wouldn't have sex on a first date.

But I stayed silent. I let the question grow and grow. *What are you doing, Irina?* My heart started thumping. I'd already come on a date with him when I knew this couldn't go anywhere. I had to come to my senses and end it now.

But the thought of seeing that broad, muscled chest without the shirt, of running my fingers down his bare abs....

The waitress asked if we wanted dessert. We both agreed we didn't. I asked for the check and he caught my eye. And we both *knew*, and, immediately, things changed. His gazes had felt like soft caresses but now they turned firm and direct: I could almost feel his hands as they slid up my sides and over my back, could feel the touch of his lips on the upper slopes of my breasts.

I went to speak, but it was suddenly difficult to get air. Part of me still couldn't believe I was about to do this on a first date. But I didn't want it to end.

"Would you like to come back to mine?" I asked. My house felt safer: familiar territory, plus Rachel would be there, just in case all my instincts were wrong and he was an axe murderer.

A smile slowly spread across his face, eyes twinkling with a mixture of joy and raw, hot lust.

He stood behind me to slip my coat on and, when it was wrapped around me, he stopped like that for a second, holding the edges tightly together in front of me so that the coat hugged me. As if, now that he was embracing me, he couldn't bear to let me go.

Then we were stepping out into the freezing night air. I looked up the street one way then the other for a cab. As I turned back to him, he stepped right up close to me, so close that his leg slipped between mine. I blinked up at him: we were so close, I had to tilt my head right back.

"I've been wanting to kiss you since I first saw you," he said. "Time's up."

I had time to open my mouth in astonishment. Then he was kissing me.

He didn't just bring his lips down to mine: he scooped an arm under the small of my back and lifted me, bringing me to him. By the time our lips touched, my toes were only just scraping the icy sidewalk.

His first touch was gentle, just a graze of his lips against mine. But I had a hand on his arm and I could feel how his whole body had gone hard with barely-restrained lust. He was fighting to go slow, forcing himself to taste me first before consuming me completely. I could feel the power of him, even in that brief touch, and it made me go weak.

His second touch was a flick of his tongue across my lips, sampling my softness. The pleasure crackled out from each millimeter he touched, rocketing its way down my body. I came alive in his arms, writhing and arching, my breasts pushing against his chest. I grabbed his other arm in my free hand and clung to him, my mind spinning. I needed more. *Now.* My whole body was throbbing, pulsing to the rhythm he'd started.

We stayed like that for a second, mouths open and lips almost touching, our panting breath forming clouds of mist around us. I could hear the blood rushing in my ears. I was almost drunk with anticipation: I wanted it more than I've ever wanted anything in my life. *Kiss me!*

He gave a low growl, one that vibrated through me. I could feel every muscle tense as he primed himself, but still he didn't move. *Kiss me!*

I had my eyes closed, but I could sense that he'd opened his. He was gazing down at me, savoring the moment. I couldn't take it any longer. "*Pozhaluysta potseluy menya!*" I panted desperately, forgetting that he wouldn't understand.

The urgency in my voice was enough. A big, warm hand slid across my cheek, fingers sinking into my hair, and then he was kissing me full-on and for keeps, lips hard against mine. I could feel every ounce of his pent-up lust: he wanted me with an intensity I'd never known, wanted to take me in every conceivable way, to know every inch of my body. But there was something else, as well, something that was so powerful it took my breath away, something that felt like it shocked him as much as me. He wanted to possess me, to wrap me up in his arms and carry me away somewhere so that no one else could have me.

And even as part of me wanted to draw back from the intensity of it, something deep inside me was rushing towards it, as if it was something I'd been missing my entire life.

It was a kiss that moved, that made me twist and slide against him as I followed it. My hands were grabbing at his arms, my cold fingers sinking into the soft cashmere of his overcoat, feeling the hard bulk of his muscles beneath the layers of clothes. His tongue found mine and danced with it and I moaned through the kiss, clutching at his shoulders. He answered with another low growl, kissing me even harder, as if my moan turned him on. And as our bodies shifted together I felt it for the first time: the hard, hot outline of his cock against my upper thigh, very close to my groin....

Movement beside us and the rattle of an engine. I opened my eyes to see a cab had pulled up beside us. We must have looked as if we needed a taxi, *now*.

Angelo reluctantly broke the kiss and lowered me gently to the sidewalk, then held the door of the cab for me. He strode around to the other side, overcoat billowing out behind him like a cape, and got in beside me, his thigh against mine, his muscled body huge in the confined space. I leaned forward to tell the driver my address and, the instant I'd finished and we were moving, Angelo's hand was on my shoulder, pressing me back in my seat. "What was it you said, back there?" he asked. His eyes darted between my eyes and my lips.

I swallowed. "*Please kiss me*," I translated.

His eyes ate me up for a second and then he pounced, twisting around so that he was in front of me, my head cupped between his hands as he pressed me back against the leather and kissed me. I panted into his mouth and kissed him back, my hands roaming over his neck and shoulders.

The cab whisked us towards my house...and whatever came next.

8

———

ANGELO

I'd never been so hot for a woman my entire life. Not just hot for her, but just totally...I couldn't even find the words.

The traffic was light and we were rushing through the city, heading God knows where: I hadn't heard the address she gave the cabbie. But it didn't matter. I didn't once glance out of the window. We could have been driving via the fucking North Pole with polar bears ambling past outside and I wouldn't have known. I couldn't take my eyes off of her.

Captivated. That was the word. I was captivated.

She was so completely unlike any woman I'd ever met. There was this...*grace* to her, even when she was still. And when she moved...Jesus, watching her walk into the restaurant had been like watching a prowling cat, and everyone in there, men and women, me included, were just yapping, clumsy dogs.

Lithe. That's what she was. Soft, smooth skin, elegant curves, but underneath it all were those toned dancer's muscles, giving her flexibility and stamina. Combined with the fire in her eyes and the way she'd panted at me to kiss her...she was going to be unbelievable in bed.

My kisses slowed down, growing purposeful as my hands

explored her. I couldn't get enough of her mouth. She was the perfect combination of sweet femininity and raw, untamed sexuality. Kissing her was like throwing myself head first into a warm, dark canyon with no bottom: my lips met hers and I was just *lost* and I didn't care at all.

She seemed to be oblivious to how insanely sexy she was, unlike the preening women I normally met. But she couldn't be: that was impossible. Every little detail must have been carefully calculated to turn me on, like she was some Soviet spy from the 80s who'd been tasked with my seduction.

Her hair, which had looked so tauntingly prim when it was up in a bun, now hung loose down her back, making her look like some ice princess off the cover of a fantasy novel. I couldn't believe how long it was and I couldn't stop thinking about what it would look like when she was naked and it was the only thing shielding her modesty. I wanted to brush it forward over her shoulders so that it covered her breasts, nipples peeking out between the strands, just so I could have the pleasure of sweeping it back and revealing her again.

Her dress, her coat, even her shoes were all black, setting off the soft tan of her skin and making that platinum-blonde hair shine even brighter. When she'd shrugged out of her coat and her back had arched a little, her high, pert breasts had lifted under the thin fabric of her dress in a way that made me catch my breath. I'd been looking at that dress and the way it hugged her body all evening. I'd been imagining cupping her bare shoulders and then following the sides of the dress all the way down.

Now I could finally do it, growling as I circled my palms on the soft warmth of her shoulders, kissing her slow and deep as my hands slid lower, lower...past her chest, the heels of my hands almost grazing her breasts, down her sides, over her hips and along her thighs.

My thumbs touched nylon and she gasped against my mouth. The feel of her smooth thighs was addictive. My kisses became hungry and open-mouthed. I sucked that gorgeous lower lip into my mouth and nibbled on it, the sound of her rapid breathing exciting me even more. *She's as turned on as I am.* My thumbs circled and stroked, my fingers nudging the fabric of her dress higher. Was she wearing nylons or—

My thumb touched a band of smooth fabric, then the soft warmth of naked skin. She was wearing stockings. My cock was harder than it had ever been. *I have to get this dress off of her. Right. Now.*

And then the cab slowed to a stop and we were there.

I threw some money at the cabbie and then we were sliding out of the seat and into the night air, still kissing, my hands on her hips. The air was shockingly cold after the warmth of the cab, rushing under my coat and down my collar. I knew it must be even worse for Irina, with her stockinged legs, so I pulled her right up against me, leaving not even a hair's width between our bodies. We stood there kissing as the cab pulled away, our fronts keeping each other warm while our backs grew colder and colder.

When she finally broke the kiss, she said, "That's my house."

For the first time, I bothered to glance around. We were in some suburb I didn't recognize, way out in the sticks. The street was quiet and it was a clear night, the stars shockingly bright overhead. "Uh-huh." And I drew her back into the kiss.

A moment later, she broke the kiss again and ran a nervous hand through her hair. Her face was flushed, her pupils huge with need, but she looked worried. "My roommate will be there."

"Uh-huh." I cupped her cheeks and brushed my thumbs through her hair, marveling at its silken softness. I was vaguely aware that something was up, but I was too busy trying to kiss her to figure it out. My lips came down on hers and she gave a soft little moan. I ran my hands down her back, tracing the shape of her through the layers. I was desperate to get her inside and undressed, but kissing her was just *too fucking good!*

She broke the kiss a third time. "My room's a mess," she said.

This time I finally forced myself to focus because I could tell something was wrong. She wasn't changing her mind: I could see it in her eyes, hear it in the husk of her voice. She wanted this as much as I did. But....

I had to fight hard to get through the fog of lust clouding my brain, but I finally got it. She was worried I was going to think she was a slut or something because she'd invited me back here on a first date.

Just as I worked it out, she opened her mouth to speak again. Immediately, I put a warning finger on her lips. She went silent, but gave me a look of outrage that was so fucking adorable I nearly forgot what I wanted to say.

"*Shh*," I said sharply. Then I leaned closer, so I could speak right into her ear. "Irina: I want you. Right now. You're driving me crazy and I've got to have you. But—"—she shifted minutely and the feel of her soft lips against my finger made me almost groan out loud—"*But, if you're not ready, tell me now and I'll go.*" The words were rolling out of my mouth before I even knew what I was saying. Was I really telling her I'd wait for her? "We can do this tomorrow or the next night or in a month's time. It's okay. I'll still be here." I felt her draw in her breath, as if what I was saying was shocking. "But if you want this *now,* like I do...then let's go inside."

I drew back a little and blinked at her. I was at least as surprised by what I'd said as she was. But it had worked. She nodded once, quickly, her mind made up, then grabbed my hand and led me inside.

I only caught brief glimpses of the interior. She rushed me through it, maybe self-conscious that it was small. I wanted to tell her that it was a hell of a lot bigger than the place I'd grown up in, but I couldn't drag my eyes from her legs, or from the curve of her ass as she walked ahead of me. Plus, I was still trying to come to terms with what I'd said to her outside. *Offer to wait? Me?* It wasn't something I'd ever done before—hell, the women I normally met didn't *expect* anything more than a one night-stand. But with Irina...I realized it was true. I would have waited, if she'd made me. *I am fucking obsessed with this woman.*

By the time we made it into her bedroom, I couldn't wait any longer. I grabbed her as she pushed the door closed and pressed her full-length against it. Then I cupped her head in my hands and ran my fingertips through her hair as I kissed her hard. The feel of her soft, supple body against the hardness of mine had me panting. I grabbed the hem of her dress and started dragging it up her thighs, still kissing her. My fingers brushed over nylon, then her stocking tops, then the soft smoothness of her thighs. She moaned into my mouth and that stoked my lust even more.

I hauled her away from the door and spun her around, pulled her coat off her arms and let it fall to the floor. Then I pulled her back against my chest until her ass was grinding against my cock. I pulled her dress higher, revealing a pair of simple, black panties. Somehow, that triangle of black fabric between those smooth golden thighs was more enticing than any elaborate lingerie.

I snaked one hand down her body and between her thighs, groaning as my fingertips pressed against her warmth. I started to stroke her there and, immediately, she clenched her thighs tight around my hand, her dancer's muscles pinning me tight for a second. *Jesus, she's going to be an incredible fuck.* I moved my hand more firmly, overpowering her, and she groaned in surprise and pleasure as I worked at her softness through the thin fabric. A minute of gasping, panting friction and she was wilting against me, thighs clenching around my hand in time with my movements. Two minutes, and I could feel her slickness wetting the fabric.

I almost hurled her onto the bed. She landed on her back, dress rucked up around her hips, and stared up at me with a look that drove me wild. It was only there for a second, but it was like looking down through layers of ice to white-hot magma. Underneath all that cold, there was a raw, powerful lust that matched my own. The idea of that, in a woman as gorgeous as her, blew my mind.

I tore off my coat and climbed onto the bed, one knee between her legs. Her dress had slid down a little and I started to push it up again, wanting to grab hold of her panties and pull them off. I wanted to see her, there, just gaze at her for a while, then I was going to spread those thighs and lick her until she screamed—

My elbow hit the little table next to her bed. A framed picture fell over and toppled over the edge. I grabbed for it and caught it before it hit the floor, then lifted it to put it back in its place—

I froze.

That's—

No, of course it fucking isn't.

I lay there willing the picture to change, but it stubbornly refused to. *Yes, it fucking is.*

The picture had been taken in a forest. There was Irina, just as gorgeous as she was in the flesh. One arm was wrapped around a kid who might be a younger sister. And her other arm....

Her other arm was wrapped around the waist of a silver-haired man in his sixties. A man I knew very well.

"Irina," I asked, fighting to keep my voice level. "What's your last name?"

She stared up at me in confusion. "Malakov." She glanced at the photo and then my horrified expression. Her voice went tight and cold. "Vasiliy is my uncle."

The picture slid from my fingers. I heard the glass break as it hit the floor.

I got up off the bed, stumbling a little. It felt as if the whole room was spinning.

Irina's eyes narrowed in anger. "What?" she snapped. She tugged her dress down over her thighs. "So what?"

Seeing her mad made my chest ache. Ruining everything we'd been building towards cut me deep...but I couldn't speak, couldn't even reassure her that it was okay—my mind was whirling too fast.

And telling her it was okay would have been a lie anyway, because it most certainly was not fucking okay.

She was Vasiliy Malakov's niece.

My body seemed to move by itself. I saw myself grab my coat and head down the stairs to the front door and then I was away, off into the night.

9

ANGELO

I had no idea where I was. I had no idea where I was going. I just
walked.

It wasn't the best neighborhood, but I'd been in worse. Plus, if
anyone got any ideas about messing with the guy in the nice suit,
they'd change their minds when they got a look at my expression.

Vasiliy Malakov. I'd been about to fuck the niece of my sworn
enemy. One of the most dangerous men in Russia and, since he
partnered with Mikhail, one of the biggest crime bosses in New York.

I'd known he had at least one kid—Luka, who'd pretty much
taken over from his dad back in Moscow. I'd had no idea he had a
niece, or that she was right here in New York.

My mind darted through images of Irina: on stage at the ballet,
frozen in midair with those long legs akimbo; glaring at me in
Central Park, eyes full of suspicion; standing outside the restaurant
watching me through the glass, her blonde hair gleaming in the
streetlights.... And finally, in my arms, looking up at me and begging
me to kiss her. I wanted her. I needed her.

You must never, ever see her again. The leaden truth of it slammed
into me so hard that I stopped dead in the middle of the sidewalk.
Don't see her. Don't call her. Just pretend it never happened. She clearly

had no idea I was *Cosa Nostra*—we'd both been as clueless as each other. As long as I disappeared into the night and never saw her again, she never needed to find out. She'd write me off as just some asshole who'd walked out on her.

That thought stabbed deep into my chest.

But the consequences, if it had gone any further, would have been unthinkable. When Vasiliy found out, it would have tipped our two sides into full-on gang war...hell, he'd probably have put a hit out on me. My own people would have lost all faith in me. How can you trust your leader when he's literally in bed with the enemy? And my bosses—the aging pack of old-school *Cosa Nostra* who oversaw New York—they would have gone fucking apeshit. They hated the Russians even more than me. I would have been busted down to errand boy or just shot in the head.

I took a deep breath. I felt as if I'd stepped on a fucking land mine and heard the sickening *click*. Now I had to back away, very carefully, and pray it didn't go off. Being a leader is about making sacrifices. I couldn't risk everything I'd built. Not even for her.

~

By the time I got to my apartment, it was the early hours. I tried to sleep, but I just lay there staring at the ceiling, trying to get Irina out of my head. I could see her lying there on her bed, looking up at me with raw lust in her eyes. God, I wanted her so much. I finally gave up on sleep, got up and drove to work.

I run most of the business from the backroom of a big, sprawling bar called *Underground*, right in the heart of my territory. A hundred years ago, when immigrants—a lot of them Italian—dug out the first subway, it was where they used to go after their shift to shake the rock dust out of their hair and sink a cold one. It's a busy place: even when it's too early for customers, some of my guys are there. There's always coffee in the pot and music playing. Being there always makes me feel better.

Not today, though. I was in a lousy mood. What the fuck was

wrong with me? It had been months since I'd been with a woman—I just hadn't had time. Now I'd met one and lost her. So what? Back to the status quo. Two days ago, I hadn't even known Irina existed.

So why was it bothering me so much?

More people arrived and the business of the day started rolling in: decisions to be made, problems to be solved. I sat back in my big leather chair and called people in one by one. A nightclub owner needed an extension on his loan after a fire: I gave it to him. Two of my guys were short on their collection runs: I leaned forward, voice low, and put the fear of God into them, telling them to hit their totals tomorrow or else. Some morons from a local motorcycle club had started dealing meth on our turf: I sent a car full of guys to remind them where the boundaries were. Just a typical morning, but I was grouchy and irritable, yelling more than I should have done. I knew better. Ruling isn't about screaming at people: calm and determined gets you a hell of a lot further. *What's wrong with me?*

Then Rico arrived with more bad news. Some guys from Mikhail and Vasiliy's gang had visited an Italian-owned bar. They'd smashed the windows and scared off the customers.

It had happened only a few hours after Rico and I had stood up to the Russians. They were sending a message: go quietly or we'll destroy you.

I'd been nursing a cup of coffee in the hope it'd make me feel better. I suddenly snapped and hurled it across the room to smash against the wall. "*Goddammit!*" I yelled.

Rico blinked at me. "Easy," he said gently. "We've had it worse. We'll figure it out."

I stared at him. Rico's always so dependable. I love the guy. For a second, I even considered telling him about Irina. I knew he'd back me up in my decision, tell me that staying away from her was the only sensible thing to do.

Thing is, I didn't know if I *wanted* to be backed up. And just that tiny admission released the brakes on something that had been building all day. All the longing, all my lust for her, started to coalesce, shrinking but concentrating, going from a hot, painful cloud that filled me to a tiny, hard point of light that sat right at my core. A seed.

No. No, don't even think about it.

A seed that I could feel starting to grow.

"Give me some space," I growled. "I gotta make a phone call."

Rico nodded and left, closing the door behind him. I grabbed my phone.

Don't do it, Angelo. Don't you fucking do it!

I'd gotten her number from her during dinner. I told myself I was just going to end things like a gentleman, to make some excuse so she didn't think it was her fault. But I could feel that seed throbbing and burning inside me, growing steadily bigger and bigger.

I drew in a long breath...and called her.

10

IRINA

I was up on the flat roof of Fenbrook Academy, lying on my back in the snow. It's not as crazy as it sounds: my coat was thick enough to insulate me from the cold and long enough to cover me down to my thighs, so my ass didn't get wet. And there wasn't much wind. Just big, soft flakes of snow fluttering straight down, invisible against the white sky until they were almost touching my face. Gazing straight up, nothing but the sky was visible. I could have been anywhere in the world. I could have been in Moscow.

For the first time since I arrived in New York, I really wanted to go home.

When Angelo had walked out, it had felt like a slap in the face. It was a million times worse because of everything I thought I'd seen in his eyes that evening: not just raw, hot lust but a hint of a deeper need.

But all of that had become irrelevant as soon as he'd found out who I was.

Bastard!

I knew it was unfair. Everyone was scared of Vasiliy. Angelo was some sort of banker and what banker in their right mind would want to get mixed up with the Malakov family? There's a reason that all the suitors I'd met were criminals themselves. Who else would want me?

And anyway, this was for the best. It was my own fault. I should never have gone to dinner with him. I'd known it couldn't go anywhere.

If he hadn't seen the photo, we would have slept together. Maybe we would have managed a few more dates but, sooner or later, he would have found out about Vasiliy or Vasiliy would have found out about him and we would have been torn apart. This way, at least we hadn't had time to get to know each other.

So why did it hurt so much?

My phone rang. I very nearly didn't answer. Whatever excuses he made would only make it worse. And yet...

And yet, when I closed my eyes and felt the snowflakes landing on my cheeks, all I could think about were those brown eyes burning into me, the feel of his lips on mine....

Without opening my eyes, I answered and put the phone to my ear. "Hello?"

Silence for several seconds. I could hear the tension in his breathing, imagined his big hands clenching and unclenching. "I'm sorry," he said at last.

Hearing him say it should have helped, but somehow it made the pain real. "It's okay," I lied.

And then I could hear it coming: an intake of breath as he braced himself for what had to be said. I screwed my eyes closed. I didn't want to hear the words. I didn't want to hear: *I think it's best if we don't see each other again.* I didn't want to be reminded that, however far I ran from Moscow, I could never, ever escape who I was.

"I want to see you again," he said.

I was braced so hard that it took a few seconds to sink in. My eyes slowly opened. "What?"

He sounded as surprised as I was. But he repeated it and his voice grew more determined with every word. "I want to see you again, Irina. I *need* to see you again."

I just breathed for a while, processing it. Then, "Why? So you can do this in person?" My voice went cold. "So you can *let me down gently?!*"

"No!" I heard him rub his face with his hand. "I want to see you. I want to keep seeing you. I'm sorry I...left. I was just...you caught me off-guard."

"And now you're okay with it?" I didn't allow my voice to warm up. "You're okay with me being a Malakov?"

Another long silence, as if a battle was going on inside him. "Yes."

A tiny flame flared into life inside me, barely enough to push back the cold. *Hope.* I wanted it to be true. But I couldn't let that hope build until tonight or tomorrow, only to have it snuffed out again. I had to know. I had to see him in person, *now.*

There was a metallic creak as the door to the stairwell opened. I sat up and saw Rachel standing there. "Irina!" she called. "Move your ass! Break was over five minutes ago. Miss Kay's about to go freaking nuclear!"

Our ballet teacher's rants are legendary. "I can meet you in front of Fenbrook in a half hour, when this class ends," I told Angelo.

"I'll be there," he said immediately. And the tiny flame flared a little brighter.

I ended the call and ran for the stairs. Rachel held the door for me and gave a long-suffering sigh, ruffling my hair affectionately as I passed. As we raced down the stairs to class, all I could think about was Angelo. In a half hour, I'd find out if this thing was real or not.

I wanted it to be real so bad it scared me.

11

ANGELO

I grabbed my coat and pulled it on. My mind was whirling: I had no idea what I was going to do about her being Vasiliy's flesh and blood and every logical part of my brain was screaming that this was *a bad idea.* But that wasn't enough to stop me. I *had* to see her, and fuck the consequences.

Jesus, what's this woman done to me?

Rico was waiting outside when I opened the door. "I'm going out," I told him before he could speak.

"Now? What about the Russians?"

Just the mention of Vasiliy and his crew made my stomach knot. "They'll still be there when I get back," I said.

"But we need to hit back! Show them we're not going to be—"

I rounded on him. "Goddammit, Rico! Later!"

He backed off, shocked more than scared. "Okay, sure," he said, a trace of hurt in his voice.

I took a long, deep breath. *What the hell's the matter with me?* Rico was like a brother. I couldn't even remember the last time we'd argued. I laid a hand on his shoulder. "There's just something I need to take care of. Okay?"

He nodded, but I could see the confusion in his eyes. Normally, nothing came before business, especially when it concerned the Russians. "You want some backup?" he asked.

I fucking loved this guy. Always there for me, even when I was behaving like an asshole. Again, I considered telling him about Irina...but I couldn't. Knowing Rico, he'd talk sense into me. I squeezed his shoulder. "Not this time," I told him. I turned away quickly, shoved open the door to the parking lot and stalked outside—

And stopped. I stood there blinking in amazement as the door swung shut behind me.

It had been snowing. It must have started right after I arrived at the bar that morning because everything was covered with a thick white carpet, untouched and perfect. After the dim interior of the bar, the sunlight on all that bright white was blinding.

The whole world looked different. *New.* And...I'd never seen snow as anything other than a pain in the ass, before, something that slowed traffic and had to be shoveled out of the way but now.....

Maybe it was because snow made me think of Russia and Irina but it looked goddamn beautiful.

I glanced back at the bar. Inside, the other guys didn't even know it had been snowing out here. *I* wouldn't have, if I hadn't called Irina. I'd still be in there, worrying about the ugly, brutal reality of the job.

I looked ahead of me, at the unbroken snow. And took a big, deliberate step.

I blasted across town and pulled up outside Fenbrook Academy in plenty of time. I sat there outside the red-brick building, watching the students milling around on the steps: musicians with instrument cases on their backs, dancers with their hair up in buns and a few cocky guys I guessed were actors, hitting on all the girls. All of them just sitting there, happily chattering away in their nice, safe world where *crime* was something you heard about on the news.

I frowned. I'd almost forgotten that world existed.

Then Irina hurried down the steps wrapped up in a long black overcoat, so beautiful it made my chest hurt. Her hair was still up in a dancer's bun from class. I pushed open the car door so she could get in, but she shook her head.

"I need to keep moving," she told me. "I have another class in ten minutes and if I sit still, my legs will stiffen up."

The air coming in through the open car door was so cold it took my breath away. "Are you serious?"

She nodded. "Walk, or don't talk."

I didn't even have to think about it. I grabbed my coat and jumped out. She'd already taken a few paces along the street by the time I caught her, her long legs eating up the distance. She hadn't been kidding about keeping moving.

Or.... I glanced over my shoulder at the students on the steps. *Or she didn't want to have this conversation in my car, right in front of them.*

She was afraid I was going to end this and reduce her to tears in front of her friends. *Jesus.* Just the idea of it made me feel ill. Even though ending it was the only smart thing to do.

I grabbed her hand, but she didn't stop walking. Wouldn't even look at me. "Irina," I said, "I'm sorry. I'm sorry I ran out on you. I shouldn't have done that."

She kept walking but she slowed just a little. Maybe something in my voice told her I meant it. "It's...understandable," she said at last. "Everyone's scared of Vasiliy."

I stared at her in horror. She thought I was *scared* of him? I'm not scared of anyone. But what explanation could I give her?

The truth, a little voice inside me urged. *Tell her the truth. Tell her that you're her uncle's number one rival...and then watch her walk off into the sunset.*

Maybe it won't be like that. Maybe she isn't loyal to him. But I couldn't risk that. This was about more than just wanting to fuck her, now. I couldn't get her out of my head and I wasn't about to give her up, not even if it meant lying.

I drew in a deep breath. "I just...I know what your uncle's like," I said slowly. "And I couldn't believe that someone as amazing as you was connected with someone like that."

I waited to see how she took it. I hoped it rang true because it *was* the truth.

She slowed a little more. And then, for the first time, she turned and looked at me. God, even now, even when we were in the middle of all this, she was heartbreakingly beautiful. Those blue eyes burned with so much emotion, so much pain. It took everything I had to stop myself just grabbing her and pulling her into my arms.

"Vasiliy has done very bad things," she said slowly.

Down in the depths of my soul, the hot black anger uncoiled and stirred. I knew exactly what *bad things* Russians were capable of. I'd had personal fucking experience. And Vasiliy was no different to the bastard who'd—

Irina's gorgeous voice cut me free from the memory that had threatened to drag me down into rage. "Sometimes because he had to," she said. "But sometimes—especially in the last few years—just to grow his empire. He didn't used to be this ruthless."

I forced the memories back down inside me before they could take over, but the bitterness remained. *Just to grow his empire.* Just another power-crazed Russian, trying to take what wasn't his. At the same time, though, I felt a tiny shred of hope. She sounded bitter, too: maybe they weren't close. Maybe she'd cut ties long ago. "Are you close?"

She nodded. "After my parents died, he practically raised me."

Shit. My disappointment must have shown on my face because she shook her head. "But I turned my back on that," she said with pride. "I don't take his money. I hate everything about his business. Vasiliy wants me to marry someone like him, a gangster. I never will."

Oh Jesus...it got worse and worse. She hated gangsters. When she found out I was *Cosa Nostra* she'd never want to see me again. *I have to end this now, before she finds out.*

I opened my mouth to say it.

But nothing would come out.

I stared at her, completely fucking helpless. *Just do it!* A moment's pain. She'd cry. Then it would be over. I had to be honest with her. I'm a vicious son of a bitch, but I'm not a complete asshole.

But I just...*couldn't.* Whenever I went to speak, the thought of losing her felt like someone crushing my fucking chest.

"What?" she asked. She finally stopped walking and turned to me. I could hear the fear in her voice—she could tell something was wrong. "What are you trying to say?" *There'll never be a better time. Do it! Tell her!*

I stared into those cornflower-blue eyes and thought of never seeing her again.

"I need you." It was out before I even knew I was going to say it. "I need to keep seeing you."

She blinked...and then a smile spread across her face. Immediately, I got a stab of something I hadn't felt in years: guilt. *What the fuck are you doing, Angelo? What happens when she finds out?*

I knew it was wrong. But every second in her presence, watching her look up at me with that little smile tugging at her lips, felt so valuable that I would have done anything just to buy a few more of them.

Something inside me snapped: I had to have those lips, had to have them *now.* I grabbed her waist and pushed her back, almost lifting her clear of the sidewalk as I slammed her up against the trunk of a tree. She yelped in surprise and then, for the first time, I heard her giggle. The sound rippled through me like champagne bubbles, light and intoxicating, fucking *glorious.* I hadn't been able to imagine her laugh: she was always so serious. Now I wanted to hear it again and again.

But I wanted something else more. I moved in close and put one hand on her cheek, heard her breathing hitch as she realized what I was about to do.

Then my lips came down on hers.

12

IRINA

As soon as his lips touched mine, I could feel the animal hunger in him. Ferocious, savage: he didn't just want me, he *needed* me. It made me go weak inside and the feeling was as unfamiliar as it was fantastic. I'd had so many years of being hard, of never showing weakness for a second, that being just...*overcome* was incredible. *This is what it's meant to be like.* This is what I'd been missing from all the Russian men Vasiliy had tried to set me up with.

His kisses were soft and brutal, tasting me and directing me, pushing me one way then the other so that he could sample every inch of my lips. The kisses got faster and I felt his hands tighten on my waist, his lips working down across my cheek and then along my jaw, tilting my head up and back. Each kiss was a little explosion of pleasure, my breathing notching faster and faster along with his. Both of us were sliding fast, out of control—

He broke the kiss and put his mouth to my ear, his stubble brushing my cheek as he pushed my head to the side. "*Sei bellissima,*" he said. I didn't know much Italian, but even I knew that meant *you're beautiful.* A warm glow rippled out from my center, slamming into the pleasure and making it flare even hotter.

His hand slid up my back, captured my hair, still in a bun, and pulled it down, his grip firm but not painful. My chin tilted up to the sky and he kissed down my throat, each touch of his lips soft and measured but full of barely-restrained power, like putting your hand on the hood of a sports car and feeling the throb of the engine. His whole body was pushed up against me from his chest to his thighs and I could feel the hard bulk of him dwarfing me. I grabbed for his upper arms and found every muscle had gone tense: God, he was having to try so hard just to hold himself back....

He pushed my head to the side again. When he spoke into my ear, the low rasp of his voice made me catch my breath. "I need you," he said. "I fucking need you. I have to have you." Then he drew back and I realized he was looking at me. I opened my eyes, stared up into his, and I saw him frowning. "What have you *done* to me?" he growled.

I didn't have an answer. I just stared up at him, my hair still gripped in his hand.

"You're making me nuts. I can't get you out of my head." He kissed me again, open-mouthed and hungry, his tongue dancing with mine for long seconds. Then he drew back and stared at me again, still frowning...but the lust was winning, those brown eyes burning with it. "I can't stop thinking about what I'm going to do to you."

I'd never heard a voice like his before: so heavy and deep, every word loaded with intent. He said something and *it was going to happen.*

He leaned very close, his lips right on my ear, his hot breath making me tremble. His voice was strained with lust. "I'm going to throw you down on your bed and strip every fucking stitch of clothing off you." His hands were hard on my waist, holding me like he never wanted to let go. "Then I'm going to kiss you. *All over.* Starting on your mouth and all the way down to here."

His free hand cupped my groin and my eyes fluttered closed. The layers of clothing between us were irrelevant: I could feel his touch throbbing straight through, his palm against the softness of my folds. My breath caught in my chest and a rippling, white-hot ribbon of pleasure snaked up inside me, making me arch. His hand pressed a little harder and I gasped...and found myself pushing back against him, the pleasure pulsing and changing, turning to hot slickness.

I suddenly remembered where we were. My eyes opened but all I could see was Angelo: he was so big, he blocked out everything behind him. Behind me was the tree. I twisted my head to the side and felt my eyes go wide as I saw the passing cars. "We can't do this," I mumbled. "Not here."

He frowned, glanced at the traffic and turned back to me. "Who gives a fuck about *them?*"

He grabbed my shoulders and spun me around, so fast and so hard that I would have lost my footing if he hadn't been holding me. Then he pushed me face-first up against the tree. He moved up tight behind me so that I was sandwiched between him and the trunk again. The hard wood pressed right against my groin.

He tugged the collar of my coat down a little so that he could kiss the back of my neck. I felt his hands at my waist, loosening the belt that held my coat closed and then diving inside. I heard his gasp of surprise when he realized I was still in my leotard: I'd just thrown a pair of jeans and my coat over the top. His hands slid over my denim-covered hips and then squeezed my ass. I groaned and pressed my thighs together, excitement and fear twisting together and merging into something stronger.

His mouth at my ear again. "You tell me if you want me to stop."

One hand started to rise, skimming up over the smooth Lycra of my leotard and tracing the shape of my breasts. I'd closed my eyes when he started kissing my neck, but they came open when I felt his fingertips on the warm skin just above my collarbone. His hand pushed down, under the edge of my leotard and its built-in bra. My breathing quickened. God...he wasn't going to—

He was. I gasped, my eyes going wide as he palmed my breast, a deep, hot throb of pleasure twisting down through me. I writhed against him, which rubbed my groin against the hard trunk of the tree and the pleasure tightened and grew. I thought about telling him to stop: *God...we're right out on the street!*

But at that moment, his other hand brushed a stray lock of hair from my cheek and stroked me there, calming me, and then his thumb slid across my lips and it felt *so good*.... I gave myself up to it, my eyes closing.

He started to lightly squeeze my breast and my breath hissed from between my parted lips in time to his rhythm. Then he began to rub his thumb across my nipple and the pleasure spiraled in on itself, thrumming through my body and pooling in my groin. My nipple stiffened more and more with every touch until it was achingly hard, each touch of his thumb making me catch my breath. I realized I was pushing my ass back against his groin and I could feel the hardness of his cock outlined through his pants.

I knew that most of what he was doing to me was hidden by our clothes and his body, but anyone looking closely would have a pretty good idea what was going on. It made my cheeks flare red...but it made the pleasure strum through me faster, as well, everything drawing inwards, becoming a heated ball of tension that demanded release. *God, if he keeps this up I'm going to—*

His voice in my ear again. "When I'm done kissing down every inch of your body, I'm going to spread your legs apart and hold them there. I want to see you. I want to just kneel there and *look* at you and tell you how beautiful you are while you get wetter and wetter. Then I'm going to put my head between your thighs and I'm not going to stop until you're screaming, *begging* for me to fuck you."

His thumb rubbing against my nipple, each pass sending pleasure arcing downward to swell my approaching orgasm. His voice painted the lurid scene in my mind: I could see those brown and amber eyes staring down at me, feel his tongue on my folds— *God, I can't come, not right here in public—*

His voice, rough and perfect. "Come for me, Irina."

His finger and thumb pinched lightly at my nipple and suddenly I was slipping over the edge, writhing between him and the tree as my climax exploded. His thumb slipped between my teeth and I bit down on it as wave after wave of pleasure broke over me. I could feel the hardness of his cock against my ass, my orgasm turning him on even more.

Then I was slumping, my legs trembling and weak, and he had to grab my waist and pull me into his arms to stop me falling. *I can't believe I just did that,* I thought, huffing ice-cold air into my lungs. But at the same time, the dark excitement at having done it made me heady. Angelo's lips touched mine and I opened, drawing strength from his kiss as I clung to his shoulders.

When he finally broke the kiss, he stared into my eyes, looking almost angry: how *dare* I turn him on this much? "How do you *do* this to me?" he rasped. Then he kissed me again. "Tonight, I'm going to do everything I just told you."

I nodded weakly...then shook my head as a memory hit me. "I can't. I have to go out tonight."

He cursed under his breath. His hands tightened on my waist again, fiercely possessive. "Tomorrow, then," he growled. "I'll call you."

I nodded. "I have to go," I said. And, with a last kiss, I broke away and set off towards Fenbrook, feeling his eyes following me. The cold wind was lashing my cheeks but it didn't do anything to cool me down. I knew I was panting and red-faced, my lips tingling and swollen from all the kissing, my hair slipping from its bun thanks to the way he'd manhandled me. I had to get to a restroom and get myself together before I went to my next class...and, at the same time, I didn't want to. I liked being this way, liked being marked by him.

This isn't like me. But I knew, deep down, that that was a lie. I'd always known there was this part of me. I'd hidden my lust away because the few guys I'd been with made me feel I had to—Russian men think sex is for *them* and expect their women to tolerate it, not enjoy it. But for Angelo, my pleasure seemed to be the whole aim.

And it was more than just sex. I'd only known him a few days but I *liked* him. I dared to let myself dream. *Maybe I can somehow talk Vasiliy around.* We wouldn't meet like this and feel like this if we were going to be separated, would we? Fate wasn't that cruel.

I was right. Fate was much, much crueller.

13

ANGELO

"It's not on straight," said Rico from behind me.

I pulled on both ends of the bow tie, trying to get it into shape, and the whole knot fell apart. "Fuck it!" I snapped. "I hate these fucking things!"

Rico sighed and twirled his finger in the air. I turned from the mirror and finally allowed him to help me. "Why do I have to go to this party, again?" I growled.

"You ask that every year, boss," said Rico. "I got the same answer for you: we got to kiss up to Heinwell." He pulled the bow tie tight, perfectly straight and balanced: how did he do that?

"I hate kissing up to Heinwell," I muttered. What I meant was, I hated kissing up to *anyone*. Even a big property developer like Heinwell who we needed on our side.

"Champagne and lobster and two hours of hanging out with all those rich chicks. I'm digging real deep but I ain't finding much sympathy," Rico told me.

I knew he was right. Going to Heinwell's charity fundraiser had been almost fun, the last few years. It *was* full of rich, eager society girls who got all wide-eyed at the prospect of meeting a real live criminal. I'd wound up taking one back to my apartment, last year.

But now I couldn't even remember her name and the idea of hanging out with them again just left me cold. The only woman I wanted to see was Irina. *Good thing she was busy tonight.* I'd forgotten all about the party until Rico had cornered me about it. He'd even picked up my tux for me. I don't know what I'd do without him.

"Fine," I grumbled. "I'll give Heinwell the fucking check and then I'm out of there."

The party was at Heinwell's place out in Long Island, a big white-painted mansion complete with columns, as if he thought he belonged in the White House. *Maybe, if I take care of Heinwell fast, I can call Irina and meet up when she gets back from wherever she is.* Just the thought of it made my cock swell in my pants...and I didn't want to admit it, but my chest got a little tight, too, like I was a fucking teenager all over again.

I threw my keys to the kid parking the cars and strode inside, feeling the eyes of the other guests on me. There must have been a hundred people there: minor politicians, some business leaders, a couple of sports stars who wanted to be seen to be doing their bit for charity. I saw a few mouths tighten as I passed. One guy dared to mutter, *what's* he *doing here?*

I stopped and pinned him with a glare. *I run half this fucking city,* my glare said. *What do you do?* I enjoyed watching the cocky piece of shit turn pale and look at his feet. It wasn't just about making them afraid. Sometimes, people need reminding that it's guys like me who keep the wheels turning.

I saw Heinwell across the room and headed towards him. I wanted to intercept him and hand him my check, then maybe I could make an excuse and leave before the actual dinner. But I was aware of someone else pushing through the crowd to my left, trying to get there first. *Oh no you don't.* I sped up, deliberately not looking at my competition. They sped up, too. We reached Heinwell at the exact same moment and I slapped him on the shoulder. "Jerry!" I gave him a big, bullshit grin. "It's been too long. Got a big fat check for you."

Jerry Heinwell tried to smile, but it wouldn't come together. His eyes kept flicking to the side, towards where my competitor for his attention was standing. "Angelo. Yeah. Haven't heard from you since last year." He swallowed, his Adam's apple bobbing nervously. "A lot's changed, since then."

"Perhaps you should stay in better touch with your partners," said a voice from my left, deep and rich and heavily accented. A voice I recognized. I finally turned towards it, my hand slipping from Heinwell's shoulder.

"Hello, Mr. Baroni," said Vasiliy Malakov coldly.

My brain froze up for a second. Vasiliy had been on my mind a lot, especially since I found out I was seeing his niece. But I couldn't wrap my head around him being here. This was *my* turf. Heinwell was *my* contact.

I watched in horror as Vasiliy put a friendly arm around Heinwell's shoulders while keeping his gaze on me. "A wise man once said, 'the only constant is change,'" he told me. "I find this is true."

My eyes flicked between the two of them. "*Jerry?*" I asked. "What the *fuck?*"

Heinwell swallowed, but then lifted his chin. "Times change, Angelo. Sorry."

Times change?! I glared at Vasiliy. It wasn't enough that he was trying to take territory from me, now he was trying to steal my contacts? Heinwell was worth tens of millions: whoever he was cozied up to got all the prime construction contracts, plus tip-offs about future projects the city was planning so they could snap up the right real estate and make a fortune. I'd had Heinwell in my pocket for years and my dad had him before that. No way was Vasiliy taking him —no *way!*

I took a step towards Vasiliy...and someone stepped between us. Big, but not some hotheaded young thug: an older guy with a scar across his cheek and a sober manner. The sort of guy who could fit right in at a posh party like this but probably knew thirty different ways to kill you.

"This is Yuri," said Vasiliy with a hint of pride. "My protection."

"I don't want any trouble tonight," said Heinwell quickly. "The fucking press is here."

Vasiliy tutted under his breath. "There will be no trouble," he said as if offended. "Mr. Baroni was just leaving."

Yuri clasped his hands behind his back and just stared at me. He didn't display any of the rage and bluster of the bratva I was used to dealing with. He seemed as calm and patient as one of those English butlers. His steady gaze seemed to say: *I'd hate to have to cause a scene by snapping your neck.*

But I wasn't backing down. I looked around Yuri at Vasiliy. "You piece of shit," I muttered. I could feel my hands bunching into fists, the rage surging and boiling inside me. "You think you can do this, you Russian bastard? There's a line and you just stepped over it."

Vasiliy casually waved Yuri out of the way so that he could step right up to me. "Mr. Baroni. Since we are face-to-face, let me deliver a message." He turned and called over his shoulder. "Mikhail!" Then he turned back to me. "A message from both me and my business partner."

There was movement in the crowd behind Vasiliy. A big, pink-faced Russian was approaching, his collar too tight around his flobbery neck. And he was pulling someone along next to him, someone smaller who I couldn't see yet through the crowd. I just got a glimpse of—

Platinum-blonde hair.

My entire body went cold, all my rage flash-frozen as everything just...stopped. *Oh no. Oh, Jesus, no. Not like this!*

For a split-second, I actually considered running. I'd never run from anything in my life but even looking like a coward in front of Vasiliy would be better than the look on her face when she—

Too late.

Mikhail pushed through the crowd and stopped beside Vasiliy, towing Irina into place beside him. The sight of his soft, pink hand around her wrist made me want to kill him.

Irina's jaw dropped as she saw me. I saw her blink in puzzlement and an iron band cinched tight around my chest: I knew what was coming.

"Who's this?" asked Irina. I could hear the strain in her voice. She wanted to be wrong.

"This is Angelo Baroni," Vasiliy told her. "Our rival."

14

IRINA

One second and my brain just failed to process. *It can't be. Of course it isn't.*

Two seconds and I realized it was true.

Three seconds and I knew I'd been staring too long. Vasiliy or Mikhail would notice, they'd guess and then Angelo would be dead. But I couldn't stop staring into those brown and amber eyes, my face threatening to crumple at any second. My tears would seal his fate. Already, Yuri was frowning at me. He'd guarded our family for years, knew me maybe even better than Vasiliy. If he guessed....

A life as a Malakov saved me. I'd had years to perfect hiding my emotions. I shook my head and looked away. "I want no part of your...*business.*"

Next to me, Vasiliy bristled. He hates it when I distance myself from the family, especially in public, but he didn't comment. On my other side, Mikhail wasn't so polite. His hand tightened on my wrist, clammy and unpleasant. "*Behave,*" he hissed, as if to a child.

It was exactly the wrong thing to say to me. "I'm going to get a drink," I told him coldly. I was desperate to get out of there before I lost it. The anger and hurt were blossoming inside me, silent explosions that made me tremble. Already, I couldn't look Angelo in the eye.

Mikhail leaned down to me. "You are supposed to be my date tonight!" he hissed, outraged. "Act like it!" He jerked my wrist, pulling me closer.

I pulled away. His fingers dug hard enough into my wrist that I knew he'd leave bruises, but I gritted my teeth and *yanked*. My wrist tore free of his grasp and then I was stalking away across the room, my anger hiding what was really going on inside my head. I heard Mikhail take a single step to follow me but then he stopped: I imagined Vasiliy putting an arm across his chest to block him. *Let her go.*

I found a door that led to the garden. Despite the cold, a few people were out there smoking. I pushed past them and into the darkness, shoes crunching on the snow-covered grass, trying to lose myself amongst the bushes and trees. The air was freezing, that sharp sort of cold that slashes right to your bones. But at least it cooled my eyes. *Don't cry, don't cry.*

A banker. I'd thought he was a banker. *Loans. Insurance.* The same sort of euphemisms Vasiliy sometimes used. How could I not have seen it? Now I knew why something about him had seemed familiar. He was a gangster. *He's just like them!*

And yet he'd seemed so utterly different. Even now, the thought of him made my chest tighten. I hated him...but I still liked him. That made the anger bubbling up inside me burn like acid. *Chyort,* I cursed. *You stupid, weak fool!*

This was all my fault. I'd known, back in Central Park, that seeing an American was impossible. But I'd tried to ignore who I was...and so fate had reminded me.

A hand on my shoulder, spinning me around. I cried out, expecting Mikhail...but it was Angelo who suddenly loomed over me.

The anger suddenly exploded. My arm was swinging before I was even aware of it. My hand cracked across his face with a noise like a gunshot. Then I instinctively tensed, ready for his fist.

"Okay." His voice was a low rumble. "I deserved that."

I stood there panting, staring up into his eyes, my body slowly relaxing as I realized he wasn't going to hit me. I'd been around Russian men for so long, I'd just assumed he'd swing at me. But as I looked into those dark, amber-flecked eyes, I didn't see even a hint of that casual, brutal violence that came so easily to Mikhail. All I saw was pain. Pain that he'd hurt *me*.

"Why didn't you tell me?" I blurted.

He just stared at me for a long time, rubbing his hand across the cheek I'd hit. "Because I couldn't stand losing you," he said at last.

He'd lied to me before and I told myself I shouldn't trust him again. But listening to him, there wasn't even a shred of doubt in my mind: he was telling the truth. I remembered the look on his face outside Fenbrook: he hadn't wanted to lie. He'd *had* to.

I shook my head. "This can't happen! You're our enemy!"

He was between me and the house. I pushed past him, my arms hugging myself against the cold. But his big hand took hold of my bare upper arm as I passed. It wasn't anything like Mikhail's cruel grip. It was firm but gentle—I could have pulled out of it if I'd wanted to. But the warmth throbbing into me felt incredible. I stopped walking and we stood there facing away from each other. I had to fight the urge to turn back to him. If I did that, I might do something stupid.

"I'm not *your* enemy," he said softly.

My stomach knotted. "You know it doesn't work like that. I'm a Malakov."

The hand on my arm pulled, a gentle pressure towing me backward until I stood in front of him again. I wanted to resist but my feet seemed to move by themselves. Then I was looking up at him, his big, muscled form blocking out the star-filled sky. When he spoke, each word was a deep growl edged in fire, burning down into my soul. "I don't fucking care."

I swallowed. I knew it was true. This man wasn't afraid of anyone: not even Vasiliy. He would move mountains to possess me. He'd start a goddamn war.

But he's a gangster. "I don't want this life," I told him, my voice bitter. "I walked away from all this." And I took a step back, intending to get some space between us and then walk around him, back to the mansion.

He followed me. Two quick strides and he'd pressed me back against a tree, his body tight against mine. Suddenly, I realized how cold I was...how much I needed the warm hardness of his chest against my breasts. *But I can't! This is crazy! Remember who he is!*

I put my palms on his chest to push him back.

He captured my wrists and pulled them up above my head, pinning them to the tree. He leaned in, his eyes searching mine. "You say you don't want this," he said. "Fine. You tell me straight, Irina. Tell me right now that you never want to see me again and I'm gone. No one ever has to know what happened."

He was giving me an out. All I had to do was say the words. I drew on everything Vasiliy had taught me, dragging up layer after layer of impenetrable Malakov ice to shield me. *Just say the words.*

But whenever I looked at him, the heat was like a blowtorch. It seared through the ice like it wasn't there. I had to look away. *I can say it if I look away—*

He released my wrists with one hand and captured my chin. He turned my head so that I had to look at him. "But you know what I think, Irina?"

I stared at him, my heart thundering.

"I think you need this as much as I do."

I didn't answer. And that was all the answer he needed. He leaned down, one big hand still holding my wrists tight against the rough trunk of the tree. He moved more gently than I would have thought possible, given his size. His lips brushed mine—

Don't! Don't let him— I felt both of us teetering on the brink of a bottomless ravine. We both knew it was wrong. We both knew how much danger this would bring and it wasn't that we didn't care. It was that we were utterly helpless to resist.

My lips parted...and I was lost. Our tongues touched and my own groan of need was matched by his. The kiss took hold of me, my whole body moving in time with the soft rhythm of his lips. Above my head, my hands tightened into fists at how good it felt. The pleasure rippled down my body, blossoming and spreading, pushing back the cold. The kiss was slow and romantic, but edged with molten heat.

I broke away, breathless. "I need to get back," I told him, my voice throaty.

He squeezed my wrists for a second, reluctant to release me...then let me go. My skin glowed warm where he'd held me and the cold air didn't seem to make it fade. "I'll call you," he told me.

I swallowed...and nodded.

As I went to step past him again, he caught my arm. "Mikhail," he growled. "Are you...*with* him?"

I shook my head. "Vasiliy wants me to marry him," I said. "I came with him to the party, to keep Vasiliy happy. But I don't feel anything for him."

Angelo gave me a slow nod. "He ever grabs you like that again, I'll kill him."

I nodded. And then I was away, walking quickly through the night, praying the freezing air would cool my face. I tried to slow my breathing, to make my face its usual cold, indifferent mask. I needed to control my emotions more than ever.

I was a Malakov. But I was kissing the enemy.

15

———

ANGELO

The sand squished between my toes, the surf tugging at my ankles as it rolled in and out. Irina hadn't seen me yet. She was looking out to sea, watching the sun sink below the horizon.

I took two running steps towards her and scooped her up into my arms. She yelped and then giggled, the sound like music. I carried her out into the waves, the water breaking over her smooth tan thighs and making them gleam. Beneath her turquoise swimsuit, her breasts were perfect, lush swells... I could feel my cock hardening in my trunks. I didn't give a shit who was watching from the beach, as soon as we got out into deeper water, that swimsuit was coming off.

My phone rang.

I waded for another step or so, frowning and looking around for the source of the noise, and then the sunset dissolved into dawn and I was lying in my bed, the sheets tangled around me. There was a sudden cold emptiness where Irina's warm, wet body had been a second before.

Fuck!

I never dreamed. Nightmares, now and again, about my folks. But not idyllic, Technicolor visions like *that*. Jesus, I could still smell the salt water and feel the wet strands of her hair against my neck.

I groped and found my phone. *"What?"* I snarled.

"Sorry, boss," said Rico meekly. "Got a call. The Saints want you to come in."

I cursed under my breath and closed my eyes. My day had started badly and it was about to get worse.

The Saints. Six old school *Cosa Nostra* guys who run New York, Boston, and a good amount of the surrounding area. The streets answer to me but I answer to them.

We'd never gotten on well. They'd never respected me, only grudgingly accepting me when I'd taken over from my dad. It didn't help that I was one of the youngest bosses around and none of The Saints were under sixty.

Sometimes, going to see them was okay. When things were going well, they'd break out the good Scotch and cigars and gently praise me. But I knew this wasn't going to be one of those times: they'd summoned me too abruptly.

The meetings were always in the big, dark mansion owned by "Saint" Nicholas Vici. Old Nicky wasn't so much the leader as the spokesperson—the six guys seemed to always agree on everything, like they were a fucking hive mind. When I walked into the room, they were all sitting around one side of the big oak table, like always, with a single chair facing them for me. Like I was a kid facing off against the Principal and five teachers.

"This thing with the Russian," Nicky said before I'd even sat down. "It's a problem."

Shit! I froze, my ass hovering above my chair. Then I told myself not to be stupid. If they knew about Irina, I would have been hauled in here at gunpoint. "I can handle Vasiliy," I told them. "*And* Mikhail."

"Doesn't seem like it. We hear he's stolen Heinwell away from you, now? And his people smashed up a restaurant? That's *public*, Angelo. That sorta shit brings the press and the cops. Everyone starts thinking you can't defend your turf."

My hands tightened into fists. "I've been holding that turf for years. The Russians aren't a problem."

"Really?" Nicky reached behind him and plucked something off the floor. "Then how the fuck do you explain *this?*"

He hurled it at me and I only caught it a second before it hit me in the face. When I lowered it, I saw Nicky smirking at me. The bastard had never liked me. He'd never liked my dad, for that matter. The only reason he hadn't replaced me was that I did too good of a job.

I turned the thing over in my hands. A handbag with shining metal buckles and the designer logo picked out in those little crystals women go nuts for.

"You *do* know about this?" asked Nicky. "I mean, you're on top of it?"

I had no fucking idea what the handbag was supposed to mean. Rico was standing by the door and, when I glanced over at him, he gave me a pained look. *Shit!* There was something he hadn't told me.

Vincenzo, a guy in his eighties with a face as brown and wrinkled as a walnut, took pity on me. "Vasiliy and Mikhail are flooding New York with these things," he told me. "Better quality than what our guys on the street are selling. Almost as good as the real thing. And not just handbags. Jeans. Jackets. Fancy shoes."

Nicky glared at him—he'd obviously been enjoying having me at a disadvantage. But I could see now why they were pissed. Counterfeit goods brought in millions in New York alone. "I'll take care of it," I told them.

Nicky leaned forward. "No fucking mercy, Angelo. *Crush* these sons of bitches. Every last one of them."

"Send 'em back to Siberia in boxes," grunted Taavetti. He was one of the oldest and needed an oxygen cylinder, these days. "Only good Russian's a dead Russian."

"Except for the women," said Nicky. "So many good-lookin' blondes. And they all come over here eager to open their legs and earn some US dollars. They breed 'em to be whores." He laughed: a long, filthy laugh, his head thrown back. Then he looked at me and scowled. "What the fuck's the matter with you?"

I was sitting there stony-faced, staring at him like a dog that's about to go for his master's throat.

"You ain't gone soft on the Russians have you, Angelo?" Nicky asked, his smile disappearing. "Your old man was never soft on them."

I was already mad. Now the rage boiled over. I jumped to my feet, slammed my palms down on the edge of the table and glared at them. "I'll deal with the fucking Russians, okay? The fake goods *and* the territory! They want a war, I'll give them a war!" The Saints went quiet and I strode from the room, Rico falling in behind me.

As I left, I heard Vincenzo mutter, "A war? Come on, no one wants a war." And then Nicky told him not to be a pussy.

"You knew about that, the handbag thing?" I asked as I got into the car. Rico's guilty expression told me he had. "Why the fuck didn't you warn me? You got my back or not?" I slammed my door.

Rico shook his head. "Sorry. It came up yesterday morning, while you were out on your...errand."

Shit. I missed it because I was outside Fenbrook Academy with Irina's breast in my hand. *What's the matter with me?* This isn't a job you can do half-assed. This is a job you give your life to. I sighed. "Don't worry about it," I muttered.

Rico put his foot down and Nicky's mansion quickly fell away behind us. But the problems remained: I stared at the handbag on my lap, turning it over and over in my hands.

"I could get some guys together," said Rico. "Go to some markets where they're selling that stuff and smash them up."

I shook my head. "That'd be like stamping on roaches. We gotta hit them at source." I examined the seams. The thing really was well made, far better than the crap our guys sold. "Vasiliy and Mikhail have to be getting this stuff into the country somehow. Probably through the docks. We're going to find out when the next shipment's coming in." I pulled out my phone and dialed Peterson, the little prick I'd threatened to push through a window.

"And then what?" asked Rico.

"And then we're going to steal it."

We were in luck: there was a container coming in at nine that night. Peterson, his voice high and tight with fear, was only too happy to give us all the details. At eight-thirty, Rico and I pulled into the docks in a rental car, followed by another car carrying five of my best men. It was a moonless night and it was snowing again, the big flakes only visible when they passed through the beams of the security lights. We parked in the thick, black shadows between two shipping containers. The Russians wouldn't even know we were there.

Rico took the men to prepare the ambush. That left me sitting alone in the car with the heater on and the snow falling all around me. It was completely silent, a warm little cocoon.

I hadn't stopped thinking about her all day. Now, I couldn't think of anything else. *Fuck it.* I had thirty minutes to kill.

I called Irina.

16

IRINA

I was lying on my bed, staring at a book but not seeing the words. *What am I doing?* Why had I given in to Angelo and kept this thing going when it was impossible and *horrifically* dangerous? If Vasiliy found out....

But I already knew the truth. I hadn't given in to *him*. I'd given in to *it,* this magnetic draw that was pulling us together, that wouldn't be blocked by family or loyalty, that had no time for sense or reason. I remembered how confused Angelo looked, sometimes, before he kissed me, how he'd asked *how do you do this to me?*

He was as powerless as I was.

My phone rang. I had it to my ear before the end of the first ring. "Hello?"

I heard his intake of breath, as if just the way I said *hello* was an immense turn-on for him. "Irina," he breathed, savoring my name. "What are you doing?"

"Reading. What are *you* doing?"

"Business." Wherever he was, it was very quiet. I could hear every breath he took: it was as if he was lying on the bed next to me. "Are you alone?"

"I'm in my room. Rachel's around."

"Is your door open?"

"A little."

"Close it."

Two innocent words, but they made a thrill of excitement go through me and I wasn't sure why. I pushed my door closed and the muted sound of Rachel's dance music disappeared completely. The silence wasn't like any I'd experienced before. It was thick and heavy, full of promise.

"Go to your bed and lie down," said Angelo.

My breathing quickened as I started to guess what he had in mind. I lay down on top of the comforter.

"What are you wearing?" he asked.

I looked down at myself and considered lying and saying *lingerie and heels.* But Angelo's voice was too real, too intimate, stroking at my mind. It would feel wrong to lie. "Jeans," I said. "Blue ones. And a thick brown sweater." I said it apologetically: I knew they weren't sexy. I'd been in slobbing-around-the-house mode. Plus, it was cold in my room—I needed that sweater.

But Angelo didn't sound disappointed at all. "Anything under the sweater?"

"My bra." My voice caught on the word *bra.* I had to lift the shoulder of the sweater to check the color. "Red."

"So the sweater's against your skin," said Angelo. "Is it soft against your stomach?"

I realized he wanted the detail so that he could imagine it. "Yes," I told him. "Very soft. Angora."

"Slide your hand under the bottom of your sweater," he said. "Run it over your stomach."

My breathing tightened. This was definitely turning into one of *those* phone calls. I'd never done something like that before, but the idea sent a hot wave down my body, making me press my thighs together. *It's nothing,* I told myself nonchalantly. *Just my hand on my stomach.* I slid my hand up under the hem of my sweater and swept it across my skin.

Except...it didn't feel like my hand, anymore. It felt like his. It felt like Angelo's big, warm hand gliding across the soft skin of my stomach, fingertips reaching towards my bra.

"Arch your back up off the bed," he said in my ear. My eyes closed. Each word was a throaty rumble that vibrated through my entire body: I thought of a slowly-throbbing engine, finished in shining Italian chrome. I arched.

"Unhook your bra," he ordered, enunciating every syllable.

I reached under me and it was *his* strong fingers that found the clasp and unhooked it.

"Run your hand higher," he said. "Over your stomach. Over your left breast. But don't touch the nipple yet."

I felt almost hypnotized. It was as if his voice was flowing into my ear and right into the very center of my brain, bypassing all my defenses. It fed into the molten core that I'd kept hidden behind layers of ice for so many years, making it glow hotter and hotter. I slid my hand over my stomach and gasped as my fingers brushed the lower slope of my breast. I went up and around, skirting the nipple as he'd instructed.

"When I next see you," Angelo said, "I'm going to take that nipple in my mouth. I'm going to lick and lick in circles along its sides, feeling it getting harder and harder against my tongue. I'm going to suck it and then I'm going to just barely let you feel the edges of my teeth."

I didn't answer. My fingers stroked around and around my breast.

"Is your nipple getting hard, Irina?" he asked.

"*Yes,*" I whispered.

"How hard?"

I could feel it straining, aching. "*Very* hard."

His voice tightened with lust. "Unfasten your jeans."

I didn't open my eyes but I turned my head on the pillow towards where I knew the bedroom door was. I don't have a lock on my door and Rachel has a habit of just barging in. *Of course I can't....*

I felt fingers popping open the button fly of my jeans. *My* fingers, but they barely seemed to be under my control.

"What sort of panties?" he asked.

"Gray ones." My voice was a hoarse whisper. "Briefs."

"Fingers under them. Now."

My fingers slid under the waistband.

"I can't wait to see you there," Angelo told me. "I've been imagining what you look like. What color the hair is. What your lips look like. How they'll part when I first slip a finger into you."

My breath caught.

"Rub yourself for me, Irina." His voice had grown even deeper, more gravelly, in his lust. It seemed to throb through me. "Two fingers, up and down."

I still had my eyes tight closed. The air was hissing between my teeth as I breathed. His fingers—*my* fingers—stroked down through soft hair and then traced the line where my lips met. It felt so good...I started to move my body to the rhythm, my ass grinding into the bed. I sped up—

"Don't speed up," Angelo told me. "Slow."

How did he know? I forced myself to slow down: long, deliberate strokes that just touched my clit at the top. I could feel my lips swelling, growing engorged and moist, and I let out a groan.

I heard his smile. "You're getting wet for me." Not a question.

"Yes," I whispered. Behind my closed eyelids, I saw him, stretched out on top of me on the bed, his knee between my thighs, his hand down the front of my jeans. I'd never done anything like this before. Russian men—at least, the ones I'd known—were simple creatures. Sex, to them, meant getting a woman naked as fast as possible, pawing at her breasts and then ramming it in. They'd never do this. They'd never wrap me up in words and ideas until it felt as if my whole body was being caressed.

"I want you to push two fingers into you, now," he said. He spoke slowly and I could hear the tension in his voice. I imagined him sitting bolt upright in his seat, eyes closed, phone clamped to his ear. Wherever he was, he wasn't *there*, any more than I was *here*. We were together in the hot, dark place we'd formed from words.

I did it, gasping as my knuckles spread my slickened lips.

"They're not as thick as my cock," said Angelo. "Or as long. But I want you to fuck yourself, now, as if it's me fucking you. That means hard, Irina. That's how I'll take you."

My fingers started to move, slow and then faster.

"Pull your knees up. Spread them wide. My hips are between your thighs, holding you open."

I rammed my jeans and panties down my hips, panting. My fingers moved faster, thumb circling my clit. I couldn't believe how wet I was.

"I'm fucking you, Irina. Right now, I'm fucking you. My ass is pumping between your legs. My cock is right up inside you.

My hand moved frantically. It didn't feel like fingers; it felt like his cock. I could see him on top of me, those brown and amber eyes burning down into mine, his broad chest looming over me. My naked ass ground and writhed against the comforter. My mouth was open and panting, my lips aching for his kiss. *God!* The pleasure was rolling through me in quick, hot waves, but the waves didn't dissipate: each one slapped up against the tight core of heat that was building at my center and added to it. It was growing hotter, tighter, making me gasp and buck.

"Faster now, Irina. Harder. I'm pounding you. My cock's stretching you and it's going *fast* and *deep*. I'm going to keep fucking you until you come your brains out."

"*Oh!*" I gasped. "*Oh, Jesus—*"

"Tell me, Irina."

"You're f—fucking me," I gasped, stumbling over the filthy words. The pleasure was tightening, tightening, turning white-hot. "H— Hard. I'm going to—" I bit my lip.

"Say it. Say it, Irina."

His cock pumped at me, the base of it grinding against my clit. "*Ya sobirayus' do orgazma!*" I screamed. Then, as I tipped over the edge, I screamed it again in English. "*I'm going to come!*"

And suddenly the pleasure exploded, every muscle going taut. I arched my back, breasts mashing against the hardness of his chest, my ass lifting off the bed as he buried himself in me. My hands dug deep into the comforter and twisted, knuckles white. I pressed my lips tight together to keep from screaming again and my climax came out as a series of long, throaty groans broken by quick little huffs of air. Then I collapsed on the bed under him, my whole body soaked with sweat....

...and realized it was just me, lying there with my jeans and panties around my ankles and my knees spread wide. I was panting and flushed and very, very wet.

My eyes opened. I realized the distant music from Rachel's room had stopped. *Chyort!* Had she heard me screaming? I quickly pulled my jeans up. Then I looked at my phone where, I realized, Angelo definitely *had* heard every groan.

It was a weird feeling, to have climaxed in front of someone before you've had sex with them. He'd shared something I'd never shared with anyone before. It should have been embarrassing. A little part of me *was* embarrassed, but....

But most of me was just deeply, deeply turned on. How could he make me feel so relaxed about sex, when the guys I'd known before had made me feel like a freak just for enjoying it? I think it was because of the relish he took in my pleasure, as if nothing made him happier than seeing—or listening to—me come.

"Tonight," Angelo told me, "when I'm finished here, we're going to do that for real."

My mind spun. It had only been a day since I'd slapped him at the party. He'd lied to me: was I ready to trust him again, to take that step with him? But just the thought of it made my ass start to grind against the bed again. *God, what's he turned me into?* "Where?" I asked, shocked at how breathless I sounded.

"I'll pick you up at your place," he said. "And then we'll go somewhere, somewhere no one knows us." His voice grew low. "And I'll find something to bend you over and—"

A hard rap of knuckles on glass, seemingly from inches away. I actually looked around, startled, before I realized it was at Angelo's end. I heard him curse. "I gotta go," he said. "I'll call you when I'm on my way." And then he was gone.

A knock at my bedroom door. I jumped up off the bed and straightened the comforter. "Come in."

Rachel pushed the door open. "What was that?" she asked cautiously.

I pushed my hair off my sweat-damp forehead. "What was what?"

"All that screaming." Her eyes narrowed.

I did my best poker face. I was a Malakov, dammit. *Ice-cold.* My expression would reveal nothing—

Rachel's eyes widened. "It's that guy from Central Park!"

Chyort! However hard I summoned the ice, it wouldn't come. Angelo had reduced me to a hot pile of mush. I sighed and nodded.

Rachel threw her arms around me. "Tell me *everything.* Only pausing to thank me for getting you together."

I hugged her. "Okay, but it'll have to be fast." A ripple of excitement shot down my body. "I'm going out."

17

ANGELO

I watched from the shadows as the huge container was lowered towards the waiting truck. It was bitterly cold—even the Russians were wrapped up in thick coats and gloves, yelling to each other to hurry. They were more concerned with keeping warm than keeping guard. *Good.*

I glanced across at Rico, who was ready to give the order to move in. He gave me a friendly nod, but I could feel the tension between us. I'd chewed him out when he'd rapped on the car window, but the truth was it was me who was in the wrong. I'd been so busy imagining Irina pumping her slender fingers into her pussy, I hadn't noticed the Russians arriving. What was *with* me? It was like the woman had cast some Russian witchcraft on me.

The container settled onto the truck and the Russians started to secure it. Rico opened his mouth, but I held up my hand: I wanted to wait as long as possible, get them to do all the work for us....

Now. I dropped my hand and Rico yelled the order. The Russians looked up in dismay as flashlights went on all around them. As they squinted against the blinding light, they heard five guns being cocked. *"Give it up!"* I yelled. *"No one has to get hurt!"*

The Russians looked at each other…and slowly raised their hands, cursing. Good. No need to make this thing bloody if we didn't have to.

Less than five minutes later, we'd collected the Russians' guns and tossed their cell phones in the water so they couldn't raise the alarm too soon. Two of my guys got into the truck and we climbed back into our cars and prepared to drive off in convoy.

"Mikhail and Vasiliy will fucking *kill you* for this," snarled one of the Russians through the car window.

I lowered the window and smiled sweetly at him. "Tell Vasiliy," I said victoriously, "A wise man once said…'*fuck you.*'"

Our little convoy moved off and I raised the window, cutting off the Russian's stream of cursing. And just like that, we stole a million dollars worth of counterfeit goods.

"That is one pissed-off Russian," said Rico, watching in the mirror from the driver's seat. "Hey, we should celebrate. Let's hit a bar. Let's hit *five* bars."

I grinned. He was right: we *did* need to celebrate. And normally I'd have liked nothing more than to sprawl around a table in one of New York's fanciest bars. But….

But I wanted to celebrate with her. "Nah. I got plans," I told him.

I saw the hurt in his eyes straightaway and felt lousy. But he rallied quickly. "Well, sure," he said. "That same chick again? Hell, I can understand that. You *should* get your dick wet."

I nodded and grinned, but just a little uneasily. It didn't feel like that, like I was just fucking her to celebrate, as I would have done in the past. It felt like much more than that.

A half hour later, the truck and its stolen cargo were safe in one of our warehouses and I'd given Rico a thick wad of cash to take the guys out on the town. I felt guilty…but the guilt evaporated as soon as I pulled up outside Irina's house and saw her hurrying down the path towards me. Her coat covered her almost to her knees, but I caught tantalizing glimpses of the firm, stocking-covered thigh as she climbed in. She'd barely closed her door when I put my hand on her cheek and turned her to me, then drew her into a long kiss. I ran my other hand down her body, feeling her through the layers of clothing, eager to unwrap her.

"We could just go inside," I growled as I broke the kiss. Less than a minute and we could be on her bed, doing for real what we'd played out on the phone.

She shook her head. "My roommate's there."

"So? Let her listen."

For the first time, I saw her flush, a delicate rose blush that made her look delectably innocent. "She already listened!" she said with feeling. "Somewhere else!"

I grinned. "I know a place. But first..." And I slipped the long, slim box out of my overcoat pocket and handed it to her.

I'd bought it that afternoon, when Rico and I were cooling our heels in the city waiting for Peterson to get back to us with the information. I'd paid a visit to an Italian jeweler I knew, a guy who'd been under my protection for years. I knew he wouldn't rip me off. And when I'd seen the necklace, it had been so perfect for Irina that I hadn't even checked the price tag.

She opened the box...and gasped as she saw the slender chain with its shining triangles of polished silver. Each one was thicker at its center than at the edge, angular and yet touchably smooth. When I helped her slip it around her neck and fasten the clasp, the triangles lay flat against her skin around the base of her throat, twinkling in the streetlights as she turned her head to examine herself in the rear view mirror. I thought they looked like ice crystals—that's why I'd picked it.

"I love it," she breathed.

I leaned close and growled in her ear. "I want to fuck you when you're wearing that necklace...and nothing else."

She stiffened...and nodded. I put the car into drive. I knew where I was going to take her: a little street that would be quiet, this time of night, while still being only a stone's throw from the Brooklyn bridge.

The Chrysler had easily enough room in the back for us to fuck in comfort, but I had something else in mind. I had a vision of Irina bent over the hood of the car, her cheek pressed against the warm metal, while I raised her skirt and drove into her from behind. I knew, from when I'd pushed her up against the tree outside Fenbrook, that public sex turned her on as much as it did me. This time, we could go all the way and it would be fucking mind-blowing.

I glanced down at her legs. Damn, but she had perfect legs. She was wearing stockings or nylons—I'd find out which soon enough—and heels. *Knee boots.* It just popped into my head. *She'd look fucking amazing in knee boots.* Maybe I'd buy her a pair.

"You seem different," she said, breaking my train of thought. "Happy."

I grinned. "Because I'm with you," I said truthfully.

She flushed again. "Not *just* that, though," she said. "Something else."

I blinked. I'd never had anyone before who could read me that easily. Other than Rico, no one ever got to know me well enough to sense my moods. It was unsettling...and *nice. Is this what a relationship's like?*

I shrugged, but couldn't stop myself smirking. "We pulled off a big score tonight."

Her voice was carefully neutral. "Oh?"

I ran it back through my mind: how shocked the Russians had been, how royally pissed they were when they realized we were taking the container. "Yeah. Big haul."

She crossed her arms. That should have been a warning, but I was too dumb, too proud.

"It's Mikhail," I blurted. "He's been bringing all this counterfeit shi—*stuff* into the city and selling it. So tonight, we stole a whole container load of it." I grinned and then glanced at her to see her reaction.

She was sitting there open-mouthed. "You *kozyol!*" she said at last.

I took my eyes off the road for a second to gape at her. I didn't know what that meant, but it didn't sound good. "I thought you hated Mikhail."

"I do!"

"So what do you care if I steal from him?"

"Because that's Mikhail's *pet project!* He's always talking about it. Have you any idea how pissed he'll be?"

I shrugged, maybe a little defensively. "He and Vasiliy started this when they moved into my territory."

She groaned, closing her eyes and slumping back in her seat. "*They started it?!* Have you listened to yourself? You sound like a child!"

Now I started to get angry, casting quick little glances at her as I drove. "Irina, you don't understand how this game is played."

Her eyes opened and she glared at me. "It's not a game!" she snapped. "That's what you don't get."

"It *is* a game. It's been played in this city for a hundred years. They push; I push back. It's the same with the Irish and the street gangs—"

"But not with us Russians! You don't understand what Mikhail and Vasiliy are *like!* This isn't going to just go back and forth, it's going to escalate! It's *already* escalating: a container full of handbags and shoes—what's that worth, a million dollars? They'll hit back, hard, and then you'll hit back and...."

I had to concentrate on the road, but I kept looking across at her. I was halfway between worried and angry, now: she was really getting worked up.

"It'll be a war," she told me. "A full-on, bloody war. People will *die.*"

I shrugged. "I don't want that," I said. "No one wants that. But what choice do I have?"

"Back down! Give some ground!"

I was so shocked I had to pull over so that I could look at her properly. "What? No! Fuck that!" I forgot to watch my language in front of her. "Vasiliy can fucking back down!"

"He won't! He's just like you!"

I shook my head. "I'm *nothing* like Vasiliy!"

She shook her head in dismay. "Why can't you just give *a little?* Sit down and talk peace?"

I thought of my mom and dad. Shards of glass, swirling in red water....

"No," I said, and I could hear the bitterness in my voice.

She must have heard it too, because her face softened for a second. She leaned a little closer, her eyes begging me to tell her why, but I shook my head. Not that. I didn't share that with anyone, not even her.

She shook her head softly, that silken hair tossing across her shoulders. "This is what I ran away from," she told me slowly. "This is what I can't stand."

I missed the warning signs. My brain was still trying to catch up. Just a few minutes ago, we'd been about to fuck. "I'm not giving up my territory," I snapped.

Too late, I saw the tears in her eyes. "Then you can give up *me*." And suddenly she was opening her door and climbing out.

"Irina!" She didn't stop. "Irina—shit!" I was just about to climb out after her when something slapped against my chest and slid down to land in my lap. The necklace. I sat there staring at it like an idiot for a few seconds. When I came to my senses and jumped out of the car, she was already across the street and getting into a cab.

"Irina!" I ran over to the cab, dodging traffic, and got there just in time to watch it pull away, Irina's tearful face looking back at me through the rear window.

18

IRINA

I *made the right decision.*

I kept repeating it. I went over and over it in my head and I knew that, logically, I'd done the only thing I could. Since the party, I'd glossed over what Angelo was: a gangster. In the car with him, I'd been forced to confront it head on. Of *course* I couldn't be with him. He was everything I'd run away from *and* he was my family's mortal enemy.

So why did breaking up with him feel so wrong? Why did I suddenly feel so cold: not cold and numb, but *painfully* cold. Maybe being alone had always hurt. Maybe I only noticed it now because I'd escaped it for a while.

I wanted to just lie in bed, huddled under the comforter. But it was Saturday and Saturday was the day Vasiliy always dropped round for breakfast. He'd stop off at a Russian bakery and bring a box of *vatrushka*—soft, glossy brown buns filled with cottage cheese and raisins—and brew tea the Russian way, with tea leaves and strawberry jam. We'd play chess, the way we'd used to back in Moscow. It was the one time I saw him without Mikhail and the one time we managed to connect like we used to, a reminder that he was the closest thing I had to a father.

But this morning, it was different. He was *pissed* and I knew why: Angelo. He tried not to let it show, but his whole body was rigid when he hugged me.

And I had to act like I had no idea what the problem was. I talked brightly about Fenbrook and helped him brew the tea and it was only when we sat down at the chess board that he suddenly thumped the table with his fist, sending the pieces jumping across the board.

I let my eyes go big and asked what the matter was. He told me about the docks and how that *bastard* Angelo had stolen their merchandise. "Mikhail should have had more security," Vasiliy grumbled. "This was his project. He's getting sloppy."

I started to put the chess pieces back into their proper positions. "What will you do now?" I asked, careful to keep my voice neutral.

"I'll kill the bastard," Vasiliy said viciously. "No one does this to me!"

I forced my fingers to pick up a knight and gently put it on its square. *You see?* said the logical part of my brain. *This is why you had to split up. This is why it could never have worked.* But it was overwhelmed by the sudden, sick fear that rose up inside me.

I couldn't stand the thought of something happening to him. It didn't matter that he was the enemy: we'd already formed too much of a connection. "Isn't there another way?" I asked. "Can't you make peace?"

Vasiliy almost spat. "*Peace?* The Italians don't want peace. They're too old-fashioned, too hot-blooded. They *want* a war!"

Had he always been like this? I was sure that I remembered him being less brutal, less ruthless when it came to expanding his empire. He'd grown colder and more bitter around the time I started to distance myself from the family, and I couldn't understand why. "Maybe they could change?" I asked in a small voice.

He sighed and shook his head. "Men like us can't change, Irina."

I closed my eyes. If that was true, there was no hope at all. "I just don't want to see people hurt."

His voice softened. "I'll be careful, *kotyonok*." That was his pet name for me when I was a child—*kitten*. "And I'll keep Mikhail and

Yuri and the rest of us safe, too." He smiled as he said it, to reassure me. "Baroni will be the one who pays."

I had to swallow hard—I thought I was going to throw up. "Can't you give a *little* ground? Work something out?"

He sighed, exasperated, and waved a hand at the apartment. "You've been wrapped up in your ballet for too long. This is how it works, how it's always worked. We crush our enemies with strength. We can't show weakness. You used to know that."

I felt as if I was being torn in two. I might try to push them away, to deny I was a Malakov, but they were family...and yet here I was trying to protect our enemy. "Sorry," I said at last, my voice tight.

He put a hand on my cheek. When I looked into his eyes, they were full of sadness. "*I'm* sorry," he said. "I know this isn't the life you would have chosen. But there *is* no choice, here. You're a Malakov, whether you want to be or not, whether you choose to play a role or not. That's why you need someone like Mikhail to protect you."

My stomach twisted. This was my future: to watch this fight escalate into war, see Angelo killed and then marry Mikhail and be drawn right back into the gangster life again.

I jumped up out of my chair and ran.

"Irina?" Vasiliy asked, sounding startled.

"I'm fine. Finish putting the pieces back, I'll be there in a minute." I raced upstairs to my bedroom, blinking back tears. I closed the door and then stood there in the middle of the room, taking deep, shuddering breaths. *Don't cry, don't cry....* I had no way of explaining red eyes to Vasiliy. I had to build up the layers of ice Angelo had broken down. I had to be cold and strong and—

Something small and hard hit the glass doors that lead onto my balcony. I walked over and threw them open, then looked down.

"Hi," said Angelo.

19

IRINA

I couldn't speak. Couldn't think. As soon as I looked into his eyes, all hopes of forgetting him, of moving on, of being a good, loyal Malakov girl, were gone.

"I'm coming up," said Angelo.

That spurred me to action. "What? *No!*" But he'd already jumped and caught the iron bars that form the front of the balcony. His muscles bunched under his suit jacket and he hauled himself up. "*Vasiliy is here!*" I hissed.

He swung himself up over the rail and landed in front of me, lithe and powerful as a panther. *God, he's gorgeous.* "Then you'd better keep quiet," he told me, "and listen to what I have to say."

Wide-eyed, I grabbed the lapels of his coat and hauled him inside before someone saw him, then closed the doors to the balcony. And then we were standing together in my bedroom. Alone. The hard, muscled bulk of him, the *presence* of him...he seemed to fill the room. The last time we'd been there, we'd very nearly had sex. Then the night before, we'd both fantasized about him fucking me, right there on the bed. I could feel myself being drawn to him, the animal heat of him melting through the layers of ice....

No! I broke up with him for a reason. This can't work! But it felt so good just to see him alive.

He took a step towards me. I took a step back, trying to stay out of range of the attraction. "You have to go!" I told him in a harsh whisper. "Vasiliy is downstairs. He wants to kill you for what you did!"

"I'm not scared of Vasiliy."

I knew it was true. He didn't seem to be scared of anyone. "Why did you come here?"

"You know why!" His voice was a low growl that I had to pray didn't carry through the door. "I need you. I want you."

My whole body seemed to sing and throb, a tuning fork responding to that bass voice. "You barely know me!"

"That's bullshit and you know it." He advanced another step, closing the distance between us. "I never met anyone like you before." He put his hand under my chin, lifting it so that I was looking up into those brown and amber eyes. He looked almost angry—angry at me for doing this to him. "You've worked some fucking spell on me, Irina. I can't let you go."

I looked up at him helplessly. I felt the same thing he did, but we *couldn't.* I opened my mouth to try to explain, but I couldn't find the words—

And then suddenly his lips were coming down on mine, his hand lifting my chin so that he could plunder my mouth. I let out a startled *mmf!* And then I was panting up into his mouth as his hands stroked through my hair.

The heat of him poured down into me, driving away the cold. It was like being brought back to life—I hadn't realized how much I needed his touch. My hands came up of their own accord, finding his neck and the hard muscles of his back. I gave myself up to it for long seconds, his tongue dancing with mine, ribbons of pleasure lashing down through my body to make my back arch and my toes dance—

I tore myself away and staggered backward. "*No!*" I told him in a harsh whisper. "*We can't do this!* You're not just a rival, you're our enemy! You're heading into a war against my uncle!"

He put his hands on my shoulders and just that simple touch felt so good I wanted to hurl myself against him again. "You don't have to get involved in it."

"I *am* involved! It's my family!" I stared desperately up into his eyes, trying to find a way to get through to him. I could feel the tension throbbing through his body, his hands like iron on my shoulders. That *intent,* utterly focused, like no one else I'd ever met. Having me was the most important thing in the world to him, I realized, and that made my head spin.

And maybe it was just enough to save him.

"I told you last night," I whispered. "We can't do this unless you make peace. Stop the war before it starts." I swallowed. "Give my uncle what he wants. Give him your territory. No one has to die!"

He shook his head. The pain on his face was as if I'd just shoved a knife deep into his guts. "Jesus, Irina...no. That's the one thing I can't give you." He stepped back from me and a floorboard creaked.

"Irina?" Vasiliy's voice from downstairs. I winced and glanced fearfully at the door. *Chyort!* "*Why?*" I whispered. "It's just...streets and businesses. Territory on a map. I don't understand!"

Angelo lowered his eyes and let out a long sigh. I recognized the look on his face because I'd felt that way many times myself. He was wishing he was someone else, a normal person with a normal life. But then he straightened and looked me in the eye again, his resolve back. "Let me help you understand," he said. He reached up and ran his fingers through my hair, tucking a strand behind my ear. "Come to Little Italy and let me show you."

"Irina?" Vasiliy again. And this time there was a creak: he was coming up the stairs!

"I'll just be a minute!" I yelled. But I knew that wouldn't hold him for long—he already sounded suspicious. "You have to go!" I whispered to Angelo.

To my horror, he shook his head. "Not until you say yes."

I gaped at him...and then heard another creak from the stairs. Vasiliy was nearly there. "*I can't!*" What could he possibly show me there that would change things?

"Irina?" God, Vasiliy was right outside my door! And when I

glanced back at Angelo, his jaw was set—he was ready to fight. I think part of him almost *wanted* Vasiliy to find him.

"*Okay!*" I whispered. "Okay, I'll come. Tomorrow. Now please, *go!*" And I pushed on his chest to get him moving, even though that was like pushing on a brick wall. Then I ran to my door...

...just as Vasiliy opened it. I caught the door when it was a foot open and gave him my best smile. "Hi! Sorry. I'm ready now."

"What's going on?" he asked. "I heard voices."

"Voices? I was on the phone. Rachel called—"

But he wasn't fooled. He stepped forward, pushing open the door and barging me out of the way. I staggered backward and looked in horror at—

Angelo was gone. The doors to the balcony were open, the drapes blowing in the breeze.

I forced my mouth to move. "I needed some air," I said.

Vasiliy strode over to the balcony and stepped onto it, looking around the small, snow-covered yard. I hurried over and stood behind him, looking over his shoulder. There was no one in sight...but Angelo couldn't have moved that fast. Where the hell was he?

Then I glanced down. The walls of my balcony are iron bars but the floor is a solid sheet of black-painted metal. Angelo, I realized, was standing right beneath Vasiliy's feet.

Vasiliy turned to face me, still suspicious. His eyes searched my face for any hint of a lie. But it was one Malakov against another—he'd taught me how to hide my emotions too well.

After a long moment, his face softened. "I'm sorry," he said. "An old man's paranoia." He reached out and lovingly stroked my cheek. "I just worry about you, Irina.

The *guilt*. I hated lying to him...but if he found out about Angelo, he'd kill him. I smiled and led him out of my bedroom, pushing him through the door first and then following behind.

Just as I left the room, I glanced back and looked out of the window. Angelo had come out from under the balcony and stepped back enough that I could see him. Our eyes locked and I felt that deep, irresistible *tug*. *Tomorrow,* he mouthed, watching my reaction.

I nodded. What else could I do? I'd go to Little Italy. I'd see whatever it was he wanted to show me. And then I'd have to break up with him all over again because there was nothing he could show me that was going to change my mind.

But I was wrong. The next day changed everything.

20

IRINA

I'd texted Angelo to tell him where and when I'd arrive. I stepped out of the cab and straight into his arms.

"Someone will recognize me," I said, my voice muffled by his chest.

His big hand smoothed down my back, calming me. "*I* barely recognize you," he murmured in my ear.

I'd tied my hair back in a bun so that there were no loose strands. With the hood of my hooded top raised, you couldn't even see I was blonde. Dark glasses covered my eyes—luckily, it was a bright day and with the sun glinting off the snow, plenty of people had opted for sunglasses so it didn't look completely ridiculous. As long as I didn't open my mouth, no one would have any idea I was Russian.

Even so, being there on Arthur Avenue—the *real* Little Italy, Angelo claimed—felt wrong. The street didn't *look* scary: it was busy despite the cold and the people looked happy, nodding to each other as they hurried between cafes and delis. But to me, this was enemy territory.

The cab pulled away but Angelo kept holding me. His big hands roamed down my back and over my ass. The embrace changed. He drew me harder against him, arms iron-hard against my back, and I felt the outline of his cock through his pants. Then he was kissing me, his tongue slipping into my mouth, and I melted against him, forgetting my fears. When he reluctantly released me, he took hold of my hand and squeezed it tight. "Come on," he said. "Let's walk."

My stomach knotted tight. What was it he wanted to show me? Whatever it was wouldn't solve the problem: we were still on opposite sides. But I fell into step beside him.

First, we passed a cafe. The owner did a double-take as we passed, then ran to the door. "Mr. Baroni!" he called. "Wait!"

We stopped and waited—Angelo relaxed, me nervous. A few seconds later, the cafe owner returned and pressed espresso cups into our hands. "Please," he said.

Angelo knocked his back and I hesitantly did the same. It was rich and perfect with a kick that hit me a beat later, warming me from the inside out, the perfect counter to the icy air. Angelo patted the cafe owner on the shoulder as he took the empty cups and the guy almost bowed.

Seconds later, we passed through an indoor market. Everyone wanted Angelo to try their fruit, or to give him a free scarf to guard against the cold, or to just say hello and tell him how they were doing.

It went on: store after store, street after street. Angelo strode along with his coat billowing out behind him, head high, regal and yet approachable...and *everyone* approached him. Some had questions. Some had concerns. Most just wanted to shake his hand.

These weren't his friends, I slowly realized. These were his subjects. And they worshipped their king. It was awe-inspiring...and weirdly familiar, but I couldn't think where I'd seen something similar.

Then Angelo put his hand on my arm, stopping me. His gaze was focused on the street corner up ahead. I couldn't figure out what he was staring at...then I saw him, a thin guy leaning against a building, hands shoved deep in his pockets. He was furtively scanning the street...looking for customers, I realized.

Then he glanced in our direction, saw Angelo...and went white. Angelo lifted his chin a millimeter, as if to say, *I've seen you.*

The guy broke and ran. And that's when I finally understood. Angelo must have seen the look on my face because he turned to me and leaned down so that he could murmur in my ear. "*Now* do you get it?"

I'd been wrong. It *wasn't* just about streets and businesses, places on a map. It was about people. His people. He helped them, lent them money, protected them from street crime. They needed their king. And he wasn't prepared to abandon them and hand them over to Vasiliy. Not even for me.

I stared up into Angelo's eyes and nodded. I got it.

And that's when I remembered where I'd seen this before. When I was a child, Vasiliy had sometimes taken me, along with his son, Luka, with him when he made his rounds of Moscow. *He'd* had people running up to shake his hand. *He'd* kept the community alive.

Angelo was Vasiliy a decade ago, before he became cold and bitter. I stumbled on along the street, trying to process it all.

A white-haired guy hurried out of a bar as we passed. "Angelo!" he said, grabbing his hand in both of his. "You gotta help me. The Russians are leaning on the liquor merchants. They won't sell to us. I'm running dry."

Angelo glanced at me for a second, then nodded. "I'll look into it," he promised.

The guy clapped him on the shoulder. "God bless you, Angelo." He disappeared back into his bar, but I just stood there staring at the place where he'd stood. Seeing it for myself made all the difference. Angelo had protected these people for years. Vasiliy and Mikhail had suddenly muscled in. Sure, Angelo had pushed back hard, but it was we Russians who were the aggressors. The war, when it happened, would be our fault. The blood would be on our hands.

I'd known Angelo and I were on opposite sides; I'd never considered, until now, that I might be on the wrong one.

And now that I realized it, I felt sick at the implications. Vasiliy and Mikhail wouldn't back down and neither would Angelo. That meant it was up to me.

If I wanted to be with Angelo, I had to stop the war.

21

___

ANGELO

She got it. She knew now why I couldn't back down and let her uncle and his thug of a partner take over. The really scary thing was that there'd been a split second, standing in her bedroom, when I'd *almost* considered it. I'd do almost anything for this woman. The power she had over me was frightening.

"How do we stop this thing?" she asked, her voice quavering.

I hugged her to me, pressing her small body against my big one and wrapping my arms around her to keep her warm. "I don't know," I said. "I don't think Vasiliy and Mikhail will stand for anything other than victory. They want this turf."

"I'll talk to Vasiliy," she said firmly. "I'll try and make him see sense."

God, she was brave. I took off her sunglasses so I could see her face. "You need to be careful. *Really* fucking careful. If he suspects we're together...." I slid my hand across her cheek. She was cold, as always. I put my other hand on her other cheek, desperate to warm her. I wasn't ready for the upswell of emotion in my chest. "I don't want anything to happen to you."

She put her hands on my hands. "I've gotten good at lying," she said, a trace of bitterness in her voice. She shook her head. "You know, Vasiliy didn't used to be like this. He was ambitious but not like *this.* He used to be like you."

Like *me?* I felt my chest tighten. *Crazy.* But I nodded.

"You need to help too," she said. "Do what you can to calm this thing down."

I sighed. And right after I'd told The Saints that I'd come down hard on the Russians. But...I looked deep into those cornflower-blue eyes and *dammit,* I couldn't deny her, even if the thought of playing nice with the Russians made me die inside. "Okay," I said at last. "I'll do what I can."

"And what about...us?" she asked quietly.

I pushed her back just far enough that I could kiss her. God, those lips tasted sweet. There was something in her soul that was clean and bright and untarnished—everything I wasn't. Kissing her was like diving into a cool mountain lake and washing away my sins...and then slipping beneath the surface into the heated, tempting depths. Within seconds, I'd lost control, pushing her back against the wall and pinning her there with my body. My hands grabbed hers, our fingers intertwining. The kiss turned open-mouthed and panting and I started to calculate how many blocks we were from my apartment.

My phone rang. *Fuck!*

I reluctantly released her and fished out my phone. Rico. I put my finger to my lips and answered. "Yeah?"

"We got a problem." He sounded worried. No, not just worried: *upset.* And it took a lot to shake Rico.

"Hold on." I covered the microphone. "I'm sorry," I said. "I gotta work. When can I see you?"

She had to think about it, which didn't bode well. "The day after tomorrow," she said at last.

What?! I was sick of these delays. I needed her naked in my bed, *now!* I'd never had to wait around like this for a woman before. But....

But for Irina, I'd wait. "Okay," I said between gritted teeth, and gave her one last kiss. Then I stepped out into the street and waved for a cab for her. When the cabbies saw who it was, they couldn't drive over fast enough.

I opened the door for her and slammed it when she was inside. Then I took the necklace from my pocket, leaned through the window and held it against her neck. Irina looked down at it, looked up into my eyes...and nodded. I fastened the clasp and smoothed the necklace against her skin...God, her skin was so soft! I gave her one last kiss and reluctantly pulled back through the window. Then I watched the cab pull away, putting the phone back to my ear only when it was halfway down the street.

This whole thing is going to be impossible, I thought. But she was worth it.

I finally uncovered the microphone and put the phone back to my ear. "Sorry," I said to Rico. "Why don't you come find me? I'm on the corner of King Street and Arthur Avenue."

"I know," said Rico's voice from behind me. "So am I."

I spun around and there he was, close enough to touch, the phone still held to his ear. He must have been walking the streets when he called me, and he'd happened across me while I was saying goodbye to Irina.

One look at his face and I knew: he'd seen me kiss her.

22

ANGELO

Rico's a big guy and, when he's riled, he barely knows his own strength. He hauled me off the street and slammed me up against the wall of an alley hard enough to whump the air out of me. "Irina Malakov?" he demanded. "Irina *fucking Malakov?!*" His hands were twisted into the front of my shirt, pulling it tight around my body as he lifted me. My feet were only barely brushing the ground. "What the fuck is the matter with you?"

I tried to pull loose. "Get the fuck off me!"

But he didn't let go. "Tell me it's a plan," he growled. "Please, Angelo, tell me it's some fucking clever plan. You're banging her to get to Vasiliy, right? She's gonna tell you all his secrets!"

"No!" I tried again to break his grip, and failed. Then I hit him with a good punch to the kidneys that would have doubled up any other man. But this was Rico, and he didn't even seem to notice. "It's not like that!"

He released me. It was so sudden that my legs buckled under me as I hit the ground and I staggered, trying to regain my balance. I glared at him, but his anger had gone...to be replaced by fear. He'd seen something in my expression, something that terrified him.

"Is it a sex thing?" he asked. "Is it about fucking over Vasiliy by fucking his niece, like revenge?"

"No! Jesus! I haven't even slept with her yet!"

Now Rico looked *really* scared. He ran a hand through his hair. "You haven't even—Oh, shit. You *like* her. You've fucking fallen for her."

I opened my mouth to snap at him, to tell him not to be so fucking stupid, but the words wouldn't come. I looked away, unable to meet his eyes.

"Oh, shit. Oh, Angelo, what the fuck am I going to do with you?"

I straightened my shirt. "You can't tell anyone."

"*Tell* anyone? Who the fuck am I going to tell? The Saints? They'd crucify you for this. You'd be *gone*. The guys? Who's going to listen to you, if they find out you're secretly banging *her*?" He took a deep breath and shook his head. "No, I'm not going to tell anyone. But you gotta end this. *Now!*"

I thought about lying and saying I would, but I'd already lied to him for too long. I shook my head.

"Angelo, what's going to happen when Vasiliy finds out you're banging his pride and joy? *Jesus Christ,* you're going to bring the whole Russian mob down on us! There'll be *war!*"

"We're heading for war anyway," I muttered.

"Oh, so you thought you'd just help things along?"

"*I didn't mean for it happen!*" My voice lashed out like a whip. I stood there for a second glaring at him, but the anger faded when I saw the hurt and confusion in his eyes. I sighed and tried to soften my gaze a little.

"You should have told me," he said.

"I didn't *know*. Not at first." I took a deep breath. "But...yeah, I should have." And then I had to struggle with it, a word I hardly ever used. "Sorry."

Rico gave a long sigh and nodded.

"You still got my back, right?"

He gave me a look. "You really gotta ask that?" He took two quick steps over to me and pulled me into a hug. It was like being crushed by a grizzly bear, but I felt better.

"So what did you call me about, anyway?" I asked when we stepped back.

Rico shook his head grimly. "It's Cinderella's," he said. "It's bad."

Cinderella's has been around for over a decade. A big old house out in Westchester with electric gates and high hedgerows for privacy, a parking lot around the back and discreet security guards. It could be a spa or perhaps an exclusive rehab clinic.

What it actually is, is a brothel. The kind where the women work in rooms plusher than any hotel, the clients are screened and the cops turn a blind eye—mostly because the Chief of Police has his own favorite girl there. The women are happy, they make a lot of money and there's very, very rarely any trouble.

Until today.

Normally, Grace, the madam, would greet me with a smile on her face and my favorite drink in her hand. This was anything but normal. She was waiting for us on the porch when we pulled up, her arms hugging herself against the cold. I'd never seen her look so shaken. "She's upstairs," she told us. "In my room. I don't want the other girls or the guests to see her."

Icy fear sluiced through my veins. I shoved open the door and led the way to the stairs.

Inside, Cinderella's is done out like a turn-of-the-century merchant's house, with lots of dark wood paneling, velvet drapes and chandeliers. There's always soft music playing and wherever you go you can hear the soft sound of female laughter. Every woman looks stunning and they walk around not in lingerie, but in sexy, tasteful gowns that cost a thousand dollars apiece. It's just about the most relaxing place a man can be. But today I hurried past the grinning guys in suits and the girls smiling and flirting with them. I needed to know, *now*.

I burst into Grace's room and saw Kirsty. And tried to control my face.

Grace and Rico trooped in behind me and closed the door. Rico cursed under his breath.

I said nothing for several seconds. Then I knelt down beside Kirsty's chair and gingerly hugged her, not wanting to cause her any more pain. After a long moment, I looked over my shoulder at Grace, my arms still wrapped around Kirsty. "Who did this?" I asked. My voice was quiet but my whole body shook with anger. "Is he still here?"

Grace shook her head.

"Why did you let him leave?!" *I am going to kill him. I am going to beat him until he's a hair's breadth from dying and then I'm going to lock the fucker in the trunk of a car and drive it into the Hudson River and drown him.*

"It didn't happen here," said Grace. "Kirsty was on an outcall. A hotel."

We don't let the girls do outcalls for precisely this reason.

Kirsty shook her head. "I'm sorry," she said. As if somehow, this was *her* fault. "I know we're not supposed to." Her voice was an agonized rasp that made my hands tighten into fists behind her back. "But he called me and said he'd give me two thousand for a few hours. He sounded okay...."

I gently released her and moved back a little. I had to look at her face, now. I couldn't avoid it any longer, not without upsetting her.

Both her eyes were swollen shut and both cheeks were bruised and bloody. There were sharp, square marks that I couldn't figure out, at first. Then my stomach lurched—they were the indentations left by the guy's rings. There were red finger marks around her throat, too —the guy must have had big hands because they wrapped almost completely around. There was a darker red mark there, too, a serpent, as if one of his rings had it carved on the inside.

She swallowed with difficulty. "It's worse lower down," she said, nodding to her robe. "He used his belt on me. And before that, he...*did* stuff to me. Stuff I don't do."

She'd been under my protection and I'd failed her. I was only barely managing to hold my anger in check. It was boiling up inside me, filling me with the need to smash, to punch, to kill. I glanced across at Rico and it was like looking into a mirror. He gave me the nod, ready to do whatever I needed him to. But this one I'd take care of myself.

I had to take a deep breath and smooth down the lapels of my suit —that calmed me enough to pull out my phone and take a couple of photos of Kirsty's face and neck. When I found the bastard, I'd shove them in his face just before I killed him, so that he knew *why*. "Who was he?" I asked.

Kirsty tried to speak but started to cough instead. Blood from her split lip dusted my shirt. "Big guy. Rich. Called himself *Simon* but I don't think that was real. He didn't say much." Her voice quavered. "He started on me as soon as I got in the room."

I looked at Grace. "Get her the best," I said. "The *very* best: doctors, plastic surgeon if she needs it. I'll pay. Be firm with the girls —no more outcalls."

Grace nodded. "Got it."

"And get the girls to talk to their friends, the ones who don't work here. They have chat rooms and forums and shit where they talk about clients. Get the word out. Let them know this guy is dangerous. And let them know I want him found. Twenty-five thousand dollars to the first person who gives us a name."

Grace nodded gratefully. "Thanks, Angelo."

"I want to be the one to do him," said Rico quietly. His face was like thunder. I couldn't remember ever seeing him so upset. "When we get a name, I'll take care of it."

I put a hand on his shoulder. "When we get a name," I told him, "you and me will do the bastard together."

23

IRINA

I pounded up the stairs and burst out onto the roof of Fenbrook Academy, my ballet slippers sliding precariously in the snow. The freezing wind whipped around me, but I welcomed it. The cold was calming, the icy air letting me breathe properly for the first time in hours.

I'd run up here the second my lesson ended, unable to take the mirrored room anymore. Every time I saw my reflection, I thought: *traitor!*

It had been two days since I'd seen Angelo. Two days of going quietly nuts, trying to figure out if I was doing the right thing. My decision to help him had changed everything. Now, instead of shying away from Vasiliy and trying to block out his conversations about crime, I listened carefully. That made Vasiliy happy, because he thought I was finally taking an interest in the family business. And that in turn made me feel even worse about betraying him.

It wasn't the worst part, though. The worst part was Mikhail. If I was to have a hope of stopping the war, I needed to be close to him—both to learn his secrets so that I could warn Angelo of danger and to try to convince him to change course. But that meant I couldn't keep pushing him away.

To save the man I was really starting to care about, I had to get friendly with the man I detested.

I'd started to smile at him, and to force myself not to pull away quite so quickly when his hands wandered. It seemed to be working but I wasn't sure how long I could keep it up. The thought of having lunch with him today was what had tipped me over the edge into panic and sent me running up to the roof. I knew that, as soon as he saw me smiling at Mikhail, Vasiliy would grin dotingly at us and comment on how well we were getting along, while I tried not to throw up. To protect Angelo, I was drifting dangerously close to the forced marriage I'd been trying so hard to run from.

So far, I hadn't learned much of value and all my attempts to try to talk peace with either of them had been ignored. *The Italians will never talk peace,* they kept saying. *We cannot show weakness.* And throughout it all, I had no clue whether I was doing the right thing. What's *right* when everyone's a criminal? Is it okay to betray your family for the right reasons or is blood sacred, as Vasiliy had always taught me? I couldn't sleep, could barely eat. There was no one I could talk to, no one who would understand—

Except....

I pulled out my phone and stared at a name in my contacts list. I stood there for almost a minute before I finally dialed.

"Hello?" said Arianna.

Arianna is an American who used to work for the CIA. She was sent by them to seduce Luka and learn his secrets. Instead, she fell for him and turned on her masters. She and Luka are inseparable, now, and she's even become close to Vasiliy. I figured that, if anyone could understand what I was going through, it was her.

"Irina?" She could tell from my silence that something was wrong. "Is everything okay?"

"I need to talk to you," I said slowly. "But this is something you can't tell anyone about. Not even Luka."

Now *she* went quiet. After all the lies she'd told Luka when she was CIA, the two of them had had to learn to trust each other. The last thing she needed was to start keeping secrets again. I knew I was putting her in an awful position and I felt shitty about it. But if I didn't talk to someone, I was going to lose it completely.

"Okay," she said at last. "Go."

I took a deep breath and told her everything. I told her about meeting Angelo and then finding out who he was. I told her about how the two sides were spinning towards war and my efforts to stop it. I told her about the lies I'd already told and the lies I'd have to tell. When I'd finished, she let out a long breath. *"Jesus, Irina...."*

I was almost in tears. "Well?" I demanded. "What do I do? What *should* I have done? Am I....evil?"

She was silent for a long time. Then she said, "You haven't told me everything."

"I have! That's everything!" I'd glossed over the details of the filthy phone call, but otherwise—

"You haven't told me how you feel about him."

That stopped me cold. And suddenly, I was struggling to get the words out. I'd had no problem admitting my sins but as soon as it came to my feelings...as a Malakov, I'd spent years keeping those trapped beneath the ice. Sometimes, I didn't even admit them to myself.

"He makes me feel..." I started. And suddenly, as I gingerly opened a path through the ice, it all came flooding out. "He makes me feel like no one else does," I said. "I know he's not a *good* man, I know he's a gangster but...he tries to do right. He protects people. He has honor. He touches me and I melt. I look at him and I feel this *pull....* It hurts when I'm not near him. And when he looks at me, it's like there's no other women in the world."

"That's how I felt about Luka," Arianna whispered. "I still do."

"So you think I'm doing the right thing?"

When she didn't answer straight away, I felt sick. I tried to imagine what it must have been like for her: thousands of miles from home, in a strange city, surrounded by people who'd kill her if they found out who she really was. She'd had every reason to change sides. "I guess at least it wasn't your family you were betraying," I said bitterly.

"It kind of was," Arianna said. "The CIA *was* my family, or as close as I had left." She sighed. "Look...are you doing the right thing? I honestly have no idea. I know how Vasiliy feels about loyalty. Luka, too. If they find out about this, it'll destroy them."

I closed my eyes, feeling them growing hot.

"But you're trying to stop a gang war that's going to get people killed...and I think you're right, Angelo probably has more in common with Vasiliy than either of them will admit. If I was in your shoes...I'd probably do the same. That's the best I can give you."

It wasn't much, but it helped. "Thanks, Arianna."

"Doesn't feel like I've helped much. What are you going to *do?*"

I thought of Mikhail and my flesh crawled as I imagined cozying up to him. But if it helped to protect Angelo.... "What I have to," I said firmly.

"Irina...even if you and he pull this off and there's some sort of peace between the Italians and the Russians...Vasiliy isn't going to let you run off with their leader. If you want a future with Angelo, you might have to abandon the family completely."

Run away together. For a second, it almost sounded tempting. But then I thought of never seeing Vasiliy or Luka or my sister, Lizaveta, again. Plus, even if I was prepared to do that, Angelo would never, ever agree to leave. A king doesn't run away from his kingdom. "One problem at a time," I said weakly.

"Agreed," said Arianna. "Keep me posted. And Irina?"

"Yes?"

"Be careful."

~

The restaurant was a big, airy place with crisp white tablecloths and a view over Central Park. The prices were eye-watering which was probably why Mikhail liked it—it was all about showing off, to him. Yuri met me at the door and showed me to our table, then returned to his position against the wall, where he could keep the entire restaurant under his watchful gaze.

Vasiliy and Mikhail were sitting on adjoining sides of the square table. Just a week before, I'd have instinctively sat down opposite Mikhail, so that he couldn't possibly touch me. We'd have faced each other like opponents, with Vasiliy trying to keep the peace between us.

Now, I sat down opposite Vasiliy, which put me right next to Mikhail. The table was small and my knee bumped his as I sat. He smirked. And Vasiliy smiled to see me so friendly.

I looked at the menu. Mikhail's knee discreetly rubbed mine beneath the tablecloth. I steeled myself and ignored it. Meanwhile, Vasiliy and Mikhail continued the conversation they'd been having.

"You need to take more care," said Vasiliy. "Show your face less. It doesn't need to be you who does these jobs." He sighed and looked to me for support. "Mikhail has been going along with his men to intimidate the Italians. Persuading suppliers to stop selling to their businesses. Threatening the bookkeepers into shutting down." He shook his head. "He should not be getting his hands dirty like this. It attracts too much attention from the police."

I gave Mikhail my best smile. "Vasiliy's right," I said obediently. "Those things are beneath you." Inside, I was thinking: *nothing is beneath you.* He wasn't a true leader, like Luka, Vasiliy or Angelo. He was just a thug who'd risen to power.

Mikhail preened under my attention. "I just want to make sure it's done right."

I knew the real reason: he enjoyed it. He enjoyed terrifying people and hurting them, instead of considering it a last resort. The thought of spending my life with this man made me die inside, but I had to smile sweetly and nod as if he was right and I was just a silly girl who didn't know any better.

Vasiliy's phone rang. He checked the screen and then cursed. "I have to take this," he said. He looked around at the other diners, then got up and headed towards the restrooms. Yuri followed discreetly behind, never letting his charge out of his sight.

As soon as they were gone, Mikhail pushed his chair back from the table and patted his lap. "Come," he told me. "Sit."

My eyes widened. Sit on his lap? Here, in the middle of an upmarket restaurant? Mikhail was almost twice my age. Not only did the idea repulse me, but people would think I was an escort.

For Angelo. I smiled at him, got up and sat gingerly down on his knee, balancing on the very edge.

"I'm glad I'm getting to know you better," said Mikhail in my ear. "When you're with me, I can take you to nice places like this all the time." He suddenly fingered my necklace—the one Angelo had given me. "You like nice things, don't you, Irina?"

I went cold inside. Did he somehow know? "Yes," I said with a calm I didn't feel.

His other arm wrapped around my waist. I was suddenly jerked back against his soft gut, and my legs fell either side of his thick thighs. I was wearing jeans, but that didn't stop it from being an uncomfortably sexual position. "Don't worry," he said, nodding to Vasiliy's empty chair. "He won't be around to interfere forever. Once we've got rid of these fucking Italians, he'll go back to Moscow and it'll be just you and me."

I felt his cock under my ass as he shifted position. My stomach lurched, but I forced my voice to be neutral. "That might take months, though. The Italians have lots of friends here, lots of allies."

Mikhail gave a nasty laugh. "We're stealing them, one by one. First the suits, like that property developer. Now the gangs." He was eager as a child to tell me his plans. "The Italians have a monthly meet with a biker gang: cash for guns. When they meet them tonight, they're going to find out that the friendship's over."

I froze in his lap. Tonight? I had to warn Angelo!

"And we'll have guys there as well, to finish the job."

My heart sank. If I didn't warn Angelo, he or his men would be killed. If I did warn them, Vasiliy's men would be killed. *Chyort!*

Then, to my horror, I felt his cock hardening under my ass. I wasn't sure if it was having me in his lap or the thought of violence that was turning him on. I instinctively tried to rise.

His arm tightened around my waist, holding me in place, and he gave a chuckle, as if he liked it when I fought him. For all his fat, he was still a strong man and he could easily overpower me. I had a sudden, sickening vision of what being married to him would be like. Crushed beneath his weight as he—

"Having fun?" Vasiliy was standing next to us. The expression on his face was uncertain: half *get your hands off my niece* and half *look at the young lovebirds.* Yuri, meanwhile, had come to high alert, his expression carefully neutral, but his whole body primed and ready to strike. He's always been very protective of me.

Mikhail grinned and released his arm. I got up as if nothing was wrong, but something must have shown in my expression because Vasiliy gave me a quizzical look. *Say something,* a voice inside me screamed. All I had to do was tell him about the groping and he'd go nuts. Yuri would snap Mikhail's arms like twigs. Vasiliy would forbid Mikhail from ever coming near me again—marriage would be off the table.

And my best source of information would be gone.

I gave Vasiliy my best smile. "Let's eat," I said.

24

ANGELO

I'd never been anywhere like it.

I'm not what you'd call the sensitive type. I sure as hell never thought I'd stand somewhere and say it's *magical* like some dewy-eyed teenage girl. But standing there in the lobby of Fenbrook Academy with the setting sun pouring through the window and lighting up drifting motes of dust, even I felt *something*.

They say places have a scent. If you go to the White House, supposedly that smells like power. Fenbrook Academy smelled like hope. Thousands of kids had come here, getting off the bus from their little towns in Nebraska or Minnesota, their entire lives up to that point packed into a battered suitcase, their entire futures resting on the guitar slung on their back or their treasured pair of ballet shoes.

I could see why Irina had traveled all the way to America to go here. It felt like a place where anything could happen. It practically made *me* want to pick up a guitar.

I shook my head and jogged up the stairs. *I'm going soft.* Before I met Irina, I wouldn't have even thought about that shit.

I prowled the empty halls looking for her, moving faster and faster. I was desperate to see her again. She was the one thing in my life that wasn't turning to shit.

The Russians were still eating away at my territory, shaking down bars and restaurants for protection money. I had Rico paying each place a visit, reassuring the owners that they were under Baroni protection and always would be, but people were *scared.* And the illegal businesses were suffering too: three different bookies had been smashed up by Russians with baseball bats, often with Mikhail himself doing most of the smashing.

Now they were going after my partners. This morning, it had been a ring of car thieves we used to steal high-end rides—they'd suddenly decided they'd be better off taking Russian money instead of ours. I'd had to swing by their garage and sweet talk them into coming back. And I had a feeling worse was to come.

I wanted revenge. I wanted to unleash an army of enforcers and goddamn hitmen and show the Russians what happened when they messed with Angelo Baroni. But once bodies started hitting the floor, the war would start and there'd be no stopping it. *I promised Irina....*

And now, on top of the Russian problem, some psycho had hurt one of my escorts. I'd had no luck tracking Kirsty's attacker down, even with the twenty-five grand reward. Either he was good at hiding or other girls had had run-ins with him in the past and they were too scared to talk. My hands tightened into fists. *When I get my hands on that son-of-a-bitch....*

The anger made me move faster. I wanted Irina and the sweet relief she would bring. Soon, I was stalking down the hallway, crashing through each set of double doors as I came to them, glancing into each practice room as I passed and grunting in disapproval as I found them empty. *Where the hell was she?* I needed to feel that silken hair against my fingers, needed to pick her up and press that sweet body against mine—

I rounded the corner and slammed straight into someone coming the other way. I got a brief glimpse of a leather jacket and long, dark hair and then she was rebounding off me. I was so much bigger than her and traveling with so much more momentum that I pretty much just came to a stop, while she went flying backwards and skidded on her ass on the linoleum.

"*Asshole!*" spat Rachel. She lay there glaring up at me for a second.

I started forward and offered her my hand, but she waved it away. She rolled back on her shoulders, long legs flexing under her jeans, and then sprang up onto her feet like a bad-tempered ninja. "You're the one from the park. The one dating Irina. Angelo, right?"

I wasn't sure how much Irina had told her. "Right. Sorry."

She narrowed her eyes and moved closer. "Irina said you were a banker. You don't look like a banker. You dress like a banker, but you don't look like one."

"You meet a lot of bankers?" I leaned in a little, looming over her. That usually scares people into shutting up.

But it didn't work with her. Her eyes had gotten big: she was afraid, but something stronger was winning out. She reminded me of someone, but I couldn't think who. "You don't *sound* like a banker, either," she said.

She had me there. I still talked like a blue-collar kid from Brooklyn. Couldn't change it and wouldn't want to if I could.

She tilted her head to one side. "You know who you *do* remind me of? Those guys that come around to our house to see Irina. Her uncle and his friend."

Why did people keep comparing me to them? "I'm not Russian."

"Yeah. Thanks. I figured that out. But what are you?" She crossed her arms. "What do you really do, Angelo?"

I suddenly realized who she reminded me of: Rico. That same iron-hard loyalty. I'd never seen it in women before. Either I never met a woman's friends because it was a one night stand, or their "friends" were back-biting bitches competing for my attention. With Irina and Rachel, it was different. I straightened up and tried not to *loom* so much. "I'm not going to hurt her," I said in a softer tone.

"You're goddamn straight, you're not," said Rachel. A lock of dark hair had fallen over her face and she blew it out of the way. She stared at me for another few seconds, arms still crossed, and then said, "She really likes you. Irina doesn't do *happy*. She's too freakin'

Russian. But I can tell when she's thinking about you because she smiles. She deserves to smile more."

I nodded.

Rachel leaned in close. "I heard the two of you on the phone. Well, *her* end of it. Anyone who makes a girl make those noises can't be all bad."

Our eyes locked. Damn, she was fiery *and* sexy as hell. I only had eyes for Irina, but some guy was going to need a reinforced bed.

"I don't care who you are," Rachel told me. "Break her heart and I'll kick your ass."

Before I could answer, she was off down the hallway. "She's in the last room on your right," she called over her shoulder.

I didn't need telling twice. I raced to the end of the hallway, grabbed the door handle...and stopped.

Irina was alone in the huge, wood-floored dance studio, balanced on one leg with her arms overhead. She was facing the windows and the setting sun painted the front of her body with reds and oranges: her platinum-blonde hair gleamed like liquid copper, her white leotard turned to polished brass. Her back was icy perfection, the Lycra stretched tight over the sensuous arch of her spine and the firm curves of her ass. My ice maiden, half consumed by fire.

I was desperate to get in there. I needed to kiss her, touch her, fuck her...but she was so perfect, standing balanced there, that interrupting her would have been like taking a sledgehammer to a priceless statue. If someone had told me, a week before, that I'd stand there and watch a woman instead of muscling straight in there, I'd have called them crazy. But then I'd never met anyone like Irina.

She slowly came out of the pose, her arms and legs descending as gracefully as ribbons drifting on the breeze. She turned and our eyes met.

Enough goddamn watching.

I threw open the door and strode across the room. I had her face between my palms before she could speak, my lips spreading her open so that I could plunge deep and—*Jesus!* Kissing her felt so good, all my anger and frustration evaporating in an instant. I didn't care about the Russians or territory or anything else. I just wanted to keep feeling those silk-soft lips against mine. The very tip of her quick, pink tongue brushed mine and I felt it all the way down to my toes.

I needed this woman. I wanted to fall into this woman and never surface. She bathed away my sins, freed me of my troubles. And all the time, the lust that had been building in me for days was burning hotter and hotter, demanding that I melt away all that icy self-control and make her scream my name.

I laid my hands on the back of her head, just under the tight bun of hair, and drew them very slowly down her neck. I broke the kiss because I wanted to hear the noise she made. At first, it was a slow pant, her mouth open and her eyes still closed. My hands reached the backs of her shoulders, strong fingers pressing firmly into her aching muscles, and it turned into a groan.

My hands carried on down, following the arch of her spine, and reached the gorgeous, upthrust curve at the top of her rump and she held her breath, biting her lip in a way that made my cock surge. I held her like that for a second...and then my hands were on her ass, squeezing hard, working the firm flesh with my fingers, and she moaned. That did it. I had to kiss her again so I covered her lips with mine, absorbing her cries as I pulled her groin tight against mine and let her feel how hard she'd made me.

When we broke the kiss again, both of us were hazy-eyed, almost drunk with it. I'd never wanted a woman so goddamn much. And I'd never wanted it like this, wanted *her* as well as her body.

This wasn't just about sex anymore. And that was going to make the sex even better.

"Where do we go?" I muttered. I had to keep my voice low because my face was so close to hers and I couldn't bear to move back.

She writhed against me. She knew what I meant: not *my place or yours, but here in the building.* Neither of us could wait.

"There's a store cupboard," she gasped, her eyes heavy-lidded. "Where they store all the old musical instruments. But it's full of spiders." Then she blinked and gave me one of those icy, imperious glares I loved so much. "*Which I'm not scared of.*"

I felt myself grin. "Uh-huh." I loved that she had a fear. She was normally so tough. "How about here?" I looked around the room: big and airy and not at all dark or private. But the building was pretty much empty.

She glanced at the door. "Someone might come in."

"Someone *might* come in," I agreed.

I watched her carefully as she thought about it, loving the battle between her fears and her lust. She kept looking from the door to me, her eyes focused on my chest. And then, suddenly, she said, "*Kakogo chyorta.*"

"What does that mean?"

"It means *the hell with it,*" she said. And pressed herself hard against me, her head tilting up for my kiss.

25

IRINA

I heard him growl deep in his throat and then his whole body was pressed to mine from shoulder to thighs, the heat of him throbbing into me. His lips were savage but they teased as much as they demanded—they'd ravish me hard and then pull back just a little, making me rise up en pointe to keep contact. Every time he did it, I felt him smile against my lips: he wanted me to be active, wanted a partner, not a passive doll. He was so different to the Russians Vasiliy had tried to pair me with in the past. Oh, they'd *say* that they wanted a woman to enjoy sex, but to them that meant she smiled before sucking their cock. If you actually showed what you wanted, they made you feel like a freak.

Not Angelo. Sex with him was like a dance and, as new partners, we were feeling each other out. His hands slid down my back, cupping my ass through the Lycra, and I could feel his chest swell against me as he drew in a breath, reveling in the feel of me. That sent a deep, hot twist of pleasure straight down to my groin—no one had ever touched me with such obvious bliss. I could feel him noting my responses, using my moans to guide him in exactly how I liked to be handled.

His hands explored my whole body through my leotard, the

material thin enough that the warmth of his hands soaked straight through to my skin as he palmed my breasts and made slow circles over them. I moved in rhythm with him, feeling my nipples harden, pressing my breasts wantonly to him and groaning to let him know when he was going at just the right speed.

He moved his head beside mine, laying a string of tiny kisses down my ear before he spoke. "I'm taking that thing off you, now."

I glanced at the door and tried to figure out how much time we had before the janitor made his rounds. But then he kissed down the length of my throat and every touch of his lips sent a pulse of heat expanding out across my skin, merging and multiplying like ripples on a pond, until I was squirming and panting, eyes closed and hands grabbing at his shoulders for support.

His hands followed behind his lips, smoothing down the length of my bare neck and throat. There's no feeling in the world like being caressed by a really big, strong set of hands that you trust to never, ever hurt you. His thumbs traced my collarbones and then, without hesitation, his fingers hooked under the shoulder straps of my leotard...and hooked them down and off. I caught my breath as my shoulders were bared. Even that tiny bit of nudity felt scandalous in the huge, light room.

But before I could get too nervous, his lips came down on my bare shoulder, kissing it gently and then working inward to my throat. I didn't protest—I forgot *how* to protest. He started to peel the leotard lower, rolling it down over itself. I could hear his breathing quicken as the upper slopes of my breasts were revealed, the Lycra stretching tighter and tighter as it neared their peaks. He must have realized, by now, that I wasn't wearing a separate bra.

Something else was happening, too: as he rolled the fabric down, the shoulder straps were trapping my arms against my body. Already, my hands had had to slide from Angelo's shoulders to his hips. Soon, my arms would be pinned and I'd be helpless. The idea only added to the building heat.

I could feel him looking at me. I opened my eyes, heavy-lidded and slow, and saw him staring with wonder at my chest—I'd never seen a more intense look of lust. His powerful hands rolled the fabric lower, lower...and with a sudden rush, my breasts spilled free, the skin throbbing in the chill air.

"Jesus," he breathed. "You're fucking perfect. I've been trying to guess how you'd look but...you're even better."

My chest went tight. "Thank you," I breathed.

He hooked the leotard an inch lower, so my breasts were completely free, and leaned in close. I felt his hot breath on me an instant before his tongue bathed my nipple—*God!* I'd been dreaming of that mouth on me, imagining what that hard upper lip and the soft, sensuous lower would feel like on my body, but my fantasies hadn't come close.

I let out a high little cry of need and that seemed to set him off. He grabbed me by the upper arms and tugged me against him, opening his mouth wide so that he could lick and suck as much of me as possible, not just the stiffening nipple and areola but the soft skin around it. He started gently and grew rougher, spurred on by my moans. He covered his teeth with his lips and gave me soft little bites that made me shudder and gasp. He twisted his tongue around the base of each nipple and spiraled upward to the tip. When his mouth wasn't enough, he used one hand to work my shining breast and moved his lips to the other.

I wanted to grab at him, to undress him, but by now the shoulder straps of the leotard were down around my elbows, trapping my arms to my sides. I clutched at his ass instead, delighting at the hardness of him. Then he was rolling the leotard lower and lower, eager to reveal all of me, lips working their way down my stomach and over the dark hollow of my navel, down towards my pelvis—

I was wearing thong panties under the leotard. Both of us looked down as he reached the waistband—would he leave them on or—

No. He rolled them down my body along with the leotard. I felt the kiss of cool air against the sensitive skin of my pubis, then through my curls of soft hair. Then my leotard and panties fell to the floor and I stood there naked and panting in the very center of the room.

For a second, he just looked at me, his eyes raking from my face to my toes in long, slow sweeps. Then his hands started to smooth over my body and I saw him look off to the side. When I followed his gaze, I gasped.

We were reflected in the mirrored wall. A dancer, naked save for her ballet shoes, her body utterly exposed, even her hair pinned up out of the way to leave her throat bare. Before her, her lover, his muscled body obvious even through his suit, his strong chest rising and falling as his hands swept over her.

I couldn't take it anymore. I had to see the body I'd been imagining.

My hands grabbed for the soft silk of his tie, suddenly frantic. He gazed down at me, brown eyes tiger-bright, as I loosened the knot and pulled it free. I leaned forward to push his suit jacket back over his shoulders and my naked breasts grazed his chest, making both of us gasp.

The jacket slid down his arms, hitting the polished floor with a soft kiss of expensive fabric. His arms...I couldn't stop looking at his arms. Men try to show off their muscles in t-shirts and tank tops but Angelo's sculpted form was perfectly, effortlessly displayed by soft, touchable cotton that flowed over every hard line. I couldn't stop myself: my hands went to his neck and then traced their way down. His shoulders were so wide, like he'd batter a hundred men out of the way to get to you. His biceps stretched out the thin white fabric, solid and warm under my fingers. His forearms, as my fingertips trailed down them, were thickly hard and ridged with veins—

I looked up into his eyes. We were breathing in sync, both of us staring at the other as if they blamed *them* for being so out of control. Then his hands were on my ass, pulling me hard to him, and he kissed me long and deep as my fingers started to work at the buttons of his shirt. I had my eyes closed as I pushed each tiny, hard disc through its hole. I had to imagine what I was revealing as his shirt opened up, visions of dark ink and tan skin exploding in my mind as his tongue danced with mine.

I undid the last button and tugged the tails of his shirt out of his pants. I had to *see!* I broke the kiss and stepped back—

And gasped.

I'd stroked my fingers over his stomach enough times that I knew the hardness there, knew each defined rise and fall of his six pack. But I wasn't ready for how the sun lit up his tan skin like gold, or the raw power that his abs suggested, the way they made me think of him *lunging* and *thrusting* and *pounding....*

I'd slid my palms across his chest, felt those big, smooth slabs of muscle that made him so *solid...*but I wasn't ready for the size of him, for how his chest filled my vision, dwarfing me, or how those dark pink nipples made me want to lick him there and make him groan.

What I really wasn't ready for, though, was the tattoo.

I'd thought it was more than one, since the shadows beneath his shirt seemed to cover him so completely. I'd imagined a confusion of women's names and symbols. What I got instead was just one thing, simple and beautiful and brutal.

A pair of angel wings, joined by a cross, had been meticulously picked out across his chest, filling both of those broadly curving pecs. Every feather was a work of art: the wings seemed to live and move as he breathed, the cross staying still and unshakeable between them. Standing there in the sunlight, the rays streaming through his outstretched shirt, he looked almost otherworldly, an angel sent from heaven or hell: I wasn't sure which. He seemed to glow with a heat and power that could melt me utterly. I looked up into his eyes, awestruck....

And something in my expression tipped him over the edge. He grabbed me around the waist and towed me over to the mirror, almost lifting me off my feet. My ass touched the smooth wood of the barre that ran horizontally just in front of the mirror. "Open your legs," he told me.

I blinked. "What?"

He moved closer. "Open those gorgeous fucking legs," he said. "I'm going to do to you what I promised I would, the first night we met."

I slowly parted my thighs, my heart pounding in my chest, and gripped the barre with both hands.

I'd never seen anyone kneel the way Angelo did. Other men kneel and it's an act of submission. He knelt the way a king would kneel, back ramrod straight. Somehow, he managed to not look any smaller. In fact, the muscled bulk of him, those wide shoulders and broad chest all moving slowly, deliberately between my spread thighs...it made it feel like *I* was the one submitting. His eyes didn't say *okay, I'll do this for you*. They said, *are you ready? Because I'm coming to get you.*

With the tip of his tongue, he licked slowly along my inner thigh and I felt the pleasure surge and sing, working its way upward towards my groin. He licked along my other leg and I began to tremble, fingers tight around the smooth wood of the barre. He looked up at me and I stared back at him, his naked chest hypnotic as it rose and fell beneath the open shirt. He moved directly below my groin, his brown-amber eyes blazing at me, his shining hair so richly black against my skin...and he spoke.

His lips were maybe an inch from my lips so each syllable buzzed and throbbed through them, his low growl like the biggest bass speaker I'd ever felt. And even as the sound of what he was saying hit from below, the sense of it penetrated my brain and spiked down to my groin in a black lightning bolt, the two elements colliding to make me pant and writhe.

"You're like something out of a dream," he said. "And guys like me don't have dreams." He took a long, slow breath and I gasped as I felt the soft suction pull at me. "When I first saw you, up on stage, I thought you were magical. Queen of the fucking elves. Not meant to be touched by mortal man. Well, I'm going to touch you. You better believe I'm going to touch you. I'm going to stroke and lick every inch of you until you're begging, *screaming* for me to let you come."

I could feel myself getting wetter and wetter. I was going to be soaked before his lips ever touched me.

"See, that's what I love about you, Irina. You're so cold. You're this ice princess, so strong and noble. But underneath...."

He raised his mouth until it was only a half-inch from my folds.

"...underneath, where it matters—"

He closed the distance again. A quarter inch away, no more.

"...underneath all that ice—"

I was heaving for breath, now, eyes tight shut. I'd never felt anything like the overwhelming pleasure from the vibrations of his voice...it was everything I could do to stop myself pressing down against his face and locking my legs around his head.

He moved his head so agonizingly close that his lips must have only just been missing me—the thickness of a butterfly's wing, a soap bubble....

"....under the ice you're just *burning*. You're *molten*. You don't let anyone see it but you're aching for someone to take you and strip you and give you a *good. Long. Fucking.*"

I felt the tip of his tongue part my folds. I just had time to open my eyes wide before his whole tongue speared up into me, hot and determined, spreading my slickened walls wide. He didn't stop until his lips were pressed hard against me, the strength of him such that he could actually rise on his knees a little and lift me, forcing me to go up en pointe for a second. The pleasure was rippling out in hot, fierce waves, rebounding and concentrating, building towards a climax.

His hands went to my ass. At first, his fingers were gentle, rubbing in slow circles as his tongue began to thrust. But as he started to speed up, his hands grew firmer, squeezing my cheeks, kneading my flesh with just the right roughness. I began to suck in air through my clenched teeth. I let go of the barre and my palms slapped against the cool surface of the mirror.

Then his mouth moved to my clit, sucking it gently into his mouth and lashing it with his tongue. The waves of pleasure rolled in faster and faster, building quicker than I could keep up with. My head rocked back, my pinned-up hair brushing the mirror behind me as I arched my back. *I'm going to—going to—*

He slid one hand up my body to capture my breast, his thumb stroking back and forth across my nipple, and I began to silently shake my head, my hair swishing across the mirror. When he began to lightly pinch the raised bud, I moaned out loud, the sound echoing around the huge room. He took two fingers of his other hand and buried them in me, sliding them deep, and my moan rose towards the ceiling as my control slipping away. I could feel my orgasm swollen and ready inside me, sucking in all rational thought and destroying it.

But instead of going fast, he moved those hard, thick fingers *slowww*. His tongue stopped flicking over my clit. My eyes flew open in horror.

I looked down into brown and amber eyes that reminded me of smoldering coals. *Oh God. He wants me to—*

Three quick breaths. Three slow pumps of his fingers before the lust overcame my shyness. "*Do it!*" I groaned low in my throat. "*Please!*"

Those gorgeous lips twisted into a filthy smirk...and he sped back up, his fingers stroking deep, his tongue circling faster and faster. He kept his eyes open, looking up the length of my body to my face, and I stared back down at him. The orgasm expanded again, growing bigger and tighter, every muscle in my body tensing in readiness, the pleasure turning from pink to scarlet to darkest black. I'd never felt so gloriously out of control.

And then it exploded, the pleasure rushing through me, my hips grinding and circling, pushing my groin towards his face. He met every movement, his tongue quick and expert, his fingers carrying me through wave after wave, until my legs weakened and started to give. Instantly his hands were under my ass, supporting me, and as he stood he lifted me into his arms. My whole body was gleaming, my breath coming in long, shaky gasps. It was almost a minute before I was able to draw back and look at him.

He was looking at me with raw lust and...*pride*. He knew, somehow, that he was the first man to ever make me really let go like that, to be so lost in sex that I'd beg for release. And even though I could feel my cheeks flushing a little at what we'd just done, I felt proud, too.

"Now," he growled. "Let's find somewhere to lie you down because I need to—"

Whistling, from the corridor. *Chyort!* I could hear the squeaky wheels of the janitor's cart, too. I ran naked across the room, legs still shaky and weak, grabbed my leotard and starting scrambling into it. I was hooking the second shoulder strap into place and Angelo was tucking in his shirt when the janitor came through the door. He said nothing, but gave us a knowing look. I grabbed my bag and pulled a smirking Angelo from the room.

In the hallway, he pushed me up against the wall, planted his hands either side of me and kissed me slow and deep, his body grinding against mine. The feel of his cock, hot and hard under his pants, made me groan. "My car's outside," he growled. "We can be at my apartment in ten."

I nodded. I wanted it as much as him. But something was hammering on the outside of my post-orgasmic bliss, something I wanted to ignore but knew I couldn't. "Wait," I said. "I need to tell you something."

He moved back a little and frowned, listening.

"I've been trying to talk to Vasiliy about peace. Mikhail, too. Neither of them will listen."

He nodded, as if unsurprised.

My chest tightened: the thing I hated most was the inevitability of it all, both sides too set in their ways to even consider change. "But I've been listening, too," I blurted. "And—" I bit my lip. *Is this right?* I couldn't figure it out. Whatever I did, I was betraying someone.

Angelo gripped my arms. "What?"

"If I tell you, you've got to promise me something. You've got to promise you only use this to protect yourself, not to attack."

He gazed into my eyes for a long time and then nodded. "Okay. I promise."

I took a deep breath. "Vasiliy and Mikhail have paid off the bikers your guys are meeting tonight."

His eyes widened. 'They've *what?* No! No way!"

"The bikers will turn on you and try to take you out. With bratva to back them up."

He shook his head slowly. I could see the hurt in his eyes, the sick sense of betrayal. *That's what Vasiliy will look like, if he ever finds out what I've done,* I thought, and the nausea rose inside me.

Angelo slammed his fist into the wall. "Damnit!" he yelled, his voice echoing down the empty hallway. He took three quick breaths and then slid his fingers and thumbs down the lapels of his jacket, straightening them. When he spoke again, his voice was level, but he was frowning. "How did you find this out? Was it Vasiliy?"

I'd hoped he wouldn't ask that. I couldn't meet his eyes.

"Was it *Mikhail?*" His voice was tight with rage.

I tried to be emotionless and cold but I couldn't, not with him. I looked at the floor.

He slowly put his palms against the wall either side of my head and leaned into me, forming a protective cage around me. I could hear the pain in every single syllable. He'd figured it out. "Did you...*do* something? To get him to talk?"

I put a hand on his chest. "I did it to save you," I whispered.

I could feel the possessive rage building like a typhoon, his muscles growing hard under my fingers. With any other man, I would have been scared he was going to hit me. Not with Angelo. All of his anger was directed at the man who'd dared to touch me. His hand covered mine. "Don't ever do that again," he told me.

I nodded. He leaned forward and kissed my forehead, then gave me a long, tender kiss on the lips. His forehead touched mine and we stayed like that for long seconds, until there could be absolutely no doubt that I was *his.*

Then he straightened up and his jaw set in that expression of absolute determination I knew so well. "I need to handle this," he told me. "I have to go." And then he was striding down the hallway.

Chyort! What have I done? "Remember what you promised," I called after him.

I saw his shoulders rise. He heard me...but he didn't look back.

26

ANGELO

I got Rico to meet me at *Underground* and we holed up in my office while I told him the bad news. His reaction was similar to mine, except, when *he* punched the wall, he took a chunk of plaster out of it. "Those guys have been buying guns from us for twenty years!" he snapped. "The whole fucking charter buys from us."

"Not anymore. Question is, what do we do about it?"

Rico considered. "The Russians don't know we know?"

I shook my head.

"Then we kill the sons of bitches. We get the bikers back on our team and we take out the bratva fucks they sent to kill us. We ambush them like they were going to ambush us."

I leaned back in my chair and thought about it. "Or...we could just call off the meet. We get the bikers buying from us again, sure. But we don't ambush the Russians."

"Why the hell would we do that? This is the perfect opportunity!" Rico stalked over to my desk. "What's *with* you? This is exactly what we need to show the Saints we can handle the Russians." He put his hands flat on my desk and leaned over me. "C'mon, boss. Now's not the time to go soft."

"I'm not going soft!" I snarled. I jumped to my feet so fast my chair hit the wall behind me. "We ambush them, maybe hurt them, maybe kill them. *Then* what? Vasiliy will be after blood! It'll be all-out war!"

"Maybe we need a war!"

We glowered at each other, our faces only a few feet apart. But the real fight wasn't between Rico and me. The real fight was going on inside, between the old me and the new me. A week ago, I would have taken the opportunity like a shot, killed as many Russians as I could and the hell with the consequences. Meeting Irina had changed everything but I couldn't figure out if she was helping me see clearly or leading me astray. I stood there for long seconds, every muscle rigid, trying to decide between betraying Irina and betraying my side.

I promised her....

But I'd made a promise to my dad, too, as he lay dying in my arms. I'd promised I'd never let his turf go to the Russians.

"Fuck it," I said, straightening up. "Get the guys. We'll go see the bikers. Then we're going to give those Russian bastards a surprise."

27

IRINA

It was just after eight when I heard a pounding at the door. I checked the door viewer and—

Oh God. *No!*

I threw the door wide. Vasiliy and Mikhail rushed inside, carrying a man between them. I didn't recognize the guy, but he had bratva tattoos on his neck and the heavy build of one of Mikhail's thugs.

And he was dying. His white shirt was soaked through with blood from a chest wound, his hands slickly red.

"Clear the table!" snapped Vasiliy. "Leave the door open. Yuri is on his way with the doctor."

I ran ahead of them and swept everything off the dining table. He didn't have to tell me to bring clean towels. I was a Malakov: this wasn't the first time I'd done this.

They laid the guy on the table and I stepped in close. He was guarding his wound with both hands and wouldn't let Vasiliy or Mikhail see. "*Shh,*" I told him. "Let me look."

Teeth gritted, he moved his hands. Fresh blood welled up—I found the place and pressed hard with my wadded-up towel. He arched off the table and howled, cursing, while Vasiliy and Mikhail helped to hold him down. *Thank God Rachel is out!* "What happened?" I asked Vasiliy.

"The Italians ambushed us!" he spat. "We barely got out."

Oh Jesus. The guy started to thrash in pain, whacking his head against the table. I grabbed the first soft thing I could see and stuffed it under his head as a pillow. "Was anyone else hurt?"

Vasiliy shook his head and then squeezed the dying man's hand. "Just Josef here."

I relaxed for a split second...and then realized that he was only talking about our side. "What about the Italians?" I asked.

Vasiliy looked at me as if I'd gone crazy. "Who gives a fuck about *them?!*"

I dropped my gaze and concentrated on Josef. Blood was soaking through the towel. *Please God, don't let him die!*

"There was a lot of shooting," said Mikhail with satisfaction. "I think we got some of them."

I have to call Angelo! But then Yuri, Vasiliy's bodyguard, burst in with the doctor, an overweight guy pushing sixty with a duffel bag full of gear. "I could use a hand," he said as soon as he saw Josef.

"Irina can help you," said Vasiliy. "She's done it before."

I had. I'd helped patch up Luka and a few others—even Vasiliy himself, once. But I'd never before done it knowing I was the one responsible for the shooting.

At first, Vasiliy and Mikhail had to hold the guy down. Once the doctor had given him something to knock him out, they were able to step back...and their voices soon rose in anger.

"Somebody talked," growled Vasiliy. "We had those bikers too scared to run to the Italians. The Italians must have gone to *them.*" He grabbed the front of Mikhail's shirt. "That means one of your men warned them."

"It was one of mine who got shot!" Mikhail wrestled out of Vasiliy's grip. "Could have been one of yours who warned them." He pointed at Yuri. "Could have been *him.*"

Vasiliy and Yuri just stared at him, stony-faced, until Mikhail dropped his gaze. Yuri was Vasiliy's bodyguard for years before he started guarding Luka. When Vasiliy came to New York and needed a man he could really trust, Yuri came with him. They're almost like brothers and Yuri is almost part of our family. He's one of the few Russian men I actually like and to question his loyalty was unthinkable.

"We will find out who talked," muttered Vasiliy. "And execute them."

My fingers slipped and I let go of the clamp I was holding. Blood spurted and ran. "Goddamnit!" snapped the doctor. "Be careful!"

"Sorry," I said quickly. I kept my eyes firmly on the wound. I wouldn't let myself look away from the horror, from the sight of his skin growing pale as the life pumped out of him. *Look at it, Irina. Look at what you've done.*

The doctor replaced the clamp and I took hold of it again, this time with a death grip. I didn't falter even when Vasiliy moved close behind me and placed his hand on my back. "I'm sorry I yelled at you," he muttered. "It's not your fault. Thank you for helping."

I nodded and said *of course.* And felt like a Moscow sewer rat.

After two long hours, the doctor said that Josef should make it. He patched him up enough to risk moving him, and Yuri and Mikhail carried him to Yuri's car. I stared at the bloodstained towels and bits of gauze that littered the floor, then got a trash bag and started to clear up. I realized that the thing I'd stuffed under Josef's head was Rachel's favorite sweater. *Chyort!* I hid it under a cushion—I'd have to hope I could get the blood out.

I was going out of my mind. I was desperate to call Angelo but I didn't dare, not with Vasiliy still in the house. If he was hurt—or worse, if someone else answered his phone and told me he was dead —I'd have no hope of holding it together.

At last, Yuri and Mikhail returned and said they were ready to go. Vasiliy nodded and hugged me, telling me again that he appreciated my help. Mikhail, though, looked suspicious. *Nothing I can do about that now. I'll just have to be careful.*

The second the door closed behind them, I grabbed my phone and dialed Angelo. I started to panic breathe. One ring. Two rings.

What if he's dead? Three rings. *He's lying dead.* Four rings. *He's lying dead because I made the wrong choice. If I hadn't—*

"Irina?"

I closed my eyes and took a long, shuddering breath. "Are you okay?"

"Yeah."

I let the breath hiss out. "Meet me at Battery Park," I told him. "We need to talk."

28

IRINA

He was waiting for me, staring out over the water at the Statue of Liberty. It wasn't snowing, but a bitter wind was whipping across the inky-black Hudson River.

"Is everyone on your side okay?" I asked as I walked up.

He turned to me. "Two hurt. Bullets winged them—they'll be okay."

The relief sluiced through me. And then I slapped his face as hard as I could.

He reeled from the blow, twisting to the side and fingering his reddened cheek. "*Svoloch!*" I yelled. I'd brought him to Battery Park specifically because I knew I could scream at him and no one would care. "You *svoloch!* You promised!"

The guilt was all over his face. "How bad was it? I know we hit one guy...."

"*Josef!* His name is Josef! He almost died!"

"I'm sorry. I just couldn't—Look, they were going to do the same thing to us!"

"That's why I warned you! But why couldn't you just walk away? Why did you have to get revenge?" I whacked him in the chest with my fist. Tears were filling my eyes. "Why can't you just—You—You *stupid*—"

"Irina—"

I began to pound on his chest with my fists. "Stupid, *svoloch, asshole!*" I bawled.

He caught my wrists. "Irina—"

"*I thought you were dead!*" I spat at him. "Don't you understand that? I thought you were dead and I couldn't even check because *you're the enemy!*" I was screaming by the end of it.

He stared into my tear-filled eyes for a long moment and then wrapped me into his arms and wouldn't let go. After a few minutes, I finally stopped struggling and nestled against his chest, my tears soaking his shirt.

"I'm sorry," he said at last. "I just...I had to."

I'd cried all the anger out of me and all I felt was tired. The freezing wind was whipping against one wet cheek, but the other was warmed by the heated slab of his chest. I didn't ever want to move away from that warmth...but I didn't see how I could stay, either. *We're just too different. Too different for me ever to convince him.* "Why?" I asked. "That's what I don't understand. Why can't you back down? Why can't you make peace? *Why?*"

I said it just to vent the hot, jagged pain inside. I didn't expect anything as simple and clear as what I heard next.

"Because Russians killed my parents," he said, his chin pressed to the top of my head.

What?!

I pushed back from his chest...and looked up into brown and amber eyes that were bitter and furious...and suddenly moist. I wrapped my arms around him and pulled myself in tight.

And he told me. He told me about being an up-and-coming captain in his dad's organization, about his mom disapproving but understanding—she'd stood by his dad every step of the way. Something about that resonated with me: it was important, but I couldn't figure out why.

He told me about the Russian gangsters eager to expand their territory, a less powerful group than Mikhail's, but determined and vicious. He told me about being in the SUV with his parents, on the way to a restaurant, and how he'd jumped out a street early to stop at an ATM, saying he'd catch them up.

He slowed down. He had to take a breath to calm himself between each sentence, the rage palpable: it was in the taut muscles of his back, in the hard bulges of his biceps. He described getting the cash and jogging down the street: his parents' SUV had stopped at a red light and he figured he could jump in there, if he was fast.

He told me how he saw the car pull up alongside his parents' car. How he'd *known*. And then the gunfire, a deafening roar, and every bit of glass in the SUV shattering. His dad had tried to drive away but had slammed into a fire hydrant after just a few seconds, unleashing a torrent of water. When Angelo reached the car, the gunmen had gone and his parents were dying, their car in a red-tinged lake of water and broken glass.

His mom died first. His dad lived just long enough to make him promise, to *swear on his life*, that he'd never let Russians take his turf.

"I hunted them," Angelo told me. "Rico helped. I wiped out every last one of their gang and then took over from my dad." He gently pushed me back and stared down at me. "Now do you get it?"

I nodded. "I do," I said, my voice catching. "And I need to tell you something. So you'll understand *me*."

And I told him about rounding the corner into our street in Moscow and seeing first the blue lights of the fire service and then the cherry red of the flames. About running down the street and realizing that it wasn't a mistake, that it was *our* townhouse that was burning, tongues of flames leaping up from every window. About searching the crowd of onlookers for my parents and not finding them.

The firefighters had already brought them out, their blackened bodies covered in sheets.

At the inquiry, the police said that my parents had passed out on a combination of booze and drugs and that's why they hadn't fled when the fire started. They showed the press photos of drug paraphernalia and empty bottles—all mysteriously unscathed by the fire—that they claimed had been found alongside my parents. My teetotal mom, who'd sworn off the booze a decade ago and my dad who was so anti-drug he'd grounded me for a solid month just because I tried weed at a party.

But no one cared about the facts. My dad was a well-known gangster. Who cared if him and his "girlfriend" (the press couldn't understand the concept of a married gangster) killed themselves with drugs?

I hugged my sister Lizaveta tight and thanked God that she'd been at a sleepover that night. And I swore I'd get as far away from the gangster life as possible. Then Vasiliy took us in and that promise became impossible...even when I ran to America.

"Jesus," muttered Angelo. His arms locked around my back, iron hard and unbreakable. His palms pumped warmth into my freezing body and his broad chest shielded me against the worst of the wind. Maybe we *were* different. But maybe we were different in just the right way. His parents' death had pushed him one way, mine had pushed me the other. But our pain had the same source.

I had to try. "That guy who got shot tonight? His name's Josef. He has a three year-old kid. A little girl. We nearly orphaned her tonight: she would have grown up wanting revenge. It'll go on forever, generation after generation, until someone's brave enough to say *enough!*"

"You want me to just walk away, like you did?" he asked.

I opened and closed my mouth a few times. *Yes,* I wanted to say. After all, that's what I'd done: distance myself as much from Vasiliy as possible and refuse to be involved, even though it meant isolating myself. But now I thought about it, something about it felt wrong. I'd never questioned my decision before, but now.... "I want you to help me figure out how to end this without people getting killed," I said instead.

He pulled away from me and paced, shoes crunching in the snow, then flung his arm out and pointed to the Statue of Liberty. "This is how it is in New York! Since the first of our guys came over on boats!

It's been going on for a hundred years! You think *we* can stop it? Just because I'm in—"

He stared at me. Drew in a shuddering breath.

"Because I've got fucking feelings for you?" he said at last.

I couldn't think about the implications of what he'd nearly said. Not now. Not with everything that was on the line. I walked over to him and took his big, warm hands in my cold ones. "We need to do it because if we don't, no one will," I told him.

We stared at each other, eyes locked and neither willing to give ground. Then I remembered how *he'd* convinced *me*. "You took me to Little Italy," I said. "Now let *me* show *you* something." I gave him a wan smile. "Please? It'll be like a date." *God, remember when this was just dating? When neither of us knew who the other one was?* So much had changed...and so little. Despite everything, the sight of him standing there, black hair ruffled by the wind, white shirt stretched tight over that magnificent chest, still reduced me to mush.

His eyes flicked over me and on each pass his gaze grew hotter until I was almost squirming. I wasn't even wearing anything special, just what I'd thrown on before running out of the house: a black dress and knee boots.

"Okay," said Angelo. "Show me."

29

ANGELO

We climbed into my car and she guided me through the streets until we reached one that was little more than an alley. I frowned because I couldn't see a sign or a doorway.

"Underground," Irina told me, grinning. She pointed at the stone steps that led down. "Best place to be, when it's cold. We have a lot of underground places in Russia."

I stepped out into ankle-deep snow—the street was too small to have been swept yet. I walked around and opened Irina's door for her...and the sight of her took my breath away. She twisted in her seat to climb out, her knees pressed demurely together. My eyes locked on the enticing slice of soft tan thigh visible between the hem of her tight black dress and the tops of her shining black knee boots. I was still getting over the knee boots. *How had she known?*

The wind was like a huge monster trying to squeeze its way down the narrow alley, shrieking as it was forced through metal fire escapes and rattling at dumpsters. It flattened our clothes against our bodies and whistled down our necks. I grimaced. I still hated winter. Irina, looking perfectly comfortable, smiled sympathetically. "Come on," she said. "Inside."

I hesitated when I saw the graffiti in Cyrillic beside the door. But I followed her down the stairs.

We emerged into a huge cellar. She was right: it *was* the best place to be. The thick stone walls stopped the cold dead: we couldn't even hear the wind. And in the center of the room there was a huge open fireplace where thick logs of wood crackled and spat, yellow flames reaching up to a big metal hood that sucked away the smoke. Near the walls, there were small wooden tables lit by candles, mostly occupied by couples. Closer to the fire, people sprawled on beanbags and cushions.

All of them were Russian. I could hear the language all around me, heavy and brutal, those long "s"s that reminded me of rusty chains dragging someone down into dark water, the hard "k"s that were like a gun being cocked as it's put to your temple. I had to stop myself reaching for my gun. My whole being was screaming at me to get out of there, telling me I was surrounded by the enemy.

There was shouting behind us. The three guys were talking in Russian but *one...two...three!* has the same feel whatever the language. I spun, expecting an ambush—

And watched as the three of them chugged their beers and then drunkenly cheered.

Irina pulled me over to the bar and got us a shot of vodka each, along with a beer. She clinked shot glasses with me and I knocked back the vodka: smooth and icy, with a scalding kick. Then she was leading me through the sea of bean bags and cushions, right into the center of a group of people. She sat us down on the one unoccupied beanbag, me sitting on my ass with her sitting between my legs. I glanced around, skittish and *pissed. Out of my comfort zone* didn't begin to describe it. These were the people who'd invaded my country, stolen my territory, killed my parents....

And for the next four hours, I got to know them.

I met a few guys who worked down at the docks and another who was in med school. I met a violinist who went to Fenbrook and a stripper who was sinking all her earnings into property. I met a couple who were opening a cafe together and a single mom on a very rare night out.

I tried to hate them. I tried to remember every bit of shit that the Saints had said about them. I reminded myself that they were cold-hearted and disloyal, that Russians would turn on each other in a heartbeat. That's why they bred gangsters who were so power-crazed and brutal.

But...none of that tallied with what I was hearing and seeing. The dock workers would have fit right in with the American guys I knew down there, bitching about the new safety laws and playing dumb pranks on each other. The stripper was smart as hell and was going to have a property empire in a few years if she kept it up, but she wasn't callous or mean: she was leasing one of her places to a homeless shelter at a crazy low rate so that they could get people in out of the cold. And the couple who were opening a cafe were just as wide-eyed and naively-optimistic as any of the hundreds of American couples who try the same thing.

All of which made the nausea build in my stomach. *They're just like us.*

And all of them were scared. The dock workers had nearly got into a fight with their Italian co-workers, because Mikhail's thugs had shut down their favorite bookie. The stripper said she didn't feel safe walking to her car anymore, because a couple of guys in the crowd—Italian guys—had called out some vicious shit when they realized she was Russian. The couple had been warned away from their first choice of cafe. They'd been told: *that's too close to Italian territory. Don't you know they hate us?*

The war was only just starting and already it was affecting civilians. What next? I could see it unfolding in my head: some riled-up Italian dock worker smashing a crowbar into one of the Russian's heads, then staggering back in shock as the guy's body went limp; the stripper trying to scream as she was pushed up against a wall by drunken Italians who'd had their businesses smashed up by Mikhail's thugs; the couple clutching at each other in fear as their brand new cafe was torched in front of them.

I suddenly stood up, shaking my head, and made for the exit. Irina scrambled after me, but I was almost outside before she caught me.

"No," I said before she could speak. "No way." I turned my back on the cellar bar, pulling my overcoat tight around me. *Jesus*, it was cold. "I can't have been wrong. My dad can't have been wrong."

"Maybe he wasn't wrong," said Irina quietly. She nestled against my side, her arm around my waist. "Did he hate Russians, or just the gangsters he was fighting?"

I said nothing, just started walking along the sidewalk, feeling her there beside me, but not able to meet her eyes. I'd started to shiver despite my suit and thick coat. Suddenly, I wasn't sure of anything, anymore.

I went back to the days growing up in our tiny house. My dad bitching about the gangsters he was fighting: the Irish and the Triads and the Russians...but not the people. Now that I forced myself to face the memories, I couldn't think of a single time where he'd looked down on someone because of where they were from.

The Saints, though...they'd been full of hate. Especially Nicky and Taavetti, even in those days. I'd gone to visit them with my dad a few times and I remembered the shit they talked about anyone who wasn't "one of us."

When my parents were killed, I'd been driven by rage. I'd slain the Russians who'd murdered them, but that wasn't enough. I needed to keep satisfying the anger or it might burn down and go out, and then I wouldn't be able to keep going. So it became about *all* Russian gangsters. And then, as The Saints whispered more and more in my ear, it became all Russians.

I stopped in my tracks, the snow scrunching under my feet. My dad hadn't hated...but I had.

I turned and looked at Irina. She looked up at me and the hope I saw in her eyes tore me up inside. "I've been an asshole," I muttered.

"You were angry. You've been manipulated. And you are *all* assholes, all of you gangsters. But you, I think, can change. Find a way to work with Vasiliy. Talk peace with him."

The whole street seemed to spin around me. Talk peace with Vasiliy?! What the fuck would I tell The Saints? Rico? The rest of my guys? Giving ground was unthinkable.

But letting this escalate into a full-blown war, with both the Italian and Russian communities paying the price...that was unthinkable, too. *Shit. What the fuck am I going to do?*

Then the wind blew Irina's hair towards me, the tips of those platinum-blonde strands just brushing my face. They were so soft, it was difficult to tell where the wind ended and the hair began. My ice queen. The one who'd started all this. Even if I made peace, being with her was going to be almost impossible. But without peace, there was no way we could be together at all.

I let out a long sigh and rubbed a hand over my face. "I'll try," I said. "I'll set up a meet."

Irina pressed her body against mine, her warmth comforting against my chest. Her arms slid under my overcoat to wrap around my back. "Thank you," she whispered.

I pulled her even closer, until her breasts were pillowed against my lower chest and the scent of her hair filled my nose. "He can't know," I murmured. "Vasiliy can't know we're together or it'll blow everything. Even afterwards. Even if we can be..."—I had to struggle with the word—"*allies*. He's still not going to like it."

She nodded quickly. "I can live with keeping this a secret. But not with one of you dying."

My arms tightened around her. God, she was so brave. I was worried about betraying my dad's memory, or pissing off Rico or The Saints. She was going against her entire family.

30

IRINA

I hadn't planned on being there for the phone call. But Vasiliy knocked at my door first thing in the morning, Mikhail by his side, to talk to me about me moving into his New York townhouse until "these problems with the Italians are dealt with." I tried to figure out how to convince Vasiliy that Angelo wasn't a threat to me without letting on why.

Then Vasiliy's phone rang and I saw him stiffen when he heard the voice at the other end. *Shit! Angelo!* I turned away quickly, terrified my expression would reveal something. I wound up looking at Mikhail, who was looking worried himself.

Vasiliy ended the call and then stood staring at the phone for a few seconds. "That was Angelo Baroni," he said, his tone neutral. "He wants to talk peace."

"It's a trick," said Mikhail immediately. "Baroni would never make peace with us."

Vasiliy looked across at him. "I thought so, too. But perhaps we misjudged him. He wants to meet, just him and us."

Mikhail slapped Vasiliy's arm with his fat, ham-like hand. "We can *crush* this fucker, Vasiliy. He's showing that he's weak. Let's finish him and take his territory." He was grinning but I could see how pale he'd turned under the bravado.

"We don't need his territory," said Vasiliy.

Mikhail's eyes bugged out. "*I* need his fucking territory! This isn't just about your guns, Vasiliy! You backed me so that I could take over his turf!"

"I backed you so that my family could have a firm foothold in New York," Vasiliy countered. "If we can do that another way..." He shook his head. "It may be a trick. But we should hear what Baroni has to say."

Hope soared in my chest—it felt as if it was going to lift me right off my feet. That sounded like the old Vasiliy, the one I remembered. The elder statesman, the diplomat, the businessman. It was everything I could do to keep from grinning. Maybe, just maybe, this could all work out.

But when I composed myself and dared to look up again, I found myself looking right into Mikhail's eyes. He was glaring at me...but then he nodded to himself, as if deciding something. "Fine," he told Vasiliy. "Let's go.

Even Vasiliy seemed surprised by the sudden about-face. But he took out his phone again to call Angelo back, already leading the way to the door.

It was when Mikhail was closing the door behind them that it happened. He glanced up at me...and smiled.

Not the lecherous smile he normally gave me, the one that told me he was imagining running his flabby hands up the insides of my thighs. A smile I'd never seen before. A smile of victory.

It was so unexpected that I didn't have time to react. The door closed and I stood there stupidly, watching them climb into Vasiliy's Mercedes. I watched them talk to Yuri, no doubt explaining the plan, then Yuri climbed out and just Vasiliy and Mikhail drove off to meet Angelo.

What did that smile mean?

Moments later, another car filled with Vasiliy's men pulled up, picked up Yuri and drove off after the Mercedes. Whatever he'd told

Angelo, Vasiliy wasn't risking showing up without backup. I wasn't disappointed. That was just the way these things were done: one hand stretched out in greeting, the other ready behind your back with a knife.

What did that smile mean?

I knew that these sort of meets could turn bad in half a second, just as the one with the bikers had. If Angelo had any sense, he'd secretly take backup too. But it seemed like Vasiliy was at least willing to talk. It was Mikhail who was the problem. Mikhail wanted all-out war. He wanted every last scrap of Angelo's territory—that's why he'd formed the alliance with Vasiliy in the first place. He stood to lose everything he'd been fighting for...so why had he smiled?

Unless....

Unless he knew the meet was going to turn bad.

Unless he knew something that would turn Vasiliy against Angelo.

Unless he knew about us!

I stood staring out at the snow-covered street, my eyes widening. *No. No way.*

I started to panic breathe. My chest was heaving but I couldn't fill my lungs. I frantically tried to rationalize it away. *It makes no sense. If he knew, why wouldn't he have told Vasiliy already? Why bother to even go to the meeting?* I turned slowly away from the window, willing my heart to slow. *Yes. That's right. Of course he doesn't know.* I walked through to the kitchen and started making myself a coffee. I thought the problem was that all the lying had made me paranoid.

I was wrong. The problem was that I'd been away from my family too long.

I'd forgotten how to think like a gangster. I didn't see it: not when I fetched a mug, not the whole time I stood there waiting for the coffee machine to whirr and hiss, not even when I was adding extra milk. It didn't hit me until I turned back towards the living room, the coffee's creamy froth just touching my lips. My eyes fell upon the chessboard. Half of the pieces were still out of position from when Vasiliy had knocked them, days ago. The black king stood exposed.

It's so that Vasiliy's alone with Angelo. That's why he waited.

The mug slipped from my fingers.

It was all so perfect: Angelo in a remote location; Vasiliy's guards just itching to pull the trigger on their hated enemy. Mikhail would reveal our relationship. A moment of rage from Vasiliy and he'd give the order, or pull a gun himself...

And Angelo would die.

The mug exploded on the tiles, coffee spraying across my jeans. I didn't even feel it. I ran into the living room, grabbed my phone and called Angelo, then paced as I waited for him to answer. One ring. *Come on.* Two rings. *Come on!*

It went to answerphone. *Chyort! Chyort, Chyort, Chyort! "Don't go to the meet!"* I screamed. "Mikhail knows about us! Vasiliy will kill you! Call me back when you get this!"

I ended the call and then stood there staring at the phone, willing it to ring. How long since Vasiliy and Mikhail had left? I didn't know when the meet was set for—it could be happening right now. What if Angelo didn't check his messages in time?

There was only one thing to do. I had to call Vasiliy and break the news myself: defuse Mikhail's weapon before he could use it. But what if I was wrong? What if Mikhail *didn't* know? I could tear our family apart and put Angelo's life in danger for no reason. I stared at the chessboard, going rapidly insane. Tactics. Strategy. Which was the right move? I was a Malakov, I was supposed to be *good* at this!

I gave a long, despairing cry of rage and kicked the table that held the chessboard, scattering pieces across the room.

Then I took a deep breath...and called Vasiliy.

31

IRINA

Vasiliy's phone rang once. Twice. *What the hell am I going to say?* Three times.

"Irina?" Vasiliy sounded annoyed. "What is it? I'm driving." *Chyort.* I'd forgotten that. And he always got stressed when he drove himself anywhere.

"Okay," I said. I dug my nails into my palms. "Listen...."

A muffled voice in the background. "Let me speak to her."

"Tell Mikhail," said Vasiliy.

"No, WAIT—" I yelled.

That disorienting, falling-through-space feeling as the microphone suddenly moved. And then I heard the fake warmth of Mikhail's voice. "Hello, Irina."

I think I knew, as soon as he spoke, that I'd been right. But I clung on to any forlorn hope. "Hi Mikhail," I said, forcing my voice level. "Could I speak to Vasiliy, please? It's private."

"What is it?" Vasiliy's voice in the background. He sounded horribly distant. Then he cursed. "*Fucking* potholes."

"It's okay," called Mikhail. "I'm dealing with it." I heard him settle his bulk back in his seat. When he spoke again, his voice was low, for my ears only. "Do you know when I first knew, Irina?"

Fuck. I closed my eyes. "No."

"The necklace. You wore it when you came to lunch with Vasiliy and me. That's not the sort of necklace a girl buys herself. That's the sort of necklace a man buys a girl because he wants to see her neck adorned. *I* could have bought you a necklace like that. But you would have thrown it back at me and laughed, wouldn't you?"

My insides flipped over. This wasn't just about him wanting all-out war with the Italians so that he could grab more territory. This was personal.

"And you kept touching it," he said. "You sat in my lap, with my cock right up against that precious, holy *cunt* of yours and you smiled at me, but you were touching your necklace because you were thinking of *him.* That's when I knew you were seeing someone else. So I had you followed...and discovered it was Angelo."

His voice was quiet, but so savage that I took a stumbling step backwards. I'd been ready for him to be evil, but I hadn't been expecting *this,* this hatred.

He hated me.

Someone else, he'd said. *You were seeing someone else.* He hated me, knew that I detested him...and yet he thought of me as *his.* In his mind, I'd cheated on him.

"It's fucking perfect, Irina. *Thank you.* Thank you for spreading your legs for our enemy, because now Vasiliy's going to kill your boyfriend and I'll get exactly what I want."

I didn't know when the tears had started, but I could feel them running down my cheeks. *Why can't Vasiliy hear this?* But then I heard Vasiliy's voice: "What are you gossiping about, back there?" And I realized Mikhail was lounging in the back seat, and that there was no hope at all.

"Please," I begged. I don't think I expected him to suddenly show mercy. I was more begging the universe for this not to be happening.

"We're here," I heard Vasiliy say from the front seat.

"*Proshchay*, Irina," said Mikhail. *Goodbye.*

And the phone went dead.

32

ANGELO

"This is a bad idea," said Rico. He was drumming his fingers on the steering wheel, but the sound was drowned out by the rain outside. After days of snow, it had warmed up just enough for the skies to unleash torrential rain. It wasn't yet noon, but it was as dark as twilight outside. He turned to me. "Just to be clear, I mean *you going alone* and *this entire fucking peace plan*. Both of them."

Usually, Rico will argue with me but know when to shut up and follow orders. The fact he was fighting me so hard on this spoke volumes.

"We've got to stop this thing," I told him. "Or it's going to get worse and worse. People are going to die. A *lot* of people."

"We're not beat!" snapped Rico. "Mikhail's got all the money from Vasiliy, sure, but we've got plenty of people loyal to us."

"It's not about being beat," I told him tiredly. "It's about being smart."

Rico glared at me, arms crossed. I noticed he'd stopped calling me *boss*. It wasn't that he'd lost any of his loyalty: his loyalty was the problem. He was trying to protect me from myself. He was smart enough not to say it, but we both knew he was thinking it: *this is all because of Irina.*

And he was right. It was. But how did I explain to him that she'd changed me for the better? How could I say that she'd made me realize I'd become twisted, over the years, and that being around her made me want to be more like her. Not *good,* because I'd never be that. But maybe I could go back to being honorable instead of being driven by hate. I couldn't figure out how to put any of that into words. When Irina had called on the way over, I'd let it go to voicemail: I knew if Rico heard me talking to her, we'd get into a full-on shouting match.

"At least let me come with you," Rico said. "You don't seriously think Vasiliy and Mikhail will have come alone?" he nodded through the windshield. "Those buildings will be *full* of Russians. *Full.*"

The place we'd chosen for the meet was a construction site, one of mafia boss Erico Fiorentini's projects. When he'd gone to jail, the whole thing had gotten bound up in red tape and now it was just an empty block of dirt and half-built buildings. With the dark sky and the pounding rain, it looked like a city that had been built and then bombed, girders reaching towards the slate gray sky like dead men's fingers and the streets nothing more than thick, glutinous mud.

"We have to show them we're serious," I told Rico. The real reason I wanted to go alone was, I didn't want to put anyone else at risk. This was my stupid gamble, not his. And if it went wrong, I wanted to take all the heat from The Saints.

I saw the headlights of a car approaching, picking its way carefully along the single gravel road that led through the site. "Now get out of here. I'll call you when they've gone."

Rico let out a long sigh and nodded. I opened my door and stepped out into hell. Freezing rain slammed into my shoulders and scalp, like being under a fucking power shower. I was soaked instantly and the rain poured down my face—I had to keep blinking it out of my eyes just to see. It was even worse than the day when I first saw Irina. The day my whole life started going wrong...and right.

I slammed my door. Rico turned the car around and headed off along the road, his tail lights quickly fading into the gloom. By now, the other car was closer, its headlights lighting me up. There was a flash of lightning overhead and then a boom of thunder so loud it sounded like the sky was splitting apart.

The car came to a stop right in front of me, but no one got out. I could see Vasiliy in the driver's seat and that prick Mikhail sprawled out in the back. He was on the phone to someone and I saw him finish the call and drop the phone into his pocket as he looked at me, a smug grin on his face.

I pantomimed looking to my left and right and held my arms up, indicating I was alone. Rico was right, of course. The buildings around me *would* be full of Russians. I'd just have to hope this went well.

Vasiliy nodded me towards the passenger door. Oh, of course, *they* didn't want to get wet, so the meeting would happen in their car. That gave them about a million advantages: I couldn't see what weapons they were carrying and they had the option of putting a gun to my head and driving me off somewhere.

But I didn't have a choice. Opening the door was almost surreal: standing in the pounding rain, looking in at the calm, clean, dry interior with the *bong bong bong* of the door chime sounding and my two enemies staring back at me. *What the fuck am I doing?*

For Irina. I climbed in, sat down in the passenger seat and slammed the door. Immediately, I could feel Mikhail's presence in the rear seat behind me. I couldn't watch both him and Vasiliy at the same time and the fat fuck could just lean forward and throttle me at any time. The hairs on the back of my neck started to rise.

"Mr. Baroni," said Vasiliy. "I was...*surprised* to receive your call. Surprised but intrigued. Let us keep this short. What are you offering?"

"How much of your territory will you give up?" Mikhail, from the rear seat. I looked in the rear view mirror, but the angle was wrong and I couldn't see him. *Shit.*

"I'm not offering territory," I said cautiously. "But—"

"You're wasting our time," snapped Mikhail. I heard his bulk shift on the rear seat, maybe getting ready to pounce.

Vasiliy held up his hand. "Let me hear what he has to say."

Mikhail cursed, but stopped moving. It was dark inside the car, especially in the back, and I didn't want to show weakness by turning around to look. But I imagined he was sitting there with his arms half extended, ready to wrap those big hands around my throat. Thank God Vasiliy was there to hold him back.

"A partnership," I began. I couldn't figure out if dad would be spinning in his grave or telling me I was doing the right thing.

"He already has partnership!" snapped Mikhail, his English fracturing in his anger.

"The way I see it," I said, keeping my eyes on Vasiliy, "you don't need more territory. You just want safe passage for your guns. You want security. I can give you that. We share the contacts: property development, politicians, the cops. Everything can run smoothly. No more fighting. No more territory grabs."

Vasiliy stared at me for a long time. I could only properly make out his face when a flash of lightning lit it up and even then it was an unreadable mask. "Why should I not just carry on and crush you, take your territory street by street?" he said at last.

I looked him right in the eye. "Because I'll give you a war you'll never forget. You've got the money, sure. I hear you've got billions in the bank. But how much of it do you want to spend to take each bar, each restaurant, each tattoo parlor? How much is it really worth to you? Because make no mistake, Vasiliy, I will turn this into your personal Vietnam. Your Iraq. You're the invading force here and we're the locals. We will fight you for every fucking inch and you'll bleed money *and* men. Do you really want that, when you could just do a deal instead?"

This time there was an even longer pause while he considered. The son of a bitch had the best poker face I'd ever seen. Eventually, he said, "A partnership is not out of the question." I heard Mikhail hiss air through his teeth behind me. "But I must be sure I can trust you. We must proceed very carefully. The first step—"

"You can't trust him," said Mikhail from behind me.

Vasiliy looked around at him, frowning angrily at being

interrupted. I noticed the car had lit up with a soft pink glow, coming from the rear seat.

"Here," said Mikhail. And passed something to Vasiliy. A smartphone. Now Vasiliy and I were both frowning. Vasiliy brought the phone into the front seat with him and stared at the screen and I stared with him. It was a porn picture. A naked guy entwined with a naked blonde, up against a mirror—

Oh Jesus.

I realized a split-second before Vasiliy. I guess my mind had been full of nothing else but Irina naked, ever since I first saw her. And you don't look at a picture like that and even consider, at first, that it might be your beloved niece.

In slow motion, I saw Vasiliy's jaw start to fall. I could actually see his face flushing, all the tiny blood vessels swelling as the scarlet spread.

"He seduced her," said Mikhail from the rear seat. "Fucked her. Used her. To get to you."

Vasiliy's head slowly turned to look at me. The look in his eyes wasn't the Vasiliy everyone fears, the cold, calculating businessman who'll murder to get what he wants. This was hot and human and very, very personal. This was betrayal and outrage and fury. There would be no reasoning with him. Not on this.

I was going to die.

I felt for the door release. Found it and pulled...but even as the door opened, Mikhail's sweat-damp hands slapped onto either side of my neck, heaved me back against the headrest and *squeezed*. He was a fat fuck but he was strong—I was pinned in place and his fingers were digging deeper and deeper, crushing as much as strangling. I clawed at them, making choking sounds in my throat, but I couldn't pry them loose. My windpipe narrowed, narrowed...and then I couldn't breathe at all.

Vasiliy pulled a gun from a shoulder holster. A second later I felt the cold kiss of the metal against my temple. I met his eyes and saw an anger I'd never seen in all my years. *He practically raised me,* I remembered Irina saying.

Shit.

There was a metallic click as Vasiliy cocked the gun.

33

ANGELO

There was a boom, but no pain. *Maybe you don't feel the one that kills you.* My head didn't hurt and even the crushing of my windpipe had stopped. *Is this heaven?*

For a second, I just sat there, dazed. Then I started to become aware of things. Mikhail was no longer gripping my neck and I could hear him screaming in the rear seat behind me. Vasiliy was trying to hunker down low in his seat, his gun still drawn but not pointed at me. And his pristine suit was sprinkled with glittering diamonds. I looked down. My suit was the same.

Then I saw the hole in the windshield. Not diamonds: glass.

I twisted and looked behind me. Mikhail was clutching his left ear, blood dripping from between his fingers. Behind him, there was a ragged hole through the leather seat at roughly head height.

I looked out of the windshield just as a flash of lightning lit up the construction site. Up on the second floor of one of the half-finished buildings was a dark shape: a man, lying full-length. Rico, with his favorite sniper rifle. He must have seen me staring at him through his scope because he lifted an arm and pointed frantically to the side. *Go! Go!*

I looked across at Vasiliy. He was still trying to hunker down beneath the level of the windshield, but he was swinging his gun around to point at me again.

I dived out of the car and staggered across the gravel road. Immediately, gunshots cracked the air around me, some close enough that I could hear the hiss of the bullet. Not Vasiliy and Mikhail, the Russians who they'd brought with them. They were all around me. *Shit!*

The road was brightly lit by the Mercedes's headlights: staying there was suicide. I ran into the darkness, panting with adrenaline, rain slicking my face. Almost immediately, I slipped and went full-length in the mud. That saved my life: a bullet aimed at my chest zipped over my head.

I started to crawl, but each time I put my hand down, it sank into the thick, black mud to the elbow. I gritted my teeth and forced my way onward, wincing as more bullets whistled overhead.

The ground was churned up by construction machinery, with countless ditches and potholes, some of them a few feet deep and many of them filled with rainwater. The storm had darkened the sky so much, I couldn't tell what was mud, what was shadow and what was water. Every few steps, I'd suddenly find there was no ground and I'd lurch down into a hole with a bone-jarring thump. Only the softness of the mud saved me from breaking something. Other times, I'd suddenly find myself chest-deep in freezing water, desperately trying to free my legs from the mud so I could lift my face clear.

And the bullets never stopped coming. The only blessing was that my overcoat was black and, as long as I stayed low, I blended in with the darkness and the mud. With the rain still hammering down, the Russians must have been guessing where I was. But that didn't mean they wouldn't get lucky. Some of the bullets hit the mud horribly close to me. And over the hammering rain, I could hear running footsteps: the Russians were spreading out, searching for me....

I tried to crawl faster, but powering through the thick, sucking mud was exhausting. Already, my limbs felt like lead. The mud coated every part of me and it had oozed through my cashmere overcoat and thousand dollar suit to squish against my skin. The rain was flowing down my face and into my ears. I had no idea where I was or where the Russians were. I just had to keep crawling, crawling—

A foot caught me under the chin and sent me sprawling backwards in the mud. I tasted blood. When I looked up, I saw Yuri, Vasiliy's personal bodyguard. A flash of lightning lit up the scars on his cheek—someone had really done a number on the guy.

He was gazing down at me with cold fury. *Shit.* I could tell immediately that he knew about Irina. How?

As if in answer, he tapped his ear and I saw the radio earpiece he wore. "I listen," he grunted. His English wasn't as good as Vasiliy's. "Car is bugged. I want to know what is going on. I want to be ready if you cross Vasiliy. But instead, I hear you use Irina. *Irina!*"

Shit. This got worse and worse. There are bodyguards and bodyguards. There are the hired guns who don't give a shit who they protect as long as they get paid and then there are the loyal ones, the guys who stay with one family so long they become part of it. Yuri was the second kind—I could hear in his voice that Irina was like a little sister to him. "No!" I shouted over the rain. "It's not like that!"

He growled and grabbed my foot, then spun and heaved me through the air like he was throwing the hammer. I crashed down on my back on the concrete floor of a part-finished building. Pain shot through my spine and I wondered if I'd broken something. Certainly, I wasn't getting up anytime soon.

Yuri came over to stand at my feet. The rain was pounding down on my upturned face and I was panting and exhausted by my desperate scramble through the mud. Another time, I could have taken him, but not now. I was *done.* "I swear," I croaked. "I love her."

It just came out. I didn't know I was going to say it until I had.

Yuri stared down at me for a moment, his hulking body outlined by the rain crashing against his shoulders and back. For a moment, his expression seemed to soften and he looked almost sad. "Then you are very stupid," he said. "And very unlucky."

He dropped to one knee and pulled a knife from his belt, then lifted it high to drive it down into my heart.

There was a *crack* and a cloud of dust exploded from the half-finished wall behind Yuri. He dived to the floor—he was ex-military, judging by how fast he reacted. A second shot rang out, this one hitting the wall right where he'd been standing. Yuri scrambled behind a waist-high pile of breeze blocks.

Rico emerged out of the darkness, rifle in his arms, covered in mud up to his knees. "How many times," he panted, "do I have to save your ass?" He swapped his rifle for a handgun and pointed it at the breeze blocks. "Get up!"

I clambered to my feet, which took a while. I was exhausted, frozen and my back and ribs were badly bruised—maybe worse. I staggered over to Rico and threw an arm around his shoulders. He supported me and we backed away into the mud, all the time keeping a watchful eye on where Yuri was hiding. Then, when darkness surrounded us, we ran.

Ten long, exhausting minutes later, we finally reached the edge of the construction site. I wanted to weep at how good the sidewalk felt under my feet. Rico helped me stumble to where he'd parked the car. A streetlight lit us up as we passed under it and I got a look at his face. There was so much anger in his eyes...and so much hurt, too. Hurt that I'd ignored his warnings. Hurt that I'd turned my back on everything he understood. Even, for some reason, hurt that I was with Irina.

But he didn't say any of it. He said, "Where to, boss?"

I tightened the arm I had around his shoulders, pulling him into a half-hug. "Home," I said. "Take me home."

A half hour later, I stood in the shower stall in my apartment, scalding water beating down on my head and shoulders. The water turned first brown as the mud rinsed off me, then red as the scrapes and cuts on my back opened up. There was a sharp pain in one side whenever I took a deep breath. When I emerged, Rico felt around and declared that I'd bust a rib, and taped it up as best he could.

I took a look at my reflection in the mirror. It looked as if I'd been through a war. My face was covered in tiny scratches where the windshield glass had hit me, my torso was bound with medical tape, my back was a mess of purple and black bruises and my normal upright posture was gone—I was slumped, dog-tired and aching.

None of which bothered me. Even the thought of what Vasiliy and Mikhail would unleash against me didn't bother me. The only thing on my mind was Irina.

I'd finally listened to her voicemail on the way to my apartment. I'd been calling her ever since. But she wasn't picking up.

                                  34

                                IRINA

ockdown
        I'd been on lockdown before. Everyone in a bratva family
has. Whenever the danger from a rival gang gets too high, whenever
there's word of a hit: *lockdown.* Everyone is moved to the most secure
house, armed guards patrol and no one's allowed to leave.

      When I was a kid, it was almost fun. I'd get to stay home from
school and Lizaveta and I would make dens under Vasiliy's kitchen
table. Now, though, it felt very different. This time, I felt like a
prisoner.

      A mud-stained Yuri had driven me to Vasiliy's townhouse. I hadn't
seen Vasiliy, yet. I'd asked to, but Yuri had simply shaken his head
sadly. That truly terrified me. How much damage had I done?

      How could I have been so stupid? How could I have thought that
Vasiliy wouldn't find out, especially when I had enemies like Mikhail?

      Worst of all, I had no idea whether Angelo was alive or dead. Yuri
had confiscated my phone.

      I sat alone on one of the huge leather couches in the living room,
hugging my legs and tipped over to the side so that I could press my
cheek against the arm. I wanted to be as small as possible. I wanted to
sink into the couch's depths. *I'd* caused this. I'd gone against my

destiny and tried to start something with an American. I'd pursued it even when I found out he was the enemy, betraying my family. I'd persuaded Angelo to try to make peace and led him straight into a trap that might have cost him his life.

The door opened and Mikhail shambled in. One side of his head was bandaged and there were drips of blood on his shirt. What the hell had happened at the meet?!

He eyed me silently for a long time, his gaze raking over my body. The familiar sick feeling started, but this time it was worse, bitter and cold. Having someone leer at you when they like you is one thing. Having someone do it when they hate you, when they'll do anything in their power to hurt you—that's unbearable.

The last thing I wanted to do was speak to him, but I needed to know. "Please," I said, looking up at him. "Please—what happened to Angelo?"

He just stared at me for another minute, making me sweat. Then he sank down onto the couch next to me, his hip brushing mine. He leaned in close and put his lips to my ear in a hideous parody of a kiss. I forced myself not to pull away because I needed to know....

He whispered, "You're a disloyal whore. And you'll get what's coming to you."

I jerked away from him as if he'd slapped me. I was still staring at him in horror when the door was flung open. Vasiliy stood there, his face thunderous. He jerked his head in the direction of his study.

Feeling numb, I got up and followed him out of the room. Behind me, I could feel Mikhail smirking.

In his study, Vasiliy wouldn't look at me. He sat down slowly behind his desk. *Too* slowly. And he picked up a pen and moved it too carefully, too deliberately. I'd been around him enough years that I could tell when he was trying to contain his rage and this was the worst I'd ever seen him. He placed his hands flat on the desktop, flexing his fingers as if he wanted to tear great handfuls out of the wood. "Why?" he asked at last.

A huge lump rose up in my throat. "Is he alive?" I whispered. "Just tell me that. Is he alive?"

Vasiliy finally looked up at me and the look he gave me made me wish I hadn't asked. He looked at me as if he didn't know me. As if I was an enemy.

"You lie to me," he said, his voice a tight little whisper. "You betray me. After all these years. After everything I've done for you. You side with my enemy and you plot against me. *Why?*"

I'd been trying to get away from Vasiliy for years. Suddenly, I was. I was no longer a Malakov, not to him. I was free...and it was agony. I'd never wanted *this,* never wanted to see the man who'd raised me torn apart. People said Vasiliy Malakov was emotionless but right then he was almost trembling, he was so wounded and angry. And it was all thanks to me.

"I didn't mean for it to happen," I croaked. "I fell in love with him." And there it was. I'd said it.

He stared at me in silence. "Did you do it to hurt me?" he said at last.

"*No!* It...it wasn't about who he was. I didn't even know, at first! It was about *him. Us.*"

"You told him about our plan with the bikers," he said. He looked off into the corner, as if he couldn't bear to look at me anymore.

I was trying not to cry, now. "I was worried he was going to get killed."

"So you turned on your family?"

"No! I told him to call off the meet!"

"But he didn't. And Josef was shot. And you stood there and let me accuse Mikhail's men. You let him accuse *Yuri!*"

"I'm *sorry!*"

"Get out."

I took a half step forward. "Vasiliy, please—"

"*Get. Out.*" And this time, I saw his knuckles whiten as his hands clawed at the desk. He wanted me to go before he lost control.

I fled. I ran to one of the guest rooms up on the top floor and buried my face in the bed. I'd lost my family. I'd lost Angelo. I cried it out with big, wracking sobs: Malakovs don't cry, but I wasn't a Malakov anymore.

It was hours later when I finally stumbled out onto the balcony. I wanted to be numb again. I wanted to not feel the deep, jagged pain where my family had been torn out of me. But as soon as the freezing air engulfed me, I wanted his hands on me, warming me. *Angelo!* I was going crazy, not knowing if he was alive or dead.

Voices below me. Mikhail and Vasiliy, standing on the patio downstairs. It was a still night and their voices carried. "—with her?" Mikhail was saying.

Vasiliy shook his head and I was glad the shadows hid his expression. "She's dead to me," he said.

I felt as if I'd been punched in the chest.

"Don't be too hard on her," said Mikhail. "Women do stupid things. That bastard seduced her. Told her what she wanted to hear."

Vasiliy looked at the ground and shook his head, but this time with sadness. "She must go back to Moscow," he said, his voice thick with emotion. "With someone who can protect her." Then he nodded towards the house. "Come on. We have a lot to do. That bastard's turf is going to burn, tonight."

They disappeared inside. I retreated into the guest room and quietly closed the doors, then leaned against them.

I'm dead to him.

For a long time, I just stood there, my heart breaking.

One thing finally got me moving again. I'd destroyed everything else: had I killed Angelo, too? I had to know.

Yuri had taken my cell phone and I didn't dare use the house phone. But I knew Yuri kept a stash of "burner" phones for when he or Vasiliy needed to make an untraceable call.

I didn't want to run into Vasiliy. I wanted to run into Mikhail even less. But I forced myself to creep out of the guest room and down the stairs to the first floor. The door to Vasiliy's office was open and I could hear him and Mikhail talking inside. I could hear Mikhail's finger sliding across a map as he outlined where he was going to attack: the restaurants and nightclubs he'd burn, the bars he'd smash…. I'd tried to stop a war and I'd started one instead. And it was worse, much worse, than if things had escalated on their own. I could hear the rage in Vasiliy's voice as they talked. This was about revenge and it would be bloody and brutal.

"Don't do it yourself," I heard him grunt. "Keep your hands clean."

"I will, I will," said Mikhail airily. He sounded almost happy. Of course he was: he'd gotten exactly what he wanted.

I took a deep breath and stole past the door and on down the hallway, then down the spiral staircase that led to the old servant quarters in the basement, where Yuri and the other live-in bodyguards had their rooms. I knew which room was Yuri's because I'd sat on his bed with him a few times while he taught me things: how to shoot a gun, for one, and how to get out of plastic zip ties. Last-resort skills, for if I was ever kidnapped. If Vasiliy was like my father, Yuri had been like an older brother to me. *Another person I've lost.*

Yuri's room was empty and, as always, immaculate. It reminded me of an army barracks, the blanket so tight on the bed you could bounce a coin off it. There were some very old books, a tiny closet and a gun rack. *Is this really all he has in his life?* It seemed so cold, so lonely.

I knelt, pulled the box of burner phones from under Yuri's bed and grabbed one. *I should take it upstairs.* But what if someone saw me with it on the way up? They'd take it off me and then I might never know….

No. I wasn't risking it. I had to know *now*. I dialed Angelo's number.

He picked up on the second ring. "Irina?"

"Angelo!" My eyes closed and I slumped against Yuri's bed in relief. At the same time, I felt a sudden, deep ache right down the front of my body: the need to press myself against him and the pain of not being able to. He sounded so far away. "Are you okay?"

"Fine. Where are you?"

I told him about being on lockdown in Vasiliy's house. How he wanted to send me back to Moscow. How he was gearing up for all-out war. "*How do we turn this off?!*" I asked, my voice quavering. "This is our fault!"

I heard him rub his face with his hands. "I know. Look, stay safe. Let me figure things out. I—"

My breath caught in my chest. I knew which two words he'd bitten back. Because he wasn't sure? Or because it was crazy to say them, with everything that was going on?

"I'll see you soon," he said at last. "I'll find a way."

I ended the call. I knew I should get out of there, but all the energy had just drained out of me. *I'll see you soon. How?!* We were at war. And I was going to be on a plane back to Moscow within a few days at most.

I was never going to see him again.

That was when I heard footsteps in the hallway. *Chyort!* I shoved the phone into my jeans, pushed the box back where it was, then looked around for an escape route. There wasn't one. The room was about eight feet square and the footsteps were too close: whoever was approaching would see me coming out....

I stood up just as Yuri walked in. I tried to come up with an explanation as to why I was there, but the way he looked at me made the excuses die in my throat.

Yuri had been a constant throughout my life. He'd been around when my parents were alive, then I'd gotten to know him even better when I went to live with Vasiliy. He'd driven me to ballet lessons, he'd kicked the ass of a boyfriend who tried to get too touchy in the back seat, he'd once stopped the car and held my hair while I leaned out of the door and threw up after drinking too much...and he hadn't told Vasiliy. He was the best.

And the way he stared at me just killed me. Vasiliy had been mad but Yuri just looked...*wounded.*

I threw myself at him and wrapped my arms around him, burying my face in his chest. He let out a long sigh and stroked my hair.

"I'm s—sorry," I sobbed.

He made *shh*-ing noises, like the ones he used to make when

Lizaveta had a nightmare and couldn't sleep. He'd always been surprisingly good at it.

"Don't hate me," I managed between sobs. "I need someone to not hate me."

His arms tightened around me and he let out a long-suffering sigh. "I could never hate you."

I squeezed him tight. When I finally got control of my voice again, I asked, "Do you think Vasiliy can ever love me again?"

"I don't think he could ever *stop* loving you," said Yuri. "But there will be changes. You will have to go back to Moscow. You must never see this man again."

Fresh tears forced their way up from the depths, scalding hot and bitter. "I love him!"

"Then you too are stupid and unlucky."

I frowned. *You too?*

Yuri shook his head. "But that does not make this right."

"I know," I said in a tiny voice. He still hadn't asked what I was doing in his room. *He thinks I came to see him,* I realized. And that made me feel even worse, because that's what I *should* have done.

He hugged me like that for a few moments, rocking me gently from side to side. "You are not like other Malakovs. Too much fire. Your mother had too much fire, too."

"Then...why did she stay?" I blurted. I pushed myself back from his chest so that I could look up at him and sniffed. "She used to tell me that she didn't want this for me. She didn't want me to be with a gangster. If she didn't like it, why did she stay?"

Yuri thought for a moment. "Because she was stubborn like you are, too. She saw she was good for your father."

"She stayed because she loved him?"

"Yes. And because he needed her."

I looked blankly at him.

He sighed and looked at the ceiling. "I am not right person to explain fucking women," he muttered to himself. "Your father...he was cold. Very cold. He could be cruel to his enemies."

I frowned. My dad had been tough, sure, but I hadn't thought of him as cold or cruel.

Yuri read my look. "I knew him in his early days, before he met your mother. She balanced him. Is same way with all Malakov men."

I thought of Luka and Arianna. Of Angelo's mother, supporting his father. Suddenly, it all started to make sense. I thought of Vasiliy: I *knew* he'd used to be warmer and kinder, when I was growing up. "Vasiliy...when his wife died, is that when he started to turn cruel?"

Yuri shook his head sadly. "No. It would have been. But he had someone else who kept him balanced. Until she pulled away."

"A lover?" I asked in wonder. "A mistress?"

Yuri gently put his hands on my shoulders and stared into my eyes.

"*Me?!*" I croaked.

He nodded.

I blinked at him and stepped back, my head spinning. He gazed at me sadly as I stumbled off down the hallway.

Me? I'd been responsible for keeping Vasiliy moderated all those years?

But it made sense. When he first took Lizaveta and me under his protection, his wife had been dead a few years and he'd seemed cold and distant. But the shock of our parents' deaths and suddenly having two girls under his roof had jolted him off the path he'd been on. And as I became involved in the business he'd gradually warmed. Yuri was right: I'd been his conscience, his light in the darkness, just as his wife had been.

I'd thought that I hated our family because I'd been constantly arguing with him. Now I realized that that was my purpose: I was his counterbalance. How many times had he stepped back from some vicious course of action because I'd told him it was too cruel? How many times had I unwittingly defused a situation, just by being there for him to vent to over a game of chess?

I'd pulled away from my family. I'd dreamed of freedom and New York and isolated myself from Vasiliy more and more. And then I'd wondered why he became colder and colder.

My whole view of the last few years twisted around, reversing itself. All those things Vasiliy had done that drove me crazy: following me to New York, visiting all the time...God, even my arranged marriage with Mikhail. They were all ways of staying close to me. Subconsciously, he knew he needed me, even if he'd never admit it. And the harder he'd tried to keep me close, the more I'd pulled away.

The realization hit me in the chest like a sledgehammer: this whole aggressive expansion into New York, the partnership with Mikhail, the gang war we were now in: none of this would have happened if I'd been there to calm him, to be his warmth and his conscience. I'd always said I didn't want to be a Malakov: I hadn't understood that I was a vital part of the mixture that made the Malakovs work.

I stopped walking and had to hold onto the wall to steady myself. *This is all my fault!*

I climbed the stairs to the first floor just in time to see Mikhail leaving, a wide grin on his face and a small army of men in tow. Some were carrying guns, some baseball bats, some cans of gasoline.

It was all my fault...and it was too late to fix it. The war had begun.

35

ANGELO

The fires were the worst. Fighting and smashed-up storefronts...I could kid myself that that was random. But when I saw the owners standing in tears in the street, watching the flames roaring through the place they'd spent twenty years building...then, I knew I'd fucked up. These were my people, this was my turf, and I'd failed utterly to protect them.

I told them all the same thing. I hugged them and said, "I'll make this right." And they took my hand and shook it and told me they trusted me. But I could hear it in their voices: they'd never fully trust me again.

The Fire Department did their best but there were too many fires and they burned too aggressively: Mikhail's thugs had smashed their way in and then poured gasoline over everything. The firefighters kept looking at me: they knew this was connected to me and they wanted to know how I could let it happen. They were probably wondering if the same thing would be happening to Russian businesses in a few hours.

I did what I could. I even joined the bucket chains at some of the fires until the overstretched Fire Department could get to them, but we saved maybe one place out of ten. Meanwhile, I was getting phone calls about cars, boats and real estate being smashed up—the Russians were destroying anything that was under our protection. It was like nothing the community had ever seen: brutal, all-out destruction. It was Mikhail and his men who lit the fires and raised the baseball bats, but I could feel Vasiliy's raw hatred behind it all. This was personal.

And it had a horrifying knock-on effect. Fights were breaking out in the streets, not just between my guys and Mikhail's men but between civilians. Russian guys who'd never dared set foot in our neighborhood suddenly got bold and came looking for trouble, in gangs or on their own. Meanwhile, the local guys were on the streets looking for payback and they took their anger out on anyone who looked or sounded like they might be Russian. I met with community leaders and reached out to the gangs, trying to calm them down, but how do you convince a hot-headed sixteen year-old to stay home when his parents' coffee shop just got torched?

I told women to stay off the streets and made sure Grace had shut down Cinderella's and sent the girls home. That's about all I could do.

By the early hours of the morning, Little Italy looked like a war zone. The police were sweeping both Russians and Italians off the streets as fast as they could, but their holding cells were full and they didn't have enough evidence to hold them. The local captain, who was on my payroll, pulled me aside and demanded to know what the fuck I was going to do. That's when you know it's bad, when the police come to the criminals for help.

I didn't have an answer for him. I was *pissed*...but the anger didn't have anywhere to go except inward. What could I do? Burn Russian businesses in revenge? It would be the civilians who'd suffer.

As I gazed around the place I loved, now lit by orange fire and blue and red lights, I kept thinking back to that day I'd first seen Irina at the ballet. *We did this. This is our fault.*

I was worried sick about her. She was still stuck in Vasiliy's townhouse, with that bastard Mikhail way too close to her. And in a few days she'd be going back to Moscow and I might never see her again.

I hadn't told her that I loved her. I hadn't been able to say the words. I've never regretted anything more in my life.

Rico found me at about eight in the morning. The sky was lightening but the smoke blotted out the sun. The streets were running with a gray, slushy mixture of soot-stained melted snow and runoff water from the hoses. Rico had been up all night too and he looked like I probably looked: soot-smeared face, filthy white shirt with a few bloodstains from the injured. Both of us had discarded our ties at some point when the heat from the fires had gotten too much.

"Let's get you out of here," he said.

I shook my head and turned away from him. "I'm staying."

He grabbed my shoulder and gently but firmly turned me back. "This isn't something you can win from here, Angelo," he told me. "Besides, The Saints want to talk."

I closed my eyes and sighed, then let him lead me to the car. I'd always liked the cool, luxurious interior of the big Chrysler. It had been a safe haven where I could escape my troubles and *think*. Now, though, the luxury felt wrong. *I shouldn't be in here while they're out there....*

Goddamn Mikhail and Vasiliy for doing this. And goddamn me for making them. If I'd had a niece and found Mikhail had been fucking her, would I have reacted any differently?

Rico dialed The Saints. I had him put them on speakerphone. Rico deserved to know what was going on.

"What the fuck is going on?" yelled Nicky. "It's fucking Iraq down there. It's all over the fucking news! What the *fuck?!*" He screamed it so loud, his voice rasped.

Rico and I looked at each other. It was clear the Saints didn't know about me and Irina. If they had, they'd have summoned me so they could put a bullet in my head.

"It's spilling over," said Vincenzo. "The Russians are getting ideas, right across the city. You don't fix this *now*, we're going to have a big fucking problem."

"You gotta kill Vasiliy. And that fat fuck Mikhail," said Taavetti. "Only way to stop them."

Immediately, he was shouted down. "You don't kill the leaders, you dumb fuck," snapped Nicky. "Someone's gotta be there to turn it off! Why do you think they haven't taken out a hit on Angelo, yet?"

He was right. That was the only reason I was still alive. The only thing worse than war was chaos, which was what we'd have without leadership.

"What you gotta do," snapped Nicky, "is show them how much this'll hurt, if they keep it up. Each step they take into our territory has gotta be like walking on razor blades, understand? Starting tonight, we burn *their* businesses—every one of them. We take out everything they own. Every backroom poker game gets smashed up. Every car dealership, those cars get totaled. *Everything.*"

I spoke for the first time. "It's out of control. People are getting drawn in. Not just our people: anyone with Italian blood."

"Good," said Nicky savagely. "Let 'em. They *should* fight for their turf, goddammit."

Fight for their turf. It all suddenly seemed so stupid. "They're *kids,*" I said. "Some of them are sixteen."

"That's plenty old enough to fight," said Taavetti. "Put baseball bats in their hands and send them into Little Odessa."

"We're outnumbered!" I snapped, finally losing it. "They have more men, more guns. Vasiliy has *billions* in the bank: he can hire mercenaries, if he has to. Even with the civilians fighting with us, we'll lose! It'll be a bloodbath!"

"So?" Yelled Taavetti. I heard him huff for air from his oxygen cylinder. "We go out fighting. Your dad spilled blood to take those streets; you can fucking spill blood to defend them!"

I shook my head silently. My dad would never have sent men to their deaths when he knew the fight was useless. The Saints were just scared of losing what they'd built up and they were willing to sacrifice every Italian life on the street in a futile bid to cling onto it.

"Fix it, Angelo," said Nicky, his voice vicious. "This is your last fucking chance. Fix it, or we'll find someone who can."

The line went dead. I could feel Rico's eyes on me from the driver's seat. It took me a long time to turn and meet his gaze.

"Angelo?" he asked. "What's going on?"

I couldn't explain. Rico had been with me for so long, since even before I took over from my dad. He'd helped me build this empire. Now he couldn't understand why I was standing by and watching while it was torn down. I tried, even though I knew it was useless. I owed him that. "They lied to us, Rico. The Saints got us fighting a war but the Russians aren't any different to us." Rico balked. "They're *not*," I insisted. "The Saints got us thinking it has to be this way, but it doesn't."

Rico slowly shook his head at me. "This is Irina," he said. "She's done a number on you."

"*No!* She just opened my eyes!"

Rico put his hands on my shoulders and slammed me back into my seat. "Okay, *listen!* I've stood by you every fucking step of the way. I've done exactly what you told me, every time. So for once, shut up and listen to me. You are about to lose everything. Okay? *Everything.* If the Russians ever were interested in peace, they sure as fuck aren't now, not now Vasiliy knows you've been banging his niece. This is *war* and you can either fight or surrender but there ain't no third option. So *snap out of it* because I need Angelo back!"

I knew he was right. But how could I explain to him that my empire didn't matter anymore, if I couldn't have her? "Drop me home," I told Rico. "Then go to *Underground* and see what needs doing there. I need to think."

Out of the corner of my eye, I could see him shaking his head, his face taut with worry. I owed him so much. I wished I could tell him not to worry, that I'd fix everything...but it wasn't true.

I stumbled through the door of my apartment, woozy with fatigue. I hadn't slept in over twenty-four hours and my muscles, worn out from crawling through the mud and then throwing buckets of water all night, had solidified into concrete.

I needed sleep, but I didn't have time. Instead, I got under the shower in the hope the hot water beating down on me would help me think. But there wasn't any solution I could see.

My instinct was to fight. That's what I always did. That's what my dad had always done. But Vasiliy was too fired up with anger: he didn't just want victory, he wanted to destroy me. To even slow his progress, I'd have to sacrifice every man I had, plus a lot of civilians. Maybe The Saints were okay with that, but I wasn't.

Peace? There'd be no peace now, not between Vasiliy and me. We were way past that. I'd foregone any hope of peace that morning when I'd first called Irina, already knowing who she was. If I could go back in time....

Who was I kidding? If I could go back in time, I'd do exactly the same thing again. I loved her.

That only left surrender. It would save some lives, but I'd be letting down all the people who'd trusted me to protect them. Vasiliy was cold, but at least he seemed professional—it wasn't him I was worried about. It was that bastard Mikhail and his thugs: they'd be the ones who'd shake down local businesses for protection money if I surrendered. No way was I unleashing them on the people I cared about.

And however hard I tried to focus on the crisis, my mind kept swerving back to Irina. I'd told her I'd find a way, but I couldn't see one. *I'm never going to see her again!*

I finally stepped from the shower and started to towel off. I had to restick some of the dressings and tape Rico had put on my back and ribs. God, I was a mess. Bruises everywhere and livid red finger marks around my neck where Mikhail had—

I frowned in the mirror and looked closer. There was a symbol in amongst the finger marks, a symbol I recognized. A serpent. I grabbed my phone and checked the photos I'd taken of Kirsty to be sure. It was reversed because I'd been choked from behind instead of in front, but it was the same mark from the same ring. It was the same person.

Mikhail. He'd been the one who'd raped Kirsty and beat her to within an inch of her life. It had never even occurred to me that it might be a Russian. *He barely spoke,* Kirsty had said. No wonder she hadn't recognized the accent. And with his bland looks, Mikhail could be any fat businessman.

At first, it made no sense—that's why I hadn't even considered it. The last place a Russian mafia boss would go was to a *Cosa Nostra* hooker: far too much potential for dangerous pillow talk and blackmail. They'd use one of their own places, where the girls were loyal to their side.

My stomach tightened. *Unless, of course, you're a perverted bastard who likes to beat women up. Then* it made perfect sense. Mikhail could keep his nasty little hobby from his comrades and he got to take his frustration with me out on poor Kirsty. No doubt he'd known she worked at Cinderella's and that therefore she was one of mine. *The bastard. He's dead, the next time I see him....*

And then my blood turned to ice water. Mikhail was right there in Vasiliy's house, with Irina.

It got worse. Mikhail was the guy Vasiliy wanted Irina to marry. Sure, Irina had said she'd never let it happen, but then she hadn't been expecting to be sent back to Moscow, either.

Fear like I'd never known twisted together with white-hot anger. *I have to get her out of there!* My head started to fill with crazy fantasies of eloping with her, just blasting out of there in my car and never looking back, of leaving it all behind....

I shook my head, walked over to my closet and took out a fresh, crisp shirt. That was batshit crazy. I couldn't run off with Irina. My empire was burning. I had to stay here and—

I stared down at the shirt as the idea broke over me like cool, fresh water. *What if I didn't?*

What if getting out was the right thing to do?

It would solve all my problems. Irina and I could be together, in some country where Vasiliy couldn't touch us. Irina would be safe from Mikhail. And I'd take Vasiliy's anger with me. Sure, he'd still be mad as hell with me, but that rage wouldn't be directed towards *Cosa Nostra* and the people we protected anymore. Whoever took over from me could negotiate peace—Vasiliy had already shown he was willing to deal, just not with me, anymore. It could all work out.

All I had to do was give up everything I'd ever worked for.

I fingered the shirt, then stared at the neat rows of identical shirts and suits hanging in my closet. It was unthinkable. Completely fucking unthinkable. My dad's legacy: gone. All my men. *Rico.* I'd never see them again. I'd never be able to come back to Little Italy—hell, I'd never be able to come back to *America.*

But I'd get to be with her.

I slowly replaced the shirt in the closet. Then I dug around and found the clothes I wore on the rare days I wasn't working: t-shirt and jeans, a sweater and a leather jacket. Then I took the framed Yankees jersey down off the wall to reveal the wall safe, opened it up and swept all the cash into a sports bag. I grabbed my passport and tucked my gun into the back of my jeans, looked around the place for maybe the last time....

And then I called Irina.

36

IRINA

Four minutes to noon.

When Angelo had called on the burner phone, I'd had to sit down fast on my bed to avoid collapsing in relief. I'd barely slept the night before, staying up all night watching rolling news coverage of the fires in Little Italy and the fighting in the streets. I was so relieved to hear his voice, I wanted to weep. And when he told me his plan: to flee the country and start fresh somewhere else, I actually did start to cry. He was giving up his whole life for me.

The plan was simple: I'd go to my house on the pretense of collecting some clothes. It would be easier for me to sneak out of there than to escape Vasiliy's house. Angelo would be waiting in a cab on the next street over at exactly noon. I'd run to him, we'd drive straight to the airport and we'd have disappeared before anyone could stop us.

Yuri had been assigned to drive me to my house and Mikhail had insisted on coming along too. He didn't dare touch me or degrade me in front of Yuri, but I'd had to suffer his thigh pressed against mine for the whole journey. And what Angelo had told me made it worse. I'd had to sit there knowing the evil that lay inside him, that the man touching me was the sort of monster who'd rape a woman and beat her half to death. Thinking of Angelo was the only thing that kept me from screaming. *Just a little longer,* I'd promised myself, *and then we can be together.*

It had worked. Yuri and Mikhail were now downstairs and I was in my bedroom. My bag was packed, my passport was in my hand. I was ready.

So why was I still sitting there, at three minutes to noon? I had to go, *now,* to meet Angelo.

This is everything you ever wanted, I told myself. Angelo was going to give up being a gangster. I would finally be free of my family. We could live out our lives somewhere where the sun could warm my skin. It could be paradise....

Two minutes to noon.

I kept thinking about what Yuri had said. As his surrogate daughter, I'd moderated Vasiliy, kept him warm—kept him *human.* When I'd pushed him away, Mikhail had stepped in to fill the void. He was gradually turning Vasiliy into a monster, no better than him. When Vasiliy had discovered my betrayal, it had pushed him even closer to Mikhail. If I walked away, soon there'd be nothing left of the man who'd raised me.

One minute to noon.

I opened the doors to the balcony and picked up my bag. I took a long look at myself in the mirror....

And then I slowly put the bag down in the middle of the floor and climbed down off the balcony without it.

~

Angelo let out a long sigh of relief when I ran up. He pushed the cab's door open for me, then slammed it as soon as I was inside. "Go!" he told the cabbie. "Airport!"

Before I could speak, he gathered me into his arms and his lips found mine. Those big, warm hands slid up to tangle in my hair and he kissed me as if to make up for every second we'd been apart. I melted against his chest, his pecs like slabs of rock. God, he felt so good!

"But where's your bag?" he asked when he finally broke the kiss. Then he shook his head. "Doesn't matter. We can buy you new stuff."

He looked so different. It was the first time I'd seen him in anything other than a suit. He looked younger, as if a massive weight had been lifted from his shoulders. How could I possibly suggest that he take it back?

The cab sped on towards the airport. It was bliss, sitting there beside him, soaking up the warmth from his body, our whole lives before us...but inside, my soul was screaming at me. Every minute that ticked by was making it worse. *Tell him, tell him, tell him!*

"We can't leave," I said at last, my face buried in his chest.

I felt him look down at me. "The hell we can't."

I swallowed. "I don't have my passport."

He pushed me back from him. "*What?!*"

I bit my lip. "I knew if I brought it, you'd talk me round. *We can't leave.*" I glanced out of the window. We were on the highway, now, and the airport was close enough that we could hear the jets in the distance. "We have to talk." I looked meaningfully at the cabbie— what I had to say, I didn't want to say in front of him.

Angelo was still staring at me, aghast. "Pull over," he told the cabbie at last.

The cabbie craned around. "*Here?*"

"Do it."

The cabbie cursed and pulled over by the side of the highway. Angelo tossed him some bills and we got out. It wasn't snowing, but a thick layer coated everything, giving even the crash barriers beside the highway a soft edge. The traffic was too loud for us to talk so I started walking up the grassy rise that lay alongside the highway. Angelo followed. "What is this bullshit?" he asked.

I shook my head. "We can't leave."

He grabbed my arm and pulled me around to face him. "*Yes we can.* We can go anywhere we want. Paris. Rome. Fucking Kuala Lumpur!"

I couldn't meet his eyes. Every cell in my body was screaming at me to just go with him and, if I looked into those brown and amber eyes one more time, I'd give in. "You always told me how important this was. How people need you in Little Italy. How it was your dad's legacy." I pulled free and started walking up the rise again.

"Fuck all that!" he snapped. "Maybe I was wrong. Maybe it's all just bullshit. *You* were right. Russians aren't any different to Italians. We shouldn't be killing each other."

My heart was breaking. He'd changed so much, he'd come around to everything I'd tried to convince him of, and now I had to undo it all. Because the truth was, we were both right. I reached the top of the rise: ahead, it sloped steeply down to an empty field covered in crisp, unbroken snow.

I took Angelo's hand and led him down the slope with me, the traffic noise dying away behind us. It felt ridiculous, leading him along: he was so big and his whole body was tense and straining with anger. He could have so easily pulled away or towed me along with him, but he followed. When I looked across at him, the need I saw in his expression almost made me crumble before I got a word out. All he wanted in the entire world was for me to run away with him. *Why can't I just go?*

Because I'd finally figured out what my destiny was. Vasiliy had been trying to tell me all along and I'd refused to listen: I was a Malakov and I had a role to play.

"We have to stay," I said, "because we're the only ones who can stop this thing. I'm the only one who can come between Mikhail and Vasiliy and get Vasiliy to talk peace. You're the only one who can control your guys and stop this getting worse and worse."

"Vasiliy hates me," Angelo said. "He'll never talk peace with me. If I leave and someone new comes in, maybe they'll do better."

We reached the bottom of the slope and stood looking out across the field. It was surprisingly quiet here, the hill doing a good job of blocking the traffic noise. "Who'll pick your replacement, if you leave?" I asked gently.

"My bosses. The Saints."

"And will they pick someone who'll talk peace? Or will they pick someone who'll keep the war going?"

I could see him struggling with it. He wanted to deny it, but he knew I was right. "They hate the Russians. Shit. They'll keep it going until we're all dead."

I nodded. "And hundreds of Russians will die, too."

Angelo stood and turned from me, his massive shoulders hunched in rage. He suddenly turned and kicked the snow, a huge fantail of it flying through the air. "I don't want this fucking job!" he bellowed. "Not anymore! I just want you!"

"I never wanted to be a Malakov," I said, lifting my chin. "But I've finally realized that the only thing worse than being involved in this stuff is running from it. We can't run because *we're part of it,* Angelo. We're holding up the freakin' building. If we run, like I tried to when I came to New York, *it all comes down.*"

He took a long breath in. "What about us?" he said at last.

"We wait. We go home and we do what we have to do. I talk Vasiliy into stopping the attacks. If you can hold your guys back from retaliating, maybe we can get a ceasefire. Then maybe, *maybe,* I can get Vasiliy to talk peace. And when it's all done...maybe we can be together. But this is more important than us."

He took my face between his hands. "*Nothing* is more important! Nothing is more important than you!" He looked away. Looked back at me. "I love you."

I wasn't ready for how hard that hit me. It struck me square in the chest and lit me up, the warmth radiating out to every cell of my body. And instead of dissipating and fading, it *glowed,* a deep, fiery heat that made me ache and pulse every time I looked at him. Despite everything, I couldn't stop myself grinning. "I love you, too," I managed, my voice breaking. And I saw his whole face soften, those brown and amber eyes suddenly vulnerable for a second.

I swallowed. "There are lives at stake. A lot of lives. We started this; we have to finish it." I lifted my chin and looked at him defiantly. "Because what's the alternative? Are you *really* going to get on a plane knowing that everything you said you'd protect is burning? Because that's not the Angelo I know. That's not the guy I fell for."

He ducked his head and pressed his cheek to mine, the heat of him warming me as the freezing wind whipped my hair against the other cheek. "*Irina,*" he said simply. But my name contained all the anger, all the pain, all the lust that I'd brought to him.

"Do you wish you'd never met me?" I asked. My eyes were suddenly wet, burning saltiness threatening to overspill.

His big hands squeezed my shoulders hard and he crushed me against his chest. "You're the best thing that ever happened to me." He kissed the soft skin below my ear, then followed the line of my jaw to my lips and kissed me, long and deep. "Alright, we'll wait. We'll sort this mess out. But you've got to promise me: when all this is done, we're going to be together."

I pressed my face to his chest and snuggled my cheek into the deep, hard line between his pecs. "I promise."

He pushed me back from him and his lips met mine, hard against my softness. The raw heat of him made me melt, my body wilting against his and my mouth flowering open. He took possession of me, hands stroking across my cheeks and into my hair, fingers sinking deep into it as if it was the best thing he'd ever felt. His tongue sought out mine and I came alive, flexing and writhing against him as we twisted and danced, my breasts soft against his chest. The kiss changed. The mood changed. I could feel the outline of his cock against his thigh, already hot and hard and still swelling.

It felt like weeks since we'd seen each other. We didn't know when we'd see each other again.

Suddenly, his hands were on the buttons of my coat, popping them one by one with quick efficiency. By the time I broke the kiss, it was already open to my waist. "We can't," I panted, looking around. We were two black-clad figures at the edge of a vast white space. We must have been visible for miles. "Not *here!*"

"Fuck 'em," panted Angelo. "If anyone's watching, let's give them a good show." And he unbuttoned my coat the rest of the way, flinging the sides open. Underneath, I was in a rust-colored sweater and black skirt with black leggings. He shoved the coat down my arms and then tossed it down on the snow.

He started kissing me again, this time open-mouthed and hungry, and I groaned as I felt his hands slide down over my ass and squeeze. Then they were rising, slipping beneath the hem of my sweater to stroke the bare skin beneath. God, his warmth felt so good, his palms sliding over my back as if sculpting it, then his thumbs circling on my stomach. "We *can't*," I gasped again, having to twist my head to the side to escape his furious kissing. "It's *freezing!*" I left a cloud of white in the air when I said it, proving my point.

"I thought you didn't mind the cold?" he growled. "Besides, I'll warm you up." And his hands rose higher, up over my back, stroking over the elastic of my bra, then around to my front, cupping my breasts, squeezing them lightly, thumbs finding the nipples through the bra and rubbing, *Oh God....*

His hands slid behind me again. Suddenly the clasp was free and my bra went loose across my breasts. His hands were on me in an instant, palming my breasts, the nipples stiffening automatically at his touch. My breath quickened, hitching faster and faster with each brush of his hands—God, I was aching for him. He never stopped kissing me, first sucking my top lip into his mouth and nibbling gently on it, then drawing my lower lip oh-so-slowly down, leaving me quivering. My nipples were between his thumbs and forefingers now, the nubs tight and hard as he rolled and stroked, the heat pumping straight down between my legs....

Angelo growled as if he couldn't wait any longer. He grabbed the hem of my sweater and drew it slowly upwards, taking my bra with it. I lifted my arms over my head to help him but he didn't speed up: he drew the fabric up over me as reverently as if he was unveiling a statue. I could feel his eyes on each inch of my bare skin as it was revealed: my stomach, my chest...when the sweater's hem reached my breasts, he slowed down almost to a stop, the fabric rising millimeter by slow millimeter.

The top of it was already over my head, trapping me in a cocoon of warmth, thin enough that it was translucent but thick enough that it mostly blindfolded me. I could see the brightness of the snow around us and the huge, dark shape of him in front of me, but not details. I didn't need to see him to know where he was looking, though. I could feel his eyes eating me up, devouring my breasts as they gradually appeared. The icy air blew across my naked back and over my breasts, my nipples throbbing and ultra-sensitive, every little gust of wind magnified a thousand fold.

The dark shape in front of me leaned forward and I squealed as a hot mouth enveloped one breast. The heat of his tongue after the freezing air was shocking, oven-hot and slickly wet. I had to press my thighs hard together, my ass describing an "S" in the air as I swayed and ground, the heat rising and building inside me.

Then the sweater was tugged up and off me, falling to the ground with my bra tangled within it. My hair fell around my shoulders, strands tickling against my bare skin. I let out a long breath, forming a soft cloud of vapor in the air between us.

He put his hands on my waist and ran them up and down my sides, the heels of his hands just brushing the sides of my breasts—it was as if he was teasing himself, drawing out the moment before he'd take them in his hands again. Those brown and amber eyes were burning, now, his gaze a scalding trail across my skin. He let a long, shuddering gasp of lust, the white cloud it left mixing with mine. Finally, when he couldn't bear it any longer, he filled his hands with my breasts and pulled me close, squeezing rhythmically, his thumbs brushing across my nipples as he kissed me hard and deep.

The wind picked up, freezing one side of my body. I pressed myself hard against him, letting the warmth of him soak into me through his clothes. My hands wound around his back and slid up under his jacket and sweater, tracing the hard lines of his muscles. I started to ease his jacket down his arms and off even as he unzipped my skirt. Both of us were frantic, now, needing to feel each other's bodies. His jacket hit the snow and then, a second later, my skirt fell around my feet.

I lifted his sweater and t-shirt up and over his head, kissing my way up his exposed chest an inch behind the rising hem. The hardness of his abs against the softness of my lips made me crazy, the heat inside me twisting, becoming tight and frantic. I kissed up his centerline, over smooth tan skin and then up to the dark ink of the angel wings tattoo, lips tracing first one broad, curved pec and then the other, my hands sliding around his shoulders.

The heat of him blazed across the space that separated us, searing away the cold. I crushed my body to his, me soft and cold and him iron hard and throbbing with warmth, and it was the best thing I'd felt in my life. He wrapped his arms around my naked back and I knew I'd never want to be cold or numb again.

His hands slid under the waistband of my leggings and panties and palmed my ass, then started rolling the fabric down my thighs. I caught my breath as the wind whipped across my exposed sex, but the cold only made the heat inside pulse faster and hotter. My hands found the belt of his jeans and I tugged the buckle open. His cock strained against the heavy fabric and then tented his jockey shorts as his jeans fell. I ran the tips of my fingers over it and saw it twitch, thick and hard and fiercely hot. I was panting, now. I needed that heat inside me.

I kicked off my shoes, stepping back onto my coat and then stripping my leggings the rest of the way off. I was naked, except for the necklace he'd given me.

"I said I'd fuck you, with you wearing just that," he murmured, brushing it with his fingers. He pushed down his jockey shorts and his cock sprang free, gorgeous and brutal, the silken head pointing at the sky. He drew it down so that it pointed right at the soft curls of blonde hair between my thighs. "Now I'm going to."

I didn't so much *lie down* as *sink*, my knees buckling at the thought of what we were going to do. He stood there naked, legs braced a little way apart, the cold wind whipping across his tattooed chest, his tan skin beautiful against the snow. I lay on my back, the outspread coat my only protection against the snow. And yet despite the freezing ground and the cold wind, I wasn't shivering. The heat inside me was now furnace-bright and expanding fast. I lifted my knees and stepped my feet apart, welcoming him in, and saw his cock twitch in response.

He knelt between my thighs, retrieved a condom from his pants and rolled it on, and then his hips were spreading my legs. The thick head of him brushed the sensitive skin of my inner thighs once, twice...and then it kissed up against the lips of my sex. God, I hadn't realized how wet I was. My breath started to come in quick little pants, the clouds of mist breaking against his chest as he lowered himself atop me, his hard body burning hot against mine.

He kissed me on the lips once, then started to kiss down my neck and across my shoulder, his tongue quick and expert on my collarbone. He kissed me with that perfect blend of care and roughness. I was a princess to be worshipped...but a princess he was going to damn well ravish and make *his*. I moved beneath him, flexing and twisting, rubbing my body against his like a cat. The hard ridges of his abs stroked along my stomach, the deep diagonal lines of his Adonis belt stroking at the tops of my thighs. With every breath I took, my chest touched his: soft, sinful breast and nipple grazing sculpted pec and heavenly angel feathers. And then I felt the head of his cock stroking, pushing, spreading me wide....

My eyes fluttered open and I stared up into a white sky as he slid into me, my arms coming up to clasp around his shoulders. My ass come up off the coat, my back arching as he stretched me just right...and then my head tilted back, chin pointed at the sky, as he filled me in a hot rush. The heat of him met my own twisting, aching need and we combined and blazed even hotter. I heard him groan in satisfaction. "Jesus," he whispered, his lips at my ear. "Jesus, Irina, you feel so good."

He began to move, stroking slowly out of me, and the feel of him against my satiny walls made me dig my toes hard into the smooth lining of my coat, the snow scrunching beneath it. I missed the heat and hardness of him inside me but I wanted that sweet friction, knew that in a second it would—

God! He slammed back into me, even deeper than before, and my head came up, eyes locking with his. We kissed, hard and hot, as my hands explored his back. He began to thrust, breaking the kiss and dipping his head to lick at my breasts, shoulders hunched like a beast, and I went wild, thrashing and gasping under him as his tongue lashed over my nipples.

The heat inside me was taking control of me, spreading out to my fingers and toes. I wrapped my legs around him, loving the feeling of his solid, muscled thighs against my heels. I grabbed his ass and immediately went weak as my fingers found the hot, solid power of him there, the tight muscles that would let him pound me for hours. The heat was folding in on itself, tightening, beginning to thrash and seek escape. And with Angelo, I didn't have to keep it under control: I could let it out.

He raised himself up on his arms, biceps bulging, and I couldn't stop myself running my hands all the way up his naked back and down his arms, melting inside as I swept my fingertips over the hard swells. The size of him made me feel small; the strength of him made me feel weak. For someone like me who'd been trying to be strong her whole life, there was no better feeling in the world.

He began to move faster and the heat inside grew too much to bear. I lifted my ass and began to shamelessly grind my hips in circles, both of us groaning as the liquid friction grew and changed. I felt Angelo's body tense, a wicked smile teasing the corners of his lips: he loved to see me like this, loved to see me lose control for him.

My head began to toss from side to side, strands of hair falling across my face as I sucked in air through my nose, jaw set and teeth gritted. I was notching higher and higher, my toes dancing against my coat, my whole world narrowing down to the hard, hot thrust of him inside me. "A—Angelo," I gasped, his name floating upward in a desperate little puff of mist.

He lowered his head and kissed my chin. "Irina," he growled. My hands clawed at his back, my heels digging into his ass....

I felt it on my breasts first: an angel's kiss, so soft I wasn't sure if I'd imagined it. An instant of cold that only made the heat more real. I opened my eyes and saw my breast shining wetly, a drop of water running down my side.

Another soft kiss, this time on my other breast, and this time I was in time to see the snowflake melt against my heated skin. I looked around: snow was falling all around us, flakes hitting Angelo's muscled back and turning instantly to jewels of water. Even when the wind whipped across our bodies and flakes dusted our sides, it didn't stop us. The cold only made the heat inside more intense. The orgasm was building and tightening inside me. I was bucking and twisting under him, the sweat standing out on my forehead. We were both so close—

He suddenly leaned back and stared right into my eyes and the look I saw there sent me over the edge. His eyes were heavy-lidded with lust, drinking in the sight of me. I was his ice princess and he'd reduced me from imperious and frozen to a melted, gasping wreck. He was my hot-headed, black-hearted gangster, driven by blood and fire, and yet I'd put him under my spell.

He owned me. And I owned him.

He thrust into me, *deep* and I saw his ass clench as I felt the first hot explosion inside me. My own climax tightened into a blazing, white-hot ball...and detonated, making me bury my face against his shoulder and shout in Russian, my lips moving against his skin. I was clenching and spasming around him, shouting and shouting—

He bit at my earlobe, nuzzling there. *"Don't stop,"* I repeated in English, all shyness gone. *"Don't stop, don't stop—"*

He didn't, burying himself in me again and again as he shot and shot, and my orgasm stretched out and out, waves of it crashing through me, until I finally wrapped him in my arms and legs and lay still, chest heaving. We lay there for long minutes, the snow covering his muscled back first with a sheen of water and then, as he cooled, with a dusting of white.

We dressed, stopping every few garments to kiss. When I lifted my coat, the snow beneath it was gone—our heat had melted it, right down to the grass below. Even now, I didn't feel cold. We were both warmed from the inside out, by what we'd done and by the possibilities ahead. It didn't matter that the odds were against us. The odds had been against us right from the start. What mattered was that we were going to face them together and head on.

Angelo called Rico, who said he'd come and pick us up. The plan was for him and Angelo to drop me back in the city, a good distance from my house, and then I'd get a cab home. I'd find Mikhail and Yuri and explain that I'd attempted to run away, but had decided my place was with my family. I wouldn't mention Angelo. Then I'd start trying to talk Vasiliy into agreeing a ceasefire. Meanwhile, Angelo would try to calm things with the *Cosa Nostra*.

Angelo pushed my hair back from my face and kissed me again as we waited. "I don't want to do this," he muttered. "I just got you again. I don't want to give you up."

"We'll be together soon," I promised him.

Moments later, Rico came over the top of the rise. He stood there for a second staring down at us...at *me*. *Does he hate me?* In his eyes, I'd taken his best friend from him....

He started down the slope towards us, shaking his head softly. "What the hell are you wearing?" he asked Angelo as he drew close. Then he nodded to me, polite but cautious.

I grabbed his hand. "Thank you," I said. I didn't just mean for picking us up. Angelo was going to need his help if we were going to pull this off.

Rico shrugged. "Yeah," he muttered, "Well—"

There was a metallic *click* and we all turned to look.

Yuri was marching down the slope, his gun leveled right at us.

37

IRINA

I figured it out pretty fast. Yuri was a master at tracking people down and he'd do anything to protect me. When I hadn't come down from my room, he would have come upstairs and found me gone. And with no way to follow *me,* he'd done the next best thing. Realizing that I'd be meeting Angelo, he'd hunted him...and when he too couldn't be found, he'd hunted down his right-hand man, Rico, then followed him here.

Yuri was almost at the bottom of the slope, now, maybe twenty feet from us. "Irina," he said sadly, "move away from him."

Instead, I moved around in front of Angelo. I wasn't sure what orders Yuri had been given—was he just here to get me back, or would he kill Angelo as soon as he had a clear shot? I wasn't taking the chance. "No!"

At that moment, Rico yelled and threw himself at Yuri. The two of them crashed down into the snow, Yuri's gun flying out of his hand. They tumbled over and over, battling for dominance. I could see Rico had the youth and strength, but Yuri had decades of training, some of it with Russia's *Spetsnaz* special forces. He slammed his fist into Rico's kidneys, then headbutted him and threw him off. Before Rico could get to his feet, Yuri was standing over him drawing a vicious-looking knife.

That launched Angelo into action. He charged Yuri from the side and knocked him to the ground again, the two of them sending up showers of snow as they landed. My chest went tight: I didn't want anything to happen to Angelo but Yuri was like a brother to me. "*Stop!*" I yelled.

But they didn't. Yuri got to his feet, crouched over in a fighting pose. Angelo ran at him again and Yuri was forced back, slashing with the knife to keep Angelo at bay, the blade flashing in the painfully-bright sunlight. By now, Rico was back on his feet and the two of them moved in together, inching Yuri back towards the slope.

"*Stop!*" I yelled again. Angelo glanced quickly back at me and Yuri used the distraction to spring at him. Angelo barely jumped back in time and then, with a growl, he charged Yuri and grabbed his knife hand, forcing it up and away from him. Yuri staggered back, hit the bottom of the slope and fell, dragging Angelo down with him—

And suddenly everything was still and silent. Yuri lay on his back on the slope. Angelo straddled him, panting hard.

I ran over. Yuri seemed to have given up: he was staring up at Angelo in dismay, his face pale. Angelo had gone almost as white, looking down at his hands in horror.

Then I followed Angelo's gaze and saw the knife, buried to the hilt in Yuri's heart.

38

IRINA

"No," I croaked. "No, no, *no!*" I ran to Yuri and fell to my knees beside him. I put my hand to his cheek and it was already clammy and gray. "*No!*"

Blood was spreading out beneath him, oozing through the snow. Angelo and I looked at each other. "I didn't—"—he shook his head—"it was an accident."

All the bits of first aid I'd picked up over the years swam into my head but my brain was fogged and slow because this was *Yuri,* the protector who'd been there for my family as long as I could remember. Yuri wasn't supposed to get hurt. Yuri was forever.

Rico knelt beside me. It was the first time we'd been this close and the glance he gave me said so much: anger and hate and distrust...and guilt. Then he focused on Yuri. "If we want to save him," he told Angelo, "we've got to go *now. Right now.*"

Angelo nodded and jumped to his feet. "Get his arms," he said.

Yuri gave a long groan of pain as we lifted him but, with all three of us helping, we managed to get him up the slope to the big Chrysler Rico had driven there. Pulled up behind it, I could see one of Vasiliy's black Mercedes with blacked-out windows—that must be how Yuri got there.

We slid Yuri into the back seat and Angelo got in with him. Rico got into the driver's seat and they both looked up at me, waiting for me to get in.

"I can't come," I told them.

"*What?*" They both said it at the same time.

"Vasiliy will kill whoever did this. If I disappear, he'll figure out it was you. I need to go home. We stick to the plan: I claim I tried to run away and then had second thoughts, nothing to do with you."

Angelo just stared at me. His instinct was to stay with me, no matter the consequences. He shook his head.

"We don't have time to argue!" I told him. "I'll take the Mercedes. Find the keys!"

Angelo shook his head again but rooted in Yuri's pocket and pulled out a key fob. He weighed it in his hand, looking at me beseechingly.

"We gotta go!" yelled Rico.

Angelo drew in a long, shuddering breath and tossed me the keys. "Be careful!"

I nodded and slammed the door before he could change his mind. The big car roared away, threading its way quickly through the highway traffic in the direction of the hospital.

Jesus. Yuri. It was difficult to breathe. *Please don't let him die!* Not Yuri. There'd been too many casualties of this war already.

I ran over to the Mercedes, got in and started it up. *How did this go so wrong, so fast?* Vasiliy would want vengeance against whoever had stabbed his beloved bodyguard. There was no question: he'd put a hit out on the attacker. The only saving grace was that no one knew it was Angelo.

"Hello, Irina," said Mikhail from the back seat.

39

ANGELO

I had Yuri's head resting on my lap, my hands slick with his blood as I tried to keep pressure on the knife wound. The knife itself was still in his chest, evidence of my crime. I wanted to throw up every time I looked at it, but I didn't dare move it because it was stopping some of the bleeding. *Please don't let him die.* Yuri's face had gone the same color as the soot-stained snow back in Little Italy, his eyes narrowed in agony, his teeth gritted. From what Irina had told me, this guy was practically family. The guilt was like nothing I'd ever felt.

And yet, each time I felt Rico glance furiously back at me, that guilt was almost worse.

"What were you doing, Angelo?" he demanded.

"Just drive," I said tightly.

"You're dressed like you're going on vacation." Rico was almost panting, he was so angry. "You're out here by the highway—what's out this way, huh? The airport?!"

"Just drive! He needs the hospital!"

"I'm fucking driving!" He banged the steering wheel. "You were running out on us. You were fucking running out on us, weren't you?"

I didn't answer, just looked down at Yuri's ashen face.

When he spoke again, Rico's voice was so full of hurt it brought a lump to my throat. "Fuck you, Angelo."

Moments later, we arrived. Rico pulled right up to the Emergency Room entrance and I ran in to get a doctor. We got Yuri onto a gurney and inside but, immediately, nurses were asking me questions: who was he, who was I, what happened?

I had Vasiliy's number in my phone from when I'd set up the peace talk. I scrawled it on a form and handed it to a nurse. "Call this man. He'll take care of everything." Then I was running back to Rico. I didn't want to leave Yuri, but there was nothing more I could do and getting myself arrested wasn't going to help.

Rico pulled away as soon as I got in the car but we didn't head towards the city. He turned and headed out of town. "What are you doing?" I asked.

"The Saints just called," Rico said. "They want to see you." He twisted in his seat and looked at me, his face drawn with worry. "Angelo...they know."

40

———

IRINA

My hands were still on the Mercedes's steering wheel. I sat there clutching it, willing it not to be true. But when I looked up into the rear view mirror, I could see the lower half of Mikhail's face, his unmistakable wide smirk almost splitting his pink, doughy face in two. With shaking hands, I adjusted the mirror and those beady, lust-filled eyes gleamed back at me.

We hadn't even considered it, when we carried Yuri to Rico and Angelo's car. The Mercedes had been sitting there with the doors closed, the blacked-out windows concealing Mikhail. We'd just assumed Yuri had come alone.

Mikhail leaned forward. "I saw everything. I took a peek over the top of the hill, just in time to see your boyfriend murder Yuri."

I wanted to throw up. When he found out, Vasiliy wouldn't rest until Angelo was dead.

"Since you're already in the driver's seat, I think you should drive," said Mikhail. He sat back in his seat. "Let's go home."

My heart pounding, I put the car into gear and drove off to Vasiliy's house to seal Angelo's fate.

41

ANGELO

It wasn't like the last time I'd seen The Saints. Last time had been like being summoned to the Principal's office. This was like the walk to the gallows.

The big, dark room was lit this time by a huge fire roaring in the fireplace, the flames turning one side of Nicky's scowling face to flickering gold. He stood, hands braced on the table, but insisted I sit down. The other Saints stood beside him, looking equally pissed. Even kindly old Vincenzo was giving me a *you're fucked, kid* look.

I sat. I figured that if they were going to kill me, it wouldn't make much difference. Rico stood in the doorway behind me. I figured that that would be my warning: if they asked him to leave, I was dead.

Nicky opened a brown envelope and tossed a sheaf of photos onto the table. They spun and spread as they landed, covering the table in a glossy fan of eyes and lips, breasts and thighs. Moments that were meant to be private.

Mikhail, you bastard....

"You arrogant, self-centered little *fuck!*" snapped Nicky. "How dare you? How dare you endanger *everything,* just to dip your dick into that little whore?"

I felt the anger start, then. It was red-hot and clean, burning upward through the cold black layers of tradition and respect as if they were so much filthy coal. "Don't talk about her like that," I grated.

Nicky groaned. "You're fucking sweet on her?" he asked incredulously. "Oh, Jesus...." All of The Saints were shaking their heads in despair, now. "We knew you'd been dumb but we thought you were smarter than *that!*"

I stared at him in confusion.

"It's a *trick,* you dumb fuck!" yelled Nicky, slamming his fist down on the table. The photos of Irina and me jumped and drifted further apart, revealing more and more of us. "Vasiliy *sent her* to get into your pants, so you'd go soft on the Russians!"

"No," I said angrily. "She's his *niece!*"

"So? He's a Russian. Russians don't have any fucking qualms about sacrificing their own. Don't they teach you history in school? World War II?" He leaned across the table at me. "That's why he brought her over here, to fucking seduce you!" He glanced down at the photos, his eyes stopping on one of Irina, her leotard rolled down to mid-thigh. "She's got a nice pussy, I'll give you that. She was probably turning tricks for Vasiliy when she was fifteen."

If I'd been standing, I would have been able to hit him. But I had to shove my chair back first and stand and, when my fist was an inch from Nicky's jaw, it slapped into Rico's hand. I twisted around and glared at Rico but he simply shook his head. He forced my fist back with me resisting every inch of the way.

"It's not like that," I told Nicky. I had to pant through my anger. I barely recognized my own voice—God, what had happened to me?

"Yeah, it's true fucking love," spat Taavetti. He coughed and adjusted the valve on his oxygen cylinder. "We got no confidence in you anymore, Angelo." He indicated the room. "That's what this is."

He nodded at Rico and my shoulders tensed. This was it. Rico would leave the room, some hired killer would come in to take me off into the woods and it would all be over.

But Rico didn't leave. He walked around to stand beside me.

Aw, shit. Shit, no.

"Did you know about him and Irina?" Nicky asked.

I willed Rico to be smart. No use both of us dying over this. Thankfully, he was. "No," he said.

"You got a problem taking over?" asked Nicky. "Make no mistake, you're inheriting a war and a fucking nasty one. We'll want you to eliminate every one of those Russian bastards. No mercy. No matter how many of ours it takes. Got it?"

Rico slowly nodded. "Got it."

"Good," said Nicky. He pushed himself off from the table and waved his hand at me. "Get rid of this piece of shit." He led the other Saints out of the room and closed the door behind him. Rico and I were left there in silence, the only noise the crackling of the fire.

I couldn't believe it. I'd been ready to give it all up...but for Irina. Not like *this*. Not to be chewed up and spat out by The Saints and replaced by my best friend.

"I had to," muttered Rico, as if he was trying to convince himself. He leaned against the fireplace, its light silhouetting his big body, and gripped the mantelpiece so hard I thought it would snap. "If I'd have said no, they'd have got someone else to do it."

I shook my head. "Don't do this. They're using you, Rico. You heard them, they'll carry on this war until we're all wiped out. They don't give a shit about us." I held out my hands. "You want my job? You got it. I don't care anymore. But you gotta make peace with Vasiliy."

"*Peace?*" Rico spun to glare at me. "Listen to yourself. Ever since I've known you, all you ever talked about was power: holding onto power, getting more power. The Saints are right, she's fucking corrupted you!"

"*No!* She's got me thinking straight! *We gotta stop this!* You and me!"

Rico suddenly hauled me out of my chair and pushed me away, sending me staggering across the room. "Since when did some woman tell you what to do?" He slammed his hands into my chest, sending me staggering again. I could feel the heat of the fire behind me. "*Think,* Angelo! Snap out of this, because I can't protect you anymore!"

I took a deep breath and went to straighten my lapels, trying to hold in my rage. But my suit jacket wasn't there, just my leather jacket and t-shirt, mocking me for dreaming of a different path. "Irina—"

"*Fuck Irina!*" Rico yelled. And he gave me another shove. My foot clattered awkwardly on the hearth and then my heels kicked against the logs in the fire, raising a cloud of sparks. Burning pain shot up my ankle as the flames licked at me. I staggered sideways, slapping at my singed jeans, just as Rico's fist caught me under the chin.

I spun and crashed down onto the table, sending pictures of Irina and me spilling onto the floor. Then Rico was hauling me up by the throat and slamming me against the wall with the fireplace again. The back of my head mashed against the big mirror that hung above the hearth. The backs of my legs prickled with heat from the roaring fire.

Rico stepped back, drew his gun and pointed it at my head. "Ever since you met her," he muttered. "Ever since the day you met her, you've been—" He was talking almost to himself, trying to justify what he was about to do. He shook his head and cocked the gun. "I never thought a woman would come between us," he said.

And I suddenly saw the jealousy in his eyes. *Shit!* How could I have done this to him? "Rico—"

He pulled the trigger.

Pain exploded in my head. The whole room seemed to shake as the gunshot reverberated. I waited for everything to go dark. But Rico just stood there, anger and hurt twisting his face, the smoke still rising from his gun.

Blood was trickling down the back of my neck. I slowly turned around and looked at the mirror. There was a bullet hole a few inches to the left of where my head had been, cracks fanning out around it. A few slivers of mirror were missing—the ones that had erupted out and slashed at my neck. I could see Rico staring at me in the mirror, just as he must have been able to see himself.

"Get out," he said coldly. "Get out of the city. Get out of the country. I'll tell The Saints I killed you, but I can't ever see you again."

There was nothing more I could say. I turned and walked out of the door without looking back.

42

IRINA

I drove slowly—putting off the inevitable, I guess. So the news about Yuri reached Vasiliy before we did. When we arrived, he was already pacing the hallways, his anger obvious in the heavy slam of his feet against the tiles. We walked through the door and heard him rushing to the top of the stairs to see who it was. I braced myself for the shouting to begin—

But for a second, he just looked relieved. "Irina!"

I'd been looking at the floor, too afraid to meet his eyes. I looked up and the expression on his face made my heart ache. He'd been so worried about me, he'd forgotten his anger for a moment. *He still loves me....*

Then he seemed to catch himself and he started down the stairs, his expression growing darker and darker. "What the *fuck* is going on? The three of you go to Irina's house to get clothes, you don't come back for hours and then the hospital calls to say Yuri's close to death!"

I braced myself again. This was where Mikhail would tell Vasiliy what happened.

"We were at Irina's house," said Mikhail calmly, "Yuri got a phone call—I don't know who from. He drove off in a cab. When he didn't come back, we took his car and came back here. What happened to him?"

I stared at him, slack-jawed. I hadn't realized what a good liar he could be.

Vasiliy's face twisted in rage. "Some bastard stabbed him, right in the heart. Probably one of the Italians. When I find out who, I'll personally gut the bastard."

Mikhail shook his head. "Why would they kill *Yuri?*" he asked. "More likely, it was someone Yuri's had dealings with in the past. He had plenty of enemies."

"*Has!*" corrected Vasiliy. He closed his eyes. "They're operating on him. But the damage to his heart was severe. He may not survive." His fists were tight, white-knuckled balls of rage. "I'll kill the man who did this," he whispered. "I'll make it fucking slow."

Mikhail nodded and put a hand on Vasiliy's shoulder. It made me sick: he'd use even this moment of horror to wheedle his way into Vasiliy's affections. "I'll help you track him down," he said. Then, while Vasiliy's eyes were still closed, he turned and looked at me.

I frowned back at him. *Why are you doing this?* Mikhail hated Angelo. Why would he cover for him? But his expression was unreadable.

Vasiliy sighed and opened his eyes. He suddenly looked very tired: of all the death and suffering I'd seen him face in his career, Yuri's stabbing was hitting him hardest of all. Only the death of his wife had broken him like this. *And me betraying him,* I reminded myself viciously. Yuri had been the one rock he'd had left to cling to. No wonder he was lost...and furious. "It is too dangerous here," he said. "Irina, you must go back to Moscow immediately."

I opened my mouth to protest but he cut me off. "No arguments." Then he turned to Mikhail. "And you will go with her. Your name is all over the news. The police want to talk to you. I told you you were getting your hands too dirty! I will handle things here. You will return when things have calmed down."

I expected Mikhail to argue—New York was *his* territory. But he slowly nodded. Some time in Moscow was better than years in jail.

I finally found my voice. "I'm not going back to Moscow," I told Vasiliy, throwing a look at Mikhail. "I—"

Mikhail put a big, possessive hand on my shoulder. I turned to snap at him but something in his eyes made me hesitate. "If I could have a word with Irina in private?" he asked.

Vasiliy sighed and waved us away. Mikhail ushered me into the sumptuously-furnished drawing room. He turned to close the door behind us. "Look," I said as we both turned to face each other. "I don't know why—"

He swung and slapped me across the face. His hands were like hams and he put all his anger and frustration into it. I flew sideways, falling into the big leather couch, my cheek blazing with pain.

"Shut the fuck up," he said.

I slowly opened my eyes and stared at him in shock and outrage. Was he *crazy?!* Vasiliy would—

"Here's what's going to happen," said Mikhail. "You *are* going to come to Moscow with me. In fact, you're going to move in with me. You and I are going to get to know each other very well."

And suddenly I saw it. How could I have been so naive?

"You're going to do exactly what I say," he said. "*Everything* I say. Or Vasiliy's going to find out that Angelo killed Yuri. He'll hunt him down like a dog and torture him. You've never seen Vasiliy when he's vengeful. Your boyfriend will *beg* for death. And he doesn't have his mafia friends to protect him anymore."

What? "What did you do?" I croaked.

"I sent photos of the two of you together to Angelo's bosses," said Mikhail sweetly. "They'll have pushed him out by now."

I opened my mouth to scream at him, but suddenly that big, clammy hand was across my mouth, pushing me back into the couch while my legs kicked uselessly in the air. "I told you to shut up!" he said testily.

I could barely breathe. His big, flabby hand half-blocked my nostrils and I couldn't suck in enough air. I stared up at him in panic. For all his being out of shape, he was much bigger than me...and now he had something he could hold over me like an axe.

"Will you be good?" he asked.

I nodded, tears in my eyes.

He released his hand.

"Vasiliy won't believe I...like you," I croaked.

Mikhail straightened his suit. "Not now," he said. "You'll tell him that you're coming to Moscow under my protection. But over the next few months, you'll start to spin him a story: you're getting to know me, you're starting to fall in love with me...in six months, you'll tell him we're getting married."

He leaned close so that he could whisper. "But actually? You'll be in my bed every night, starting tonight. I'm going to enjoy violating his little princess in every way there is, and I'll teach you to fucking *obey*. I don't really care if you ever love me or not. But you'll marry me into Vasiliy's fortune and you'll give me a couple of kids to seal the deal. Within a few years, I'll run New York *and* Moscow."

"I can't do it," I said. "I can't make him believe that."

"Oh, yes you can, Irina. You've already shown me what a good liar you are. You managed to string me along while you were really fucking that Italian piece of shit. I think you can convince Vasiliy of anything you want...and you'd better, or Angelo's going to die."

We stared at each other. I knew he was right. I *would* lie to Vasiliy and I'd do a good job of it, too. I had to.

The nightmare I'd always feared was coming to pass, but it was far worse than I'd ever imagined. I was going back to Moscow and marrying a gangster...but it wasn't just some suitor I didn't love. It was a man who hated me as much as he lusted after me, who'd spend every night finding new ways to cause me pain. And I couldn't tell anyone, couldn't complain, or the man I did love would die.

I drew in a long, shuddering breath and willed the tears to draw back from my eyes. I had to use every scrap of Malakov ice to get through this. I had to wear that mask like never before. "Is my face red?" I asked Mikhail.

"What?"

"Is my face red, you son of a bitch? Where you slapped me?"

He slowly grinned. "Only a little. It hasn't bruised yet."

I stood up. "Then I should do this now."

He didn't try to stop me rising. He knew I was under his control, now. He sprawled on the couch as I walked to the door, his eyes on my ass.

I found Vasiliy in his study, looking at a map of New York. He was already planning where he was going to strike the Italians next: which businesses to burn, which politicians and police to bribe or threaten to bring their empire down. I remembered what I'd said to Angelo: this was going to turn into a bloodbath without him as leader...and now that had actually come to pass.

Why hadn't I run with him when I had the chance? By now, we could have been in the air, on our way to another country. I'd given that up to try to do the right thing and now the war was beyond our control anyway.

Vasiliy turned and looked at me. "What?" he snapped, still leaning over the table. Then he frowned at my expression and straightened up, turning to face me properly. "What?" he asked again, his voice softer.

Just tell him. If he knew how Mikhail was blackmailing me, he'd *destroy* him.

But not before Mikhail could tell him what happened to Yuri. Mikhail would die, but so would Angelo.

"I've thought about it," I said. "I'll go to Moscow. But I don't want to be all by myself, in your house. I want to go to Mikhail's place."

Vasiliy's brow knitted. "Irina, you hate Mikhail. Don't think I don't see it in your face, every time you look at him."

I took a deep breath. "I've realized I need to make sacrifices. And I need someone who can protect me. I might even grow to like him."

He looked at me doubtfully. "I know I tried to push you together. But I want you to be happy."

I shook my head and pulled him into a hug. It was the only way I could hide my tears. "I will be," I said. It horrified me that I could lie so well to someone I loved so much.

But it was nothing compared to what I'd have to do next.

43

ANGELO

I walked. I guess I could have called a cab but I was too broken, too emotionally wrung-out, to get my phone out. The highways were plowed, but not the grass beside them where I had to walk. The snow was knee deep and, as the afternoon wore on, it started to snow again. My leather jacket and the sweater beneath it turned white but I didn't even bother to zip the jacket closed. The cold felt good. Numbing.

The fire that had always driven me had gone out. I'd failed my dad—his territory might stay in Italian hands but it would be a wasteland by the end of it, a ghetto where no one wanted to raise their kids or run a business. I'd failed Rico, my best friend, abandoned him for a woman and put him in an unwinnable position. He'd likely die, in the war to come. As would all my men.

I'd lost everything. I'd been fighting my whole life and now I couldn't fight at all. I didn't have anything to fight *for*. I felt utterly cold inside, save for one bright spark.

Irina.

We couldn't stop the war, now, but maybe, when this was all over, I could contact her and convince her to run away with me. It was a slim hope, but it was all that kept me going.

My phone rang. I pulled it out. "Yeah?"

I knew it was her as soon as she breathed. That's how well I knew her, now: I could see the tremble of her lips as she inhaled, feel the rise of her firm breasts against my chest. I knew it was her and I knew she was on the edge of tears. "Irina?"

"...I need to go away," she said at last. Her voice was haunting, deep dark pain dredged up from her soul and shaped into words. "Back to Moscow." She inhaled again and I heard her voice catch. "I can't see you again."

What? There was an iron band around my chest and it was slowly constricting. I sank down and sat on the grass, the snow soaking through my jeans. "Why?"

She took a deep, pained breath. "Too many people are going to die. Yuri will probably die. Because of *us.*"

"But...us being apart: that won't change anything!"

"No. But maybe it'll make it right. We should never have been together. I should be with a Russian. You should find some Italian girl."

"I don't *want* some Italian girl!"

"We don't get to choose, Angelo. This isn't a fairy tale and people like us don't get happy endings. We do what we have to do." Her voice caught again. "I'm going. Stay safe."

"*Irina*—"

"Goodbye." And the line went dead. I sat there staring at the phone, snowflakes drifting down to melt on the screen. *What?!*

I called her back. She didn't answer. I tried again and again until she finally turned her phone off.

It made no sense. Not unless the others—Rico and Vasiliy and Yuri—had been right all along. Not unless this thing we had was stupid and impossible and she'd finally woken up to all that.

What if they *were* right? What if I'd been lost in some fucking romantic dream that was never going to end well? What if I'd lost everything...for nothing? *People like us don't get happy endings.*

That last spark of light and warmth went out and I just went...cold.

I got up and started to walk towards the city, but I'd stopped noticing how tired my legs were, or how bitterly cold the air was. I started to see why Irina liked the cold so much. If you got cold enough, you stopped feeling anything.

It was late morning by the time I stumbled into Little Italy. I saw the smoke and the blue and red lights long before I got there. Russian gangs were out: not just Mikhail's people but the street rats, the hangers-on, anyone who had an axe to grind or who just wanted a good fight. They ran straight past me. I was covered in snow, my neck was bloody and I was stumbling along on legs I could barely feel anymore. They probably mistook me for a homeless guy who'd been mugged.

I looked at the streets I'd once ruled. There was the coffee shop where the owner had given Irina and me an espresso. There was the indoor market where a lady had wrapped a scarf around my neck. Everything was either burning, smashed or daubed with graffiti.

I had to know why. I didn't understand what Irina had done to me. I remembered being strong, being unbeatable. I'd once accused her of working witchcraft on me and that's what it felt like, like she'd reached right down into my heart and rewired it so I only cared about her. She was gone, but that didn't change the way I felt. I needed to understand.

Two hours later, my feet numb from trudging through the snow, I reached her house. I knew she wouldn't be there but maybe her roommate would know how to get in touch with her. I hammered on the door until it finally swung open.

"*Jesus,*" said Rachel when she saw me. I guess I've looked better.

"Where's Irina?" I asked. "What happened to her?"

"What happened to *you?*" She looked me up and down.

I followed her gaze. My jeans and jacket were covered in snow and soaked through. My neck was caked in dried blood and I was still covered in bruises and cuts from what had happened at the construction site. I wasn't intimidating, anymore. That day when I'd met her at the ballet felt like a million years ago.

"I thought you guys always wore suits?" Rachel asked before I could speak again.

I blinked. "Us guys?"

"*Gangsters.*" She looked me dead in the eye. "I'm not a complete moron. I know what you are. And I know what those Russian guys are. And since one of them is Irina's uncle, I guess she's one, too." She crossed her arms. "Is she okay?"

Irina had underestimated her. I had, too. "I don't think so," I said at last. And as I said it, I realized it was true. "Something's wrong. She broke up with me, but...I think she was lying." I winced. I sounded like a deluded ex who couldn't take the bad news. Every time I met this woman, I came across like some crazy stalker.

But Rachel didn't slam the door in my face. She looked at me steadily, appraisingly. "You might be right," she said. "She came back here to pack her bags a few hours ago. With that Russian guy."

"Vasiliy? Her uncle?"

"No. The creepy one."

"*Mikhail?*"

"Yeah. And they were going to his place next, so he could pack. They're going to Moscow together."

I balked. "You mean...traveling together?"

But she shook her head. "No, like *together,* together. Like she's moving in with him. I heard him telling her what to pack. Like, *you won't need those. I'll buy you a better pair of those.*"

The room seemed to tilt and spin. Irina was with *Mikhail?* That made no sense. I'd seen how much she hated him. She wouldn't agree to be with him unless....

I replayed her phone call in my head. *We do what we have to do,* she'd said.

I suddenly wanted to throw up. She was being forced into it. *Blackmailed* into it. And given that Vasiliy knew about Irina and me, there was only one bit of information Mikhail could be holding over her: he knew I'd stabbed Yuri.

That tiny spark of light inside me re-ignited and this time it flared and caught, expanding until it filled me with scalding, raging fire. I had something to fight for again.

I stood up straight for the first time in hours, ignoring the pain in my back, and grabbed Rachel's shoulders. "You said they went to Mikhail's place?" I snapped.

She nodded. And swallowed. I was back to being intimidating again.

"Do you know where it is?" I tried to soften my voice a little. "Rachel, you have to trust me: she doesn't want to be with that guy."

She hesitated, then nodded. "I know," she said in a small voice. "She wants to be with you. But I don't know where Mikhail lives. I'm sorry."

I nodded. "It's okay. I'll find her." I turned to go.

"Angelo?"

I looked back over my shoulder.

"Please get her back."

I nodded once and strode off into the night, already pulling out my phone.

Finding out where Mikhail lived would have been easy if I was still the boss. Without my old connections, it would take too long. Irina would be out of the country before I tracked him down.

I needed help. And there was only one person who could help me.

44

IRINA

Mikhail had one of his thugs drive us to the mansion, which meant Mikhail was free to lounge in the back seat with me. He no longer had to make it look accidental when he touched me. The whole journey, his thigh had been pressed up against mine, his arm possessively around my shoulders. I let my head rest submissively against his thick, flabby neck but I knew he must be able to feel how tense I was.

"I'd fuck you right here," he rasped in my ear. "Bounce you in my lap like a toy. But then the driver might want to join in and I'm not ready to share you. *Yet.*"

I tried not to scream. I knew that the more I showed fear, the more he'd taunt me.

It was a relief when we pulled up outside his mansion with a scrunch of gravel. It really was a mansion, not much smaller than the one Heinwell, the property developer, owned. But that had at least been tasteful: this was hideous, a mess of pillars, elaborate fountains and statues.

Mikhail led me inside and up to the master bedroom. I sat numbly on the huge bed while he started to throw clothes into several big suitcases. When he turned and saw me sitting there, he shook his head and then snapped his fingers in the air, as if I was a dog. "Make yourself useful," he said. "Go and empty that closet into a case."

I walked over to it and opened the doors. It was a large closet but it was full, end to end, with women's lingerie. Only *lingerie* was too polite a term for it. Tiny outfits made of skintight latex and leather. Masks and blindfolds and stockings. Ridiculous heels no one could walk in. All things that he'd bought for his prostitutes to wear. All things that had been *worn*. That he expected me to now wear. I wanted to throw up.

I could feel his eyes on me. "Hurry along, Irina," he chided. He seemed to get off on using my name. "Or should I make a phone call to Vasiliy?"

I took the first few items and tossed them in the case, shaking with silent rage and humiliation.

"We have a few hours before our flight," said Mikhail. I could hear the growing lust in his voice—seeing me angry and powerless seemed to be a turn on for him. "When you're done packing, we'll have some fun."

45

ANGELO

Rico had the bar on lockdown. Eddie, one of our best, was guarding the door and he drew his gun as soon as he saw me moving in the shadows. "Hey!" he called. "Who is that?"

I stepped into the light. I'd gotten a cab back to my apartment to pick up a gun, and I'd taken a few minutes to wash off the blood and put on a suit and overcoat. I looked like *me* again.

Eddie balked. His gun wavered. "I thought you were gone!"

I looked him right in the eye. "I'm back. Is Rico inside?"

I stepped forward and he put his hand on his gun. I could see the indecision in his eyes: he'd probably heard all sorts of shit about me in the last twenty-four hours. The poor guy didn't know what to think or who to respect.

I put my face inches from his. "Eddie," I said quietly, "I'm walking through that door. You want to shoot me, then shoot me. But know exactly who you're shooting. I'm the guy who brought you in when you were a skinny kid stealing cars. I'm the guy who made you a made man. This is my territory and nobody else's." My lips drew back into a snarl. "I'm Angelo *fucking* Baroni."

Eddie withdrew his hand from his jacket. "Sorry, boss."

I slapped him on the shoulder and went inside.

I found Rico in my office, sitting at my desk. When he saw me, he reached one hand under the desk, where I kept a loaded Beretta in a little pouch made of duct tape.

I didn't try to stop him. I just stood there, our eyes locked on each other.

I saw his arm tense once, twice, ready to pull the gun...then he sighed and his arm went limp. He brought his other fist down on the desk so hard that the whole room shook *"Goddammit, Angelo!"*

"I need your help." I told him what had happened to Irina. "I just need to make sure she's safe. Then I'm gone. You can keep the job."

He glared at me for another few seconds and then his gaze slowly softened. He stood up and came around the desk. "I don't want the fucking job," he muttered. "I never did. I just—I want things back how they were." He stopped a few feet from me and looked me up and down. "Nothing's been the same since she came along!"

I nodded. He was right, it hadn't.

"But now I see how you are *without* her." He stared at me. "You need her. Don't you?"

I nodded again. Nodding would have to do because I couldn't put into words how much I needed her.

Rico gave a long, despairing sigh. "Then let's get her back, you mad son of a bitch." And he pulled me into a hug. Every second he held it made my cracked rib scream but I welcomed the pain: it meant we were back.

Rico made some calls. Ten minutes later, we had a couple of crooked cops, half the cab drivers in the city and a hacker all searching for the same information. The cab drivers got there first: a guy knew a guy who worked part-time as a limo driver and he'd driven Mikhail to his mansion a couple of times.

"Get the car," I told Rico. "And let's go."

46

———

IRINA

I made the packing go as slow as possible, removing each scrap of the obscene lingerie from the closet as if it was a treasured wedding dress. But all too quickly, I was staring at nothing but empty hangers.

Behind me, Mikhail made a show of closing his suitcases one by one with heavy, victorious thumps. I didn't turn around. Not even when he came right up behind me, slid his arms around my waist and pulled me to him. I could feel his cock hardening against my ass.

"You didn't leave one to wear?" he asked, sounding disappointed. "No matter. I will pick for you." His mouth was almost touching my ear, his breath hot and horribly moist. "Or perhaps I'll just have you naked, this time." He brushed a lock of my hair back from my face and I forced myself not to tremble, still staring fixedly at the empty closet. "There's no need to be shy, Irina. I've seen what you can do in bed. I studied those photos of you for a *long* time. And now you're going to be just as enthusiastic when it's me f—"

The sound of metal being torn apart cut him off. We both looked towards the front of the mansion. Shouting. Tires on gravel.

Angelo. It could only be Angelo. My stomach lurched. Part of me was overjoyed he'd come for me. Part of me was terrified he'd be killed.

Mikhail pulled his gun, ran to the bedroom door and looked out just as the mansion's front door was kicked in. There was gunfire outside: handguns and the boom of a shotgun.

Mikhail cursed, shouted orders to his guards and then slammed the bedroom door and locked it with heavy bolts. He grabbed my hand and pulled me with him to a bureau, then opened it to reveal a bank of security monitors showing the view from cameras around the mansion. The room was obviously designed as a safe room, with a reinforced door to hold off intruders. In the world I'd grown up in, that was considered normal.

More gunfire from downstairs. And then my heart nearly stopped when I saw Angelo on a monitor, striding through the chaos in a suit and overcoat. Beside him, his friend, Rico.

"They don't stand a chance," muttered Mikhail to himself. He'd started sweating. "The guards will stop them."

On the monitors, I saw men in black military fatigues running down hallways. *Chyort!* These were ex-military men, well trained....

But Angelo and Rico, together seemed unstoppable. The guards they didn't shoot, they battered out of the way. The hallways grew quieter and quieter as Mikhail's men fell. And then they were marching towards a door I realized was ours—

There was a heavy bang on the door. "*Irina?*" yelled Angelo.

"I'm here!" I yelled. "He has a gun!" I tried to pull free of Mikhail's hand—if I could just break free, I could run to the door and throw the bolts—

But I'd forgotten how strong Mikhail was. He yanked on my hand and I screamed, my shoulder burning as I was snapped back towards him. As I reached him, he backhanded me across the face. I cried out and fell to my knees, the room blurry. I realized I'd been lucky he'd caught me with his hand, not his gun, or I'd be unconscious at best.

"*Irina!*" yelled Angelo again. I could hear the anger in his voice: he must have heard my cry. The door shook in its frame but didn't give. Mikhail and I both looked toward the security monitors and saw

Angelo kick the door again. Rico stood next to him, shotgun at the ready.

Mikhail cursed, looked around, looked at me...and then suddenly clamped a hand over my mouth. It took me by surprise and I panicked, screaming into his palm, but it made almost no noise at all. He had big hands and an iron grip. When he pulled me back against his chest, controlling me easily, I realized he was good at this. He'd had plenty of practice controlling struggling women and stopping them from screaming. My stomach knotted. *And this is the man I'll be with forever....*

He walked us backward across the room, our feet making no sound on the deep carpet and my mewls covered by Angelo's banging at the door. Mikhail pressed a piece of the molding beside a full-length mirror and the whole thing swung open: a hidden door. Mikhail backed us into the passage and closed the mirror behind us. A secret escape route: Vasiliy's house in Moscow had one, too. I struggled frantically. *Angelo won't be able to find us!*

But it was much worse than I thought.

Mikhail edged us sideways along the narrow passage until we came to another door. He cautiously opened it and we emerged into the next bedroom. Then he snuck a glance out into the hallway, still with me held tight against his chest. I could see Angelo and Rico at the end of the hall still battering at the door, their backs to us.

Mikhail checked his gun.

My eyes went wide. I craned my head as best I could to look round at him, desperately trying to shake it. *I'll come with you,* I tried to communicate. *I'll do whatever you want! Just don't kill them!* We had a clear path to the stairs—we could easily sneak behind them and escape.

But Mikhail looked deep into my eyes...and smirked. Then he pulled me out into the hallway and leveled his gun at Angelo.

He wasn't going to kill him in spite of my protests; he was going to kill him because of them. He wanted to cause me as much pain as possible.

I tried to scream a warning but Mikhail's soft palm formed an airtight seal against my mouth and Angelo's banging at the door made far too much noise. I saw the gun barrel waver and settle on the middle of Angelo's back. Mikhail's finger tightened on the trigger....

I lifted my foot and stamped as hard as I could. My heel gouged a line straight down Mikhail's shin and instep. His hand lifted off my mouth for a split second as he tensed in agony.

"A—" I yelled.

Angelo and Rico both turned. Rico was closer to us and saw the danger first. He dived towards Angelo....

And the gun went off.

47

___

IRINA

The gun had been close to my ear when it went off. The flash and smoke blinded me for a few seconds, the boom reverberating around my head.

By the time I recovered, Mikhail was pulling me along the hallway by the hand, his gun still leveled. As we got closer, I saw Angelo on the floor. Rico was lying half on top of him—he must have knocked him to the ground when he dived in front of the bullet. Rico's face was pale, his hands clutched to his chest. Angelo's hands covered Rico's, embracing his friend from behind as they both looked down at the wound in horror. "No," said Angelo in a choked voice. "No!"

Mikhail smirked as we walked up. "See what happens when you try to take something that doesn't belong to you?" he asked. And pointed his gun right at Angelo's head.

"No!" I screamed, and grabbed at the hand holding the gun. "*Wait!*"

Mikhail half-looked at me, keeping a wary eye on Angelo. He looked amused: I think he enjoyed watching me beg.

I took a deep breath and tried to be *Russian*. Coldly logical. "If you kill him," I said, "you have no leverage over me."

He considered it for a moment. "Vasiliy is half-convinced already." He put his fingers to my face and brushed the bruise that was forming from where he'd slapped me. "I have other ways to make you obey."

Angelo let out a low growl. I wanted him to save me. I wanted nothing more in the world. But if he tried to make a move, Mikhail would kill him in a heartbeat. I forced myself not to look at him because I didn't know if I could get through this if I looked into those brown and amber eyes. "But wouldn't you rather have me willing?" I asked Mikhail.

"Don't, Irina," spat Angelo. "Don't do this!"

"Let him live," I told Mikhail, "and I'll come with you. I won't try to escape. I'll convince Vasiliy. I'll have your children. I'll do everything you want."

I heard Angelo draw in a long, shuddering breath of pure fury.

Mikhail looked at me, his smirk widening, looked at Angelo...and nodded. "Fine," he said. He took Angelo and Rico's guns. "Come. I'll have someone follow with the cases." And he started to drag me away down the hallway.

Then he stopped, remembering that he didn't have to do that anymore. He released me and then offered me his hand.

I stared at it...and then clasped it gently. When I looked back over my shoulder, Angelo looked as if someone was tearing out his heart. *Don't!* he mouthed.

It was the only way I could save him. I looked away, tears in my eyes, and walked with my husband-to-be to the door.

48

ANGELO

I stared after her for as long as I could, until she descended the stairs. I heard her and Mikhail cross the marble entrance hall and then the scrunch of their feet on the gravel outside. A moment later, a car roared away.

I'd failed.

Rico's breathing was a wet rasp, his shirt soaked with blood. Now that I didn't have Mikhail's gun on me, in theory I could try to get him to the hospital. But then I heard footsteps coming up the stairs. One of the guards who'd survived our attack, a big ex-military type. "He said to kill you as soon as he and the Malakov whore were gone," the guard told me, drawing his gun.

So Mikhail had double-crossed Irina on top of everything else. She'd have to live out her life as the perfect subservient wife to that asshole, thinking she was saving my life, and I'd already be in a shallow grave somewhere.

The guard took his time walking over to us. I wasn't any sort of threat, lying there. I tried to heave Rico off me, but my cracked rib made the movement agony. *Shit! This is how it ends.*

The guard touched his gun to my head. "*Arrivederci*, Mr. Baroni," he said, as if it was the funniest thing in the world.

And I got mad. It wasn't just me, or even Rico, or the loss of my entire fucking empire. It was the thought of Irina, living out her life in Moscow with that evil bastard. *She deserves better.* I glared up at the grinning Russian, the rage building and building. *She deserves better!*

I let out a yell, grabbed the gun barrel and pushed it away from me. It went off, narrowly missing my ear. The guard panicked and tried to back up, out of range. But it was too late: I'd grabbed two big handfuls of his shirt with my bloody hands and heaved him down toward me.

"Fuck you," I spat. "I'm not dead yet." And I headbutted him as hard as I could.

His legs folded and he landed on top of Rico and me. My cracked rib screamed at the added weight and for a second I had to just lie there, panting. Then I rolled the unconscious guard's body off us, heaved myself out from under Rico and checked his pulse.

His heart was still beating...just.

I bent, got my shoulder under him and heaved him up into a fireman's carry. I staggered a little getting him downstairs: Rico's even bigger than I am and my cracked rib turned every step into a jolting, jarring agony. But I wasn't going to leave him behind.

Outside, Mikhail had driven off in his Mercedes and our Chrysler was a wreck, its radiator caved in from when Rico had rammed through the gates. *Shit!* I found a black SUV in the garage and dumped Rico in the passenger seat, then frantically hunted for the keys, finally finding them in the guards' quarters. By now, Rico's face was deathly pale, his breathing a barely-audible hiss.

I grabbed his shoulder. "Don't you fucking die on me," I snarled. "Don't you dare!"

His breathing grew a little deeper. I threw the car into gear and screeched off towards the hospital.

49

IRINA

"Champagne?"

I turned towards the stewardess. "What?"

She smiled at me. "Champagne, madam?" She must have seen something in my expression because she frowned. "Is everything alright?"

"Yes," said Mikhail, taking the glass for me and another for himself. "She's a nervous flier." He gave her a big, wide grin and she set off down the aisle of the first class cabin, unaware that he was twisting in his seat to stare at her ass.

I'd have to get used to that: the Russian norm of watching your husband leer at other women. Even sleep with them.

Married. I'd be married. New horrors kept leaking into my brain like ice water oozing through a jagged crack. There'd be a ceremony. A dress. Vasiliy would give me away to him.

And I'd have to smile in every photo. The thought of that got to me more than the thought of what would happen that night...and every night.

Mikhail passed me my glass of champagne. "Drink," he said. He was smiling but there was an edge to his voice. *Remember your promise.*

I put the glass to my lips and drank, trying not to gag. *A wedding. A honeymoon.*

Children. I'd promised him children.

We flew on towards Moscow and I tried to hold back my tears.

50

ANGELO

At the hospital, I sat for four hours in a plastic chair while they operated on Rico. I overheard the staff talking about notifying the cops, since it was a gunshot wound, so I put a pre-emptive call in to one of the guys at the local precinct, to make sure the police report got lost. It gave me something to do aside from curse myself for getting Rico hurt.

I was going to personally gut Mikhail for what he'd done to my friend. For what he planned to do to Irina. For what he might be doing to her *right now*—

"Sir?"

I looked up into the face of a nurse. I stood up so fast that she almost got whiplash following my face. "How is he?"

"He should be fine. He was lucky: he must have been standing almost sideways because the bullet went *across* more than in. Tore up a lot of muscle but, um…"—she blushed—"he's a big guy. It's going to leave two big scars, though."

I let out a long sigh of relief. "Yeah, well, the ladies love a scar. Can I see him?"

She showed me through to his room. He was bandaged from his

neck down to almost his navel but his color was better. "He'll sleep for a couple more hours," said the nurse, and left me to it.

I sank down into the chair that faced his bed. He looked peaceful, for the moment, eyes closed and head thrown back like he didn't have a care in the world. I envied him. I thought for a long time about all the apologies I wanted to make and how the fuck I was going to explain it.

"I'm sorry," I said at last. "I was an asshole."

I had no idea what I was going to do. Irina was by now in a strange country where I had no contacts and no power, a place where I didn't even speak the fucking language. I wouldn't even be able to find out where Mikhail's Russian home was.

My head felt like it was going to explode: hate for Mikhail, hate for Vasiliy for trying to take my territory and starting all this, hate at myself for being weak and falling for a woman. I stood up and strode over to the window, pulling back the drapes. The sun was going down, the last rays lighting up fresh snow as it blew against the glass. By now, Irina and Mikhail would be in the air, on their way to Moscow. *Fuck!*

I couldn't fix this with violence or intimidation or the vicious hatred The Saints had had me believing. Maybe I needed to think more like the Russians. More like Irina. Cool and calm and logical. I shut my eyes and tried to imagine her next to me, silken strands of hair blowing against my neck in the wind. Her presence calming me, guiding me....

I opened my eyes. There was only one move I could make, only one person I could go to for help. And it would mean going against everything I'd ever known.

Abandoning the SUV at the hospital, I got a cab to Vasiliy's townhouse. He was still on lockdown, so there were guards at every window. They came alert as the cab pulled up, then did a double take as I stepped out. Several of them drew their guns.

Moving slower than I've ever moved in my life, I took the edge of my suit jacket between thumb and forefinger and drew it open, showing my gun. Then I lifted it from its holster with two fingers and tossed it away. I laced my fingers on top of my head and sank to my knees in the snow. I took a deep breath and yelled as hard as I could.

"Tell Vasiliy I surrender."

51

ANGELO

They searched me thoroughly. First, in a yard at the back of the house, with a gun barrel against my forehead, in case I'd strapped a bomb to my body in an assassination attempt. Then they pulled me inside and patted me down for guns. Finally, they had me strip off and went through my clothes looking for knives or bugs.

At last I was shown in Vasiliy's study and pushed into a chair. The guards looked at Vasiliy, wondering if they should stay, but he waved them away. When the door closed, he took a big, mean-looking handgun from his desk drawer and set it on the desk, right next to a chessboard. He nodded at the board. "Do you play?"

I shook my head. "I have no fucking idea how to play chess. It's a Russian thing."

He blinked once and then smiled. "Perhaps it is. A pity. So, tell me, Mr. Baroni...why have you given yourself up to me? Were you hoping for mercy?" He leaned forward. "I fear you will be disappointed. I couldn't kill you when you were head of your organization but from what I hear, that's no longer the case."

"I came because I need your help."

He was too surprised to even laugh, at first. There was a second of stunned silence where my words just hung in the air. Only then did he throw himself back in his chair and roar with laughter.

I took a deep breath. "Irina is in danger."

He tilted his head to one side. "Really, Mr. Baroni—you can do better than that. As I'm sure you know, Irina is where no one can hurt her, including you."

Now *I* leaned forward. "She's in danger because you sent her off with a perverted, violent son of a bitch." I pulled out my phone and showed him the photos of Kirsty. "This is what he did to one of my escorts. Look at her. *Look!* See the mark from his ring?"

I could see it break across his face in slow motion. Every cell in his body was telling him it couldn't be true. If we'd been talking about any other woman, he would have just denied it. But this was Irina...and whatever differences I'd thrown up between them, he had a father's need to make sure she was okay. And the more he looked, the more he thought about it, the more everything he thought he knew was thrown into doubt.

"Impossible," he said at last. "Irina went with him willingly."

"He's blackmailing her."

Vasiliy frowned, then let out a sigh of exasperation. "What could he possibly have to blackmail her with? I already know about...*you.*" He made me sound like a filthy drug habit.

And here it was. The moment where I sealed my own fate. I had to tell him: it was the only way I could convince him. "She had to go with Mikhail," I said, "or he was going to tell you that it was me who stabbed Yuri."

There was a half-second of stunned silence. Then the gun was in his hands and pointed right at my forehead, his hand trembling in his rage.

I talked fast. "There's no reason you shouldn't kill me," I told him. "It was an accident. We were fighting, we fell together...but that doesn't matter. I get that."

"You sliced right into his heart, you *svoloch!*" Vasiliy panted. His face had turned scarlet.

"You can kill me," I said. "But *think.* Think what this means. I'm telling the truth about Mikhail. He blackmailed her. He lied to you. He took her from right under your nose. He's going to make her life a living hell and *she's with him right now.* I can't get her back. But you can."

Vasiliy's hand flexed on the gun as he adjusted his grip. I thought about closing my eyes but I've always thought that's the coward's option. If I was going to die, I was going to look him right in the eye while he pulled the trigger. I watched his finger tighten, tighten, the chromed trigger easing back and back—

"Have you any idea what she means to me?" Vasiliy whispered.

I stared right back at him. "As much as she means to me."

He held my gaze for another few seconds...then the gun hit the desk, the heavy thump almost drowned out by a tirade of Russian curses. "Killing you would break her heart," he snapped. "Get out. Don't ever let me see you again. I will go to Russia and get Irina."

I frowned. "Now that you know...can't you just call him and tell him it's over?"

He shook his head. "Perhaps that would work with men *you* know, Mr. Baroni. But Mikhail is one of us. You don't know how we operate. By doing this, Mikhail has made himself an enemy of the Malakovs. His life is over. If he finds out we know, he will run and take Irina with him as a hostage. We may never find them again."

I leaned across the desk. "Then I want to come with you."

He stared at me, aghast. "You think I'd let you fight alongside me and my men? You think I'd let you near her again?"

"Mikhail had at least ten men just at his place in New York. How many does he have at his place in Russia? Twenty? Thirty? You need all the help you can get!"

We glared at each other, neither willing to give ground. "We have to move," I pressed. "They're hours ahead of us!"

Vasiliy rose to his feet and straightened his tie. "We will catch them up," he said. "We have jet."

Less than an hour later, we were aboard the Malakov private jet, throttling back for take-off. Luka—Vasiliy's son and Irina's cousin—was gathering a force of men in Moscow and would meet us there.

We could then refuel and quickly set off again for a small airstrip close to Mikhail's mansion, way out in the sticks. Irina and Mikhail would have had to travel from Moscow airport by road, so we'd arrive not far behind them.

I just hoped we were in time.

52

IRINA

It took hours to drive from the airport to Mikhail's mansion, most of it on winding roads through thick forest. It had been an overnight flight and I hadn't managed to sleep on the plane, so I was exhausted. But I couldn't sleep while I felt Mikhail's eyes on me in the darkness.

Thankfully, Mikhail eventually dozed off himself, lulled by the gentle roll and bounce of the SUV's suspension. With my head cushioned on a sweater against the window, I let myself drift off into a fitful sleep, haunted by nightmares where Angelo was hunted down and shot because I was weak, or where I tried to protect my children from a drunken, violent Mikhail.

I jerked awake when the car bumped over a tree branch...and when I opened my eyes, dawn was breaking and I was looking out over paradise. We'd been climbing up into the mountains for hours and the twisting road we were following clung to the side of one of the peaks, letting us look down across its steep slopes to a verdant valley below. The sunrise was turning the early-morning mist pink as it crept between the snow-covered firs, with dazzling beams of golden sunlight punching through the gaps between the clouds.

I felt a deep, unexpected swell in my heart. I'd forgotten how beautiful Russia could be. I'd deliberately put it out of my mind when I'd torn myself away from my family. Now I was back...but in a way I'd never wanted.

It didn't seem right that Mikhail should live somewhere so beautiful. He should live in some dark, concrete fortress in a world lit by lava and fire. But his mansion was a huge, stone-walled house atop a rocky peak. At least from the exterior, it looked as if it hadn't changed in centuries: it was the sort of place a Tsar might have had as a summer retreat.

Inside, the place was a mixture of the very old and the ultra-modern. Thick oak beams, wood paneling and slabs of exposed stone gave the hallways a medieval feel, with wood fires burning in many of the fireplaces. But the rooms themselves had been lavishly appointed with big screen TVs and leather couches. A staff of cooks and maids greeted us, together with an army of guards. Mikhail spent almost an hour giving me the full tour, preening at my compliments and grabbing my ass. I spun it out as long as I could: anything to prolong the inevitable. But all too soon, he said it was time to go upstairs.

Mikhail showed me to the master bedroom. The bed was an emperor-sized monstrosity, too big for even the huge room, and two walls were covered by mirror-fronted closets. I knew immediately that he hadn't intended this room for sleeping, or cuddling, or spending time together. The entire room was focused on the bed.

I ran my hand down one of the metal bed posts. There were scratches in the black paint: circular ones that ran right around the post and cut deep enough to reveal the metal beneath. Scratches from handcuffs, made as some woman had desperately thrashed and pulled against them. I wondered if the room was soundproof or if he just paid his staff enough to ignore the screams.

Mikhail came up behind me, pushed my hair aside and laid a kiss on the back of my neck. "Undress, Irina" he said quietly.

If I didn't do it, he'd tear the clothes off me. And if I resisted, Angelo was dead.

When I stood in just my underwear, he drew one wrist back

towards him. I felt the kiss of cold metal and then the cruel rasp of the handcuff's ratchet as it locked tight.

Be cold. Be numb. You can get through this, Irina.

He pushed me towards the bed, still clutching the free end of the handcuffs. My eyes were locked on the scratched bedpost as it came closer and closer. How many more scratches would I carve in it, over the next few decades?

I closed my eyes just as an explosion rocked the house.

53

———

ANGELO

All of us ducked as the SUV exploded. One of Vasiliy's men had crept up to the house and rigged it to blow to act as a diversion, drawing everyone to the front. Meanwhile, we'd go in the back.

We'd been joined at Moscow airport by five of Vasiliy's men from Moscow and Luka, his son. Luka, six-foot-something of chiseled muscle in a suit, had spent most of the short flight up into the mountains glaring at me. At one point, he'd muttered something to Vasiliy in Russian. I didn't understand it, but I was pretty sure from the tone that it involved wanting to kill me.

Vasiliy had glanced across at me and muttered what I guessed was *get in line.* If we came through this alive, my life expectancy was not looking good. *Fine.* I was past caring. The only thing that mattered was getting Irina out.

As we crept towards the house, Vasiliy started snapping out orders to his men. He was the experienced general, rallying his troops, and Luka was the young captain leading the charge. It reminded me of something but I couldn't figure out what.

Gunfire ate away at the brickwork just ahead of us and we ducked back behind cover. Luka looked at Vasiliy for orders and that's when I got it: they reminded me of myself and my dad, back when he was alive.

"Forward," snapped Vasiliy. "He knows we're here. We have to do this fast. Two men go forward, the rest will cover them. Luka, take Yuri—"

He broke off, catching himself.

Shit.

Vasiliy didn't look at me. He was very studiously avoiding looking at me, but I could see his powerful shoulders shaking with rage. If he looked at me, he'd likely shoot me. Luka, meanwhile, was looking right at me, his knuckles white where he gripped his gun. He was only held back by his father's word, and then only barely.

I stepped forward. "I'll do it. I'll go in with Luka."

Vasiliy spun and glared at me...then nodded. Luka grunted in displeasure but readied himself.

Then we were running for the house, Vasiliy and the other men covering us. Bullets hissed through the air all around us, but we made it to the cover of the house and I kicked in the door and ran inside.

It was some sort of games room with a huge pool table and a bar. The room rose the full height of the mansion, with a wooden gallery stretching across it high above, the sort of place minstrels sat playing lutes in old King Arthur movies. At the other end of the room, through a hallway, I could see an ornate wooden staircase leading upwards. *That's where we need to be.* I was guessing Mikhail would have Irina upstairs.

Before we could move, the guards inside the house opened up with automatic weapons. Fluttering tufts of green fluff and lethal shards of pool ball filled the air as gunfire chewed up the baize. We fired back, but there were too many of them: we were forced to take cover behind the pool table. For a second, we sat side by side, our backs pressed against the wood, as we reloaded. Pool balls rolled off the table and hit the floor between us. *Shit!* Vasiliy and his men were still outside, so we were on our own.

I was still reloading when one of Mikhail's men raced around the corner of the table and pointed his gun at me. I scrambled to rise but there was no way I could get out of the way in time—

There was a shot and the guy staggered backward. Next to me, Luka lowered his smoking gun.

"Thanks," I said, finally getting my own gun loaded.

Luka frowned and grunted. "He would have shot me next."

The guy he'd shot staggered back another step and fell right into one of the huge, open fires Mikhail seemed to like so much. Flaming logs went rolling across the wooden floor, a few of them hitting the drapes. Flames licked hungrily at the fabric, quickly spreading up it. *Shit!* I told myself it didn't matter, that we'd be out of there long before the fire really took hold. But half the place seemed to be made of wood and we were still pinned down. Vasiliy's men seemed to be more experienced and better trained but Mikhail had the advantage of numbers.

What if Mikhail was escaping with Irina right this moment?

54

IRINA

My eyes flew open. Mikhail had let go of the free end of the handcuffs and was turning, open-mouthed in shock, trying to determine the direction of the explosion. Then he stalked towards the door. "Stay there!" he ordered.

My mind spun. Was this a rescue? Had Angelo somehow found me, all the way out here in the wilds of Russia?

I heard Mikhail yelling orders to his guards and my heart sank when I saw men grabbing machine guns and running downstairs. This wasn't like the mansion back in New York. This was Mikhail's personal fortress. If Angelo had come, he'd be killed.

Mikhail ran back into the room, pulling his gun.

"What is it?" I asked. "What's going on?"

He glared at me. "It's Vasiliy. Come here!"

Vasiliy?! That made no sense. As far as Vasiliy knew, I was here of my own free will. Unless....*had Vasiliy somehow found out about the blackmail? About Yuri?* If that was true then Angelo was dead. *No! Please no!*

When I just stood there, too shocked to move, Mikhail grabbed the free end of the handcuffs and jerked me towards him, making me stagger. "Let me put my clothes on," I said desperately. I was trying to assemble a plan in my head: get a gun or a knife, get away from him and *run*. But I couldn't run out into a Russian winter in a bra and panties.

"You don't need clothes," he spat. He stared at the handcuffs for a moment, then locked the free end around one of his wrists so that we were bound together.

Chyort! I looked down at the metal chain in horror. "Vasiliy must know what you've done," I croaked. "You can't marry me now. It's over. You don't need me."

"Vasiliy will hunt me down and kill me...but he won't shoot at his niece. If my men can't hold them, you're my way out of here." His eyes gleamed. "There are plenty of places I can take you, far from Russia. And Vasiliy has enough enemies around the world who'd love to play with you, just to get to him. I'm sure I can sell you, once I get tired of you."

He dragged me out into the hallway and then started making his way towards the stairs. I didn't have a choice: when I hung back, he simply jerked on the handcuffs and the metal cut into my skin.

Our progress was slow: whenever he heard gunfire ahead, Mikhail would backtrack and find another route through the huge building. Even with me as a hostage, he preferred to take the coward's way out and slip away from the fight rather than face Vasiliy. The mansion was big enough that he might just be able to pull it off. What if Vasiliy didn't find us in time? I had no doubt Mikhail could make good on his threat: with his Swiss bank accounts and homes around the world, he could take me almost anywhere. No one would ever find us.

I staggered onward, my wrist already scraped and bruised from the cuff, my shoulder aching from the constant jerking. I looked around for something I could grab with my free hand to hit Mikhail with, but there was nothing. And however much I tried to stay calm and efficient, as Vasiliy had taught me, my eyes still blurred with tears. *Angelo. Angelo is dead.*

The air started to grow hazy with white smoke: it was rising up the staircases, filling the upper floors. It got worse as we descended through the mansion and I could hear the roar of flames below. *The house is on fire!*

By the time we reached the next landing, the heat was ferocious and the smoke seemed to fill every square inch of space, even low to the ground. I could barely breathe and I was sweating, even in my underwear.

We reached the next door and Mikhail swung it open, then quickly slammed it: the next room was engulfed in orange flame. "This way!" he snapped, pulling me back towards the stairs. I could barely see and I was having to fight for every breath of air. Mikhail pulled out his phone and called someone, muttering orders I couldn't hear.

"We have to find a way downstairs!" I told him. I heard timber creaking and giving way beneath us. "Mikhail, the whole place is going to come down!"

But he shook his head and jerked on the handcuffs again, leading me back upstairs instead. Whatever his plan was, it was going to get us both killed.

55

ANGELO

We'd made it up to the top floor and were going room-to-room. The fighting had died down: two of Vasiliy's men had been injured but overall we seemed to be winning. The problem was that progress was painfully slow. There was still no sign of Mikhail or Irina and the fire was turning the mansion into a smoke-filled, blazing death trap. "This is no good!" I told the Russians. "We need to move faster!"

Luka muttered something to Vasiliy in Russian and he nodded. Then, for my benefit, he grudgingly repeated it in English. "We split up," he said. "Two groups. Find her quicker." He nodded to the remaining one of Vasiliy's men—the other two were still downstairs, mopping up the defenders. "He and I will go together. You and Vasiliy go together."

Vasiliy and I glared at each other. I've never been a soldier, but I've been in fights often enough to know that you need someone to watch your back. He trusted me about as much as I trusted him. In the smoke-filled hallways, with no witnesses, he could easily kill me and then tell Irina whatever story he wanted. He'd been reluctant to kill me himself, but if he could blame it on one of Mikhail's men....

It didn't matter. I didn't have a choice and there was no time to argue anyway, not if I wanted to save Irina. "Sure," I said. "I'll go in front." And I led the way into the smoke, already feeling Vasiliy's gun on my back.

Visibility was down to a few feet. I could only see faint outlines and the glow of flames. Several times, a wall loomed up out of nowhere and I barely stopped before I ran into it. *Goddammit!* I could feel the sweat pouring down my face. *How the hell did I wind up here?* Thousands of miles from home, my mortal enemy right behind me with a gun aimed at my back—

Irina. That's how. And she was worth it.

I forged on, the heat growing even more intense. We were moving closer and closer to the fire, now: we must be close to the games room where it had first started. I could hear breaking glass and explosions and remembered the bar: all the whiskey and vodka must be going up. Then there was an enormous crash that shook the whole house. As we passed through the next door, all I could see was billowing white smoke, lit up orange by the flames. I took another step and—

The carpet beneath me dipped under my weight, turning into a ramp. *What the fuck?!* I fell onto my back, sliding, grabbing for anything that would stop me—

My hand found the edge of the carpet and I clung to it, my feet kicking in space. *Where the fuck is the floor?!*

There was the sound of shattering glass below. The fire must have gotten hot enough to break the windows in the games room and a freezing winter wind blew through the room, snowflakes hissing as they hit the flames. The smoke cleared for a second and my stomach lurched when I saw what had happened.

There was no floor.

The "room" we'd been about to walk through had once been the wooden gallery that looked down on the games room. The entire middle section had collapsed, leaving a few feet of carpet sticking out into space. That's what I'd stepped on. Now I was hanging twenty feet above an inferno, the flames singing my legs. I twisted around to look for Vasiliy.

He'd backed up a few feet and was looking down at me. So many emotions played across his face: rage, hatred, jealousy...and something else.

I saw his hand lift, as if he was going to grab me. I reached for him—

Vasiliy's hand dropped back to his side. Indecision played across his face. His hand rose again—

There was a splintering, cracking sound and the remainder of the gallery came away from the wall. Both of us cursed as it slumped sideways, tilted at a crazy angle. Vasiliy hit what was left of the handrail but his muscled body was too big and the rail was too weak. He went smashing through it and fell. He would have fallen straight down to the floor far below, but his fingers caught the edge and clung. Now we were *both* dangling, and in another few minutes the whole gallery would collapse into the fire.

The smoke was curling down into my chest, making me cough and rasp. Every gulp of red-hot air I took in scorched my lungs. I tried to use the carpet to haul myself up but, as soon as I pulled, I heard the distant sound of ripping. It was only held in place by carpet tacks and my struggles were tearing it free. *Shit!* I started climbing, hand over hand, but the edge of a carpet isn't the easiest thing to hang onto. I heaved myself inch by inch back onto the gallery, but I could feel the tacks letting go: *pop, pop, pop—*

The whole carpet suddenly slid with me still on it. I was just high enough to make a grab for one of the handrail supports and it creaked...but held. Beneath me, the carpet hissed past, carried by its momentum, and fell into the fire.

I crawled on hands and knees towards Vasiliy. He was a tough old guy but his strength was fading. One hand slipped from the wood. *Shit.* I tried to crawl faster.

He looked up as he saw me. A wry smile crept onto his face.

I wasn't going to reach him in time. "No," I gasped.

"Tell Irina—" he panted.

I forced my limbs to move faster. *"No! Hang on, you stupid Russian bastard!"*

His fingers squeaked as they lost their grip and slid along the wood. "Tell Irina I love her."

I lunged for him. "*No!*"

56

———————

ANGELO

P *ain.*

First a hard, ringing pain as my head hit the wooden floor of the gallery. Then, as my head cleared, a tearing, burning pain in my shoulder. It came in waves, as if a giant was standing on my shoulder and rocking back and forth. I looked down.

Vasiliy was dangling from my hand, his fingers just barely hooked in mine.

The gallery creaked beneath us. "*Climb,* you asshole!" I yelled.

Vasiliy heaved and swung himself up, grabbing my arm with his other hand. It felt as though he was going to tear the damn thing off. Then he got hold of my back and the edge of the gallery and finally he could pull himself up. He hauled me to my feet and we staggered together through the door we'd first come through and back down the hallway. No more than thirty seconds later, we heard the remains of the gallery crash down into the fire.

Vasiliy turned and looked at me. He looked as if he wanted to say something, but he didn't know how.

He was saved by Luka, who ran up out of the smoke. "She's not that way," he panted, pointing behind him.

The games room and the minstrel's gallery were the back of the building—there was nothing else in that direction. "Then she's not on this floor," I said.

"She must be," said Vasiliy. "We've searched every room below. This is the top floor."

There was a sickening groan as the timbers that supported the house began to give up their fight. Flames were breaking through the floor in several places. The whole place was coming down. We looked at each other. "The bastard slipped past us," said Luka. "He got past us and took a car. He could be miles away!"

He started to run for the stairs but I grabbed his jacket. "Wait!" I snapped.

"What?" He shook free of me. "We have to go! They're getting away!"

"*Listen!*"

He glared at me but listened. And then he heard it: the dull whump of helicopter blades.

"They didn't get past us," I said. "They're on the roof!"

57

IRINA

The roof of the mansion was a good facsimile of hell.

Mikhail and I were standing on a narrow stone walkway formed by the top of the walls. It ran all the way around the building and it was the only stable part left: the whole center of the roof was rapidly collapsing, the timbers and sagging as they gave, every one of the ancient slate tiles edged with cherry-red light as the fire broke through from below.

A bitter wind was blasting snow almost horizontally across us. It would have been freezing even in clothes: I was in my underwear. While one side of our bodies froze, the other roasted in the flames that were erupting through the roof. All of the smoke that had choked us inside was pouring up into the sky in a pillar so thick it almost looked solid: when the wind whipped it towards us, we couldn't see.

And the walkway had no walls. It was only a few feet wide, with a sheer drop to one side of us and an inferno to the other.

I heard the helicopter before I saw it. Then I scanned the sky, squinting against the wind, and finally made out its lights in the distance. It was coming straight towards us, fighting the side winds. If it could hover above us, we might just be able to climb aboard to safety....

Safety and a life as Mikhail's prisoner. And all for nothing. *Angelo is dead.*

I looked at the edge of the roof. Even death was better than what Mikhail had planned for me. He'd taken the only man I'd ever loved from me. If I did it right, I could take him with me when I died. I was a lot lighter than Mikhail but, if I threw myself suddenly enough, just as he was off balance, I should be able to pull him with me off the roof.

I glanced across at him. His eyes were fixed on the helicopter. I sidled a little closer to him, so that the handcuff chain went slack. I didn't want it to hold me back. I wanted it to snap taut with as much energy as possible. I took a deep breath. Bent my knees. *I love you, Angelo.*

There was a *clang* as the metal hatch that led onto the roof flew open. My head whipped around...and my jaw dropped. The hatch was almost halfway around the mansion from the walkway where we now stood, but I would have recognized him from a mile away. *"Angelo!"* I screamed in delight.

Mikhail cursed and raised his gun, narrowing his eyes and squinting as the wind whipped snow and smoke into his face. I grabbed for his gun hand, but I was on the wrong side and there was no room on the narrow walkway to step around him. I looked at Angelo. He was heaving himself up onto the roof, but that meant both hands were occupied: he couldn't shoot back. He was a sitting duck.

There was only one thing to do.

I jumped off the roof.

58

___

ANGELO

I saw Mikhail take aim at me. *Shit!* I couldn't go back: Luka was behind me on the ladder. I'd hoped to climb up silently and take the bastard by surprise, but the wind had whipped the hatch cover out of my hands. All I could do was heave myself up onto the roof as fast as possible and hope he missed...but even at this distance, it was an easy shot.

Then I saw Irina tense her legs. I realized what she was going to do a split second before she did it. "*No!*" I screamed.

She jumped. Hung there in that magical, weightless way she had, as graceful as if she was on stage. Her hair fanned out around her, rising and then sinking in slow motion....

And then she fell. Down, down, down, her head disappearing below the roof.

Mikhail cried out and jerked as the handcuffs went taut and he was pulled off his feet. His shot went high and he fell back towards the edge....

My heart stopped. I forgot how to breathe.

Mikhail thumped down on his back, still on the stone walkway that ran around the edge of the roof. Irina's momentum had been enough to pull him over but not quite enough to pull him with her.

His arm stretched out above his head and he grunted as he took her weight. I could see his arm flex and twist—she must be swinging from side to side.

I scrambled the rest of the way out of the hatch and ran along the stone walkway towards them. That's when I found that the whole roof was covered in a slick layer of ice. Towards the center, the fire had melted it away but the cold stone at the edges was still slippery as hell. My legs shot out from under me and I almost went over the edge into the blackness beyond. *Shit!* I started moving more carefully, but that slowed me down. Irina and Mikhail were on the far side of the fucking building. It was going to take forever to work my way around the edge.

And I saw to my horror that Mikhail wasn't just lying there, supporting Irina, as I'd thought. He was moving, inch by inch, towards the edge. The weight of Irina's swinging body was dragging him over. He was trying to stop himself, but he only had one hand free to grab with and there was nothing to hang onto but smooth, icy stone.

There was no way I could get there in time, not if I followed the walkway all the way around. The only chance was to go straight across the middle of the flat roof, right over the fire.

I changed course and stepped onto the tiles. The timbers beneath my feet sunk sickeningly, throwing fresh sparks into the air, and tiles tumbled down into the fire, opening up holes that led straight down into hell. *Fuck.*

Behind me, I heard Luka and then Vasiliy climb out of the hatch. "Stop!" yelled Luka.

Vasiliy cursed in Russian. I could hear the frustration in his voice: he wanted to do whatever it took to save Irina, too, but what I was trying was suicide. "It'll collapse, you crazy bastard!"

He was right. It probably was suicide. And I probably was crazy. But I was crazy for her. And if she died, life wasn't going to be worth living anyway.

I stared right at Mikhail's sliding body, shut out everything else and *ran.*

The first few steps weren't so bad. The tiles sunk and cracked but I was past them too quickly for it to matter. But then my weight made one of the big roof timbers shift and it tipped to the side, tearing a hole the size of a sedan in the roof. Flames and heat blasted up, so bright I couldn't look at them. I fell sideways and rolled. *Shit!* The tiles were as hot as a griddle pan! I could see steam rise from my clothes. I put out a hand to push myself up and—

Fuck. I actually heard the sizzle. I staggered to my feet and ran on. The tiles I was stepping on didn't feel like they were attached to anything, anymore: they just pushed down into nothingness as I stepped on them and I could see the light growing around me as more and more of the roof disintegrated. *Don't look down. Don't look down.* I sprinted towards Mikhail. The bastard's head and shoulders were off the roof, now, and he was picking up speed. *Fuck!*

I felt my feet start to fall through the roof. I launched myself forward with everything I had and landed on Mikhail's legs, stopping his slide just in time.

I lay there for a second panting, clutching at him like a lover. Then I started to haul him in. It wasn't easy, because I was moving his weight and Irina's, but I slowly got his shoulders back onto the ledge and then his head—

He spat at me. I wanted to slug him but I needed both hands just to stop him slipping off the roof. I wondered why he hadn't shot me with his free hand—had he lost his gun? Why wasn't he trying to hit me?

Then I saw that his free hand was stretched out over his head, alongside the one that was chained to Irina. He was fiddling with something that glinted in the darkness. A key.

He was trying to open the handcuffs.

59

IRINA

Chyort!

It was difficult to think through the pain. All of my weight was hanging from one wrist and the sharp metal cuff was pressing so hard into my flesh that I couldn't feel my hand anymore. I was trying to keep still because every tiny movement made me swing, and when I swung it felt like my arm was being ripped out of its socket.

Most of the heat from the fire was rising straight up through the mansion, so now I was completely at the mercy of the wind. My almost-naked body was splattered with snow and I couldn't stop shaking.

Then I saw Mikhail start to fiddle with the handcuff lock. *No!* I made the mistake of looking down. The fire was throwing out just enough light that I could see the jagged rocks three stories below. Mikhail almost had the tiny key in the lock: I could see it scraping all around the dark hole. In another second he'd get it in—

Angelo's head appeared over the edge of the roof. He'd thrown himself atop Mikhail's chest, using his body weight to try to pin the big Russian in place. Like an avenging angel, silhouetted by the blazing roof behind him, his fists swung down in arcs and slammed into Mikhail's face: right, then left, then right again. Mikhail grunted, his head whipping from side to side.

I willed him to drop the handcuff key...but he didn't. His head lolled for a second and then he turned to the side and spat out a tooth. "Fuck you," he yelled over the wind. And I saw the key finally slot into the hole. And twist. The cuff around Mikhail's wrist loosened, the tiny *click* of the mechanism reverberating through my whole body.

Angelo launched himself forward, scrambling along Mikhail's body.

"*No!*" I yelled. "*Don't!*" I could feel Mikhail resume his slide off the building as Angelo moved. *He's going to get himself killed!*

Angelo ignored me. He was face-to-face with Mikhail, now, his arm stretching down towards me....

Mikhail shook his wrist and the cuff popped open. I screamed as I fell into space.

Angelo made a final lunge, his fingers brushed my wrist...and then that big, warm hand I loved so much was holding mine in a death grip. But all three of us were now sliding off the roof: Mikhail's big body was slipping on the ice and Angelo was still lying atop him, riding him over the edge with no way to stop their forward momentum.

"Let me go!" I screamed, desperately trying to open my fingers. "*You have to let me go!*"

Angelo shook his head, his jaw set like iron. "No fucking way."

I looked up into those brown and amber eyes and tightened my fingers around his, my heart swelling. But Mikhail and Angelo's slide continued, a slow-motion car crash none of us could stop. More and more of them passed over the edge: torsos, then hips, then legs...I screamed again as their feet slipped over and all three of us plunged.

Then we jerked to a stop. My shoulder, which had had a second or so of sweet relief, wrenched again as it took my weight. I looked up in bewilderment.

A big, broad shouldered beast of a man was leaning over the ledge, grasping Angelo's ankles. He lifted his head and I gasped as I saw his face. *Luka! Luka is here too?* My brain couldn't even process him and Angelo being there together. But maybe, just maybe, there was hope now. If he could pull us up—

A hand grabbed my left ankle and my shoulder exploded with white-hot pain as I was jerked down hard, my body stretched between Angelo's hand and whatever was below me. I looked down....

Mikhail. All three of us had slid off the roof together, but Angelo had been stopped by Luka and I was attached to Angelo. Mikhail had fallen right on past us and would have plunged to his death...except he'd caught my ankle on the way down. He started to swing and twist and my shoulder hurt so much I thought I was going to pass out.

"*Fuck!*" I heard Angelo say above me.

I tried to kick Mikhail but each time I moved, the agony it caused in my shoulder made me stop instantly. All I could do was hang there and weep and pray for it to be over. Angelo was grunting with the strain of supporting both of us: I could see every muscle in his back standing out, his biceps hard as rock. Higher up, Luka was starting to lose his grip on Angelo's ankles: even he couldn't support three people for long.

Then another figure joined Luka at the ledge. As big as him, but the light from the fire gleamed off silver strands amongst the black. *Vasiliy!* Between them, they took the weight of Angelo, me and Mikhail. Now it was a question of which would give out first: Angelo's grip or my arm. Either way, Mikhail was going to take me with him.

Angelo drew his gun and tried to aim at Mikhail, but my body blocked most of his view. He cursed. And I was running out of time. The pain was so intense that my vision was starting to narrow, my view of Angelo seeming to recede. I was slipping away from everything: his warmth, his light, his love...down into the cold, dark numbness I'd known before him.

I closed my eyes. Somewhere, distantly, I could feel my fingers loosening. I'd let go of him and then I'd be alone. I'd always been alone.

"*No!*" yelled Angelo. "*You hang on!*"

"Fuck you, Vasiliy," yelled Mikhail victoriously. "You should have just let me fuck her and join the family!"

For some reason, that bit deep. Everything that he'd planned to do to me, the years of hell he'd been willing to put me through, all to join us...and yet he still had no idea, no idea at all....

I loved Angelo. I was *his*. I would always be his.

But I was something else, as well.

I opened my eyes and looked down at Mikhail. "Fuck *you*," I grunted through the pain. "You don't have what it takes to be a Malakov."

And I looked up at Angelo, stretched out my free arm and motioned for the gun. He stared down at me in shock and then dropped it into my hand. I swung my arm down and pointed the gun right at Mikhail's head.

His eyes went wide in shock and outrage. His mouth opened, but I didn't give him time to insult me again. I squeezed the trigger, the hand on my ankle released and he disappeared down into the darkness.

"But I do," I panted.

With Mikhail's weight gone, Angelo was able to lift me higher, high enough that he could grab my other arm and finally take some of the load off of my injured shoulder. Even that change made it flare with pain again and I suddenly started to cry, hot tears of agony flooding down my face. Luka and Vasiliy pulled us higher and higher and then Angelo and I were being dragged up onto the walkway and, for the first time in what felt like hours, my arm wasn't being stretched at all. I went woozy with how good it felt, even though the slightest movement made the pain start all over again.

There was a crash as another part of the roof gave way. Even the stone walkway we were on was starting to crumble and tilt. The mansion was little more than the walls, now, the whole interior having mostly collapsed. We could jump forward into the fire, follow Mikhail down onto the rocks or wait until the entire place fell.

But when you're a Malakov, there's always a way.

Vasiliy reached into his jacket, withdrew a wad of banknotes thick enough to buy a high-end Mercedes, and waved it slowly back and forth above his head. A searchlight came on, picking him out in the darkness: Mikhail's helicopter, which had been circling as we fought. It came closer and the side door slid open. I saw the pilot and crewman look at each other and shrug, then wave us forward. Russian mercenaries: not terribly loyal but outstandingly practical.

Luka got in first, then Angelo lifted me and passed me to him, so that I didn't have to use my injured arm to haul myself in. That left Vasiliy and Angelo on the ledge. I saw Vasiliy's eyes flick from the helicopter to Angelo to the edge of the roof. Killing his rival would take only a quick shove.... I grabbed Luka's hand, my heart suddenly in my mouth.

Angelo stared back at Vasiliy...and lifted his chin, unafraid. He glanced at me, then back at Vasiliy. *You can do it,* his expression said, *but I'm not going to stop loving her.*

Vasiliy let out a long sigh and looked down into the darkness where Mikhail's body lay. "Perhaps I have enough enemies," he said wearily. And he waved Angelo into the helicopter before climbing in himself.

EPILOGUE
ANGELO

It was a long trip home.

First, we flew to Moscow and a private clinic that Vasiliy knew. There, Irina was dosed up on morphine so that the doctors could reset her dislocated shoulder. Even with the morphine, she squeezed my hand so hard it hurt.

I didn't care one bit. The pain meant it was real: I had her back.

With her arm in a sling, Irina fell asleep before we even left the clinic's parking lot. She dozed all the way to the airport, where the Malakov jet met us. I carried her aboard in my arms, laid her in one of the big leather seats, put a blanket over her and strapped her in.

And then, for the next nine hours, Vasiliy, Luka and I talked.

It was a careful negotiation, the verbal equivalent of circling each other with swords drawn and shields up. None of us was prepared to show weakness. But for the first time, we talked to each other with respect, and what I had with Irina felt like it brought us closer, instead of setting us at each other's throats.

There was no way I was going to give up the territory I'd fought so hard for and there was no way that Vasiliy was going to abandon his plans. But with Mikhail out of the picture, there was the opportunity to rework things. Vasiliy didn't *need* to expand: that had been

Mikhail's power-hungry scheme. He just wanted security for his guns. There hadn't been any way he could trust that responsibility to anyone but a Russian. But with me....

We eventually decided that Vasiliy would keep Mikhail's existing territory, but wouldn't expand into mine. Since Vasiliy couldn't be in New York full time, I'd help him with the day-to-day running of it in his absence. With an Italian and a Russian in control, we'd be sending a strong message to the communities that there'd be no more violence. It amounted to a near-doubling of my territory and I'd receive a hefty cut. In return, I'd provide Vasiliy's arms traffic clear passage. It was a great deal.

But that didn't mean everyone would be happy with it.

Nicky sprang to his feet in shock as soon as I walked through the door. He'd been expecting Rico, since he'd been the one who'd asked for the meet. "*You?*" He glared at Rico. "I told you to finish this son of a bitch!"

"Yeah," said Rico calmly. "You did." And he stepped back out of the way.

Nicky was so mad, little drops of spit flew from his lips as he screamed at me. "You'd better be here to get down on your knees and *pray* you fucker, because you're—"

I punched him as hard as I could in the face. He spun fully around, tripped over his chair and crashed to the floor. The other Saints gaped. Some of them cursed...but quietly.

"Have you got any idea what you've just done?" asked Taavetti.

"Yeah," I said, straightening my tie. "What I should have done years ago."

And I laid it out for them: how I was back in power, with Rico's agreement. How I now controlled more territory than any other single boss in New York. How I wasn't going to take their shit anymore. Italians and Russians were going to live side by side in peace, and if the Saints didn't like it, we were going to have a problem.

Vasiliy had taught me something: you don't rule a kingdom by trying to keep everything the same; you rule it by nursing it on its journey to be something better.

Nicky climbed to his feet, bleeding from his lip. "You cock*sucker!*" he snarled. "I'll finish you myself for this!"

Vincenzo cut in. "We'll vote on it," he told me. "Give us the room, please, Angelo."

Three minutes later, when Rico and I went back in, Nicky was gone. Taavetti looked miserable, but the other Saints crowded around to congratulate me. Rico slapped me on the back and we embraced.

"You sure about this?" I muttered as we walked back to the car. "Do I need to watch my back, now you've had a taste of the big chair?"

"Fuck the big chair," said Rico. He rubbed his chest, wincing a little. He had two big scars, just like the nurse had promised, and he'd be dosed up on painkillers for a while, but he'd be okay. "Sitting around giving orders drove me nuts in one morning. I'm happy when I'm *doing* something. Just promise me you're never going to go crazy like this again."

I thought about it. "Don't need to," I said. "Got my woman, now. Keeping her."

We reached the Chrysler, a brand new replacement for the one we'd totaled, still with that showroom smell. We'd got the exact same model: you don't mess with a classic. I patted the roof affectionately and then climbed in. "The next thing we gotta worry about is *you* going nuts because *you* meet someone."

Rico gave me a look. "Get a grip. *Me?*"

$\sim$

I hadn't planned to be there. It felt like it should be a family thing, but Irina wanted to go to the hospital as soon as we heard and there was no way I was leaving her side. Of course, when we got there, Luka and Vasiliy were standing over the bed. They didn't smile when they saw me, but they didn't scowl at me either and that practically felt like a hug.

"The nurse said he woke," said Vasiliy. "But he's been sleeping since we got here."

I moved closer and leaned over Yuri. His chest was much more extensively bandaged than even Rico's had been and his epic surgery had apparently been a real marathon. But he'd made it through. Now we just had to wait until—

A hand shot out and grabbed me around the throat. Yuri's eyes were still closed but none of his strength had gone. It felt as though I was being throttled by a fucking bear. With his other hand, Yuri groped on his nightstand for a weapon. Thankfully, his hand only found a water glass. *Whew.*

He struck the water glass on the edge of the nightstand, leaving it with a curved, razor-sharp edge, and shoved it towards my jugular. *Shit!* I grabbed his wrists and tried to pry myself free. Luka and Vasiliy helped and we finally got him under control. His eyes opened, bleary and scrunched half shut against the bright overhead lights, but locked on me.

Vasiliy pushed me out of the way, then leaned down and embraced his friend. "It is good to have you back," he said, his voice thick with emotion. He glanced at me. "There is much to talk about."

Irina
One Month Later

The sand fascinated me. Above the surf it was white and soft, roasting your toes as it dusted them with fine power. At the waterline it scrunched and sunk as you walked, every footstep leaving a perfect impression. Then, where it mixed equally with the warm water, it became a sucking, swirling wonder, like mud but *clean.*

I lifted my face to the sun and felt the heat seep into me. First it lit up my skin, making it glow and tingle. Then it soaked through my flesh, relaxing every muscle and sending waves of sweet pleasure down my body to pool in my groin. Finally, it heated my bones, even the deepest, darkest places that had been hard-packed ice for years. I was *warm*.

"You act like you've never been on a beach before," said Angelo from behind me.

I turned. He looked gorgeous: stripped to the waist, his tattoo gleaming blackly, a pair of shorts hanging low enough on his hips that I could see the hard line of his Adonis belt disappearing beneath them.

"I haven't," I said, grinning. Holidays had always been taken somewhere Vasiliy or my dad had business, and that never involved beaches. Or sun. I spun slowly around. Or palm trees, or little beach huts with thatched roofs, or half-naked Italian-American boyfriends.

Back home, things had settled into enough of a routine that we'd felt okay coming on vacation. I'd had an emotional reunion with Rachel and spilled everything about my family, slightly shocked to learn how much she'd figured out on her own. We'd done a lot of hugging and sworn not to keep stuff from each other in the future. We were still sharing the house, but I was thinking about moving into Angelo's apartment next semester.

Things between Vasiliy and Angelo were thawing fast. Vasiliy had taken to speaking fondly of "his New York connection," or "my Italian friend," when he wasn't around, even if he was still gruff to his face. He'd even tried to teach Angelo chess, and Angelo—to his credit— was trying to learn. Luka, too, was beginning to cautiously talk to him. I'd caught the two of them out on the patio a few times, whiskeys in hand, with Luka muttering questions about Arianna and Angelo trying to help him understand American women.

And me? I'd finally found my place. I'd come full circle, from trying to escape the gangster lifestyle to embracing it...but on my terms. I'd taken on the role my mom had played for my dad and that Vasiliy's late wife had played for him: I was the voice of diplomacy and reason, talking Vasiliy down, reigning in his worst excesses. I could already see the changes in him: he was back to being the Vasiliy I knew, tough but honorable. I was the warmth that humanized him, just as Arianna was the warmth that humanized Luka. And I had a second role to play: I had Angelo to support too, the cool logic that complimented his hot-headed arrogance.

I was a Malakov. And I was also a Baroni.

I screamed in delight as Angelo scooped me up into his arms, one big hand coming down to squeeze my ass through the turquoise swimsuit he'd bought me. Then he carried me out into the water, the surf stroking past our knees, then our thighs, then our hips. He pushed off and we floated, face to face, in water that was slowly turning gold in the sunset. He swept a lock of hair back off my cheek and stared into my eyes.

"What?" I asked.

"Just looking at you," he said, and kissed me. Then his brow furrowed in concentration. "*Ya lyublyu tebya.*"

I blinked. The Russian words, wrapped up in that bass growl of his, melted straight to my core and detonated there. When had he learned that? I'd heard it in English, but hearing it in Russian made it real. I could feel my cheeks going hot, tears of happiness suddenly filling my eyes. *Malakovs don't cry!*

Maybe just this once.

Fortunately, he wasn't the only one who'd been studying. "*Ti amo anch'io,*" I told him. *I love you, too.*

With my accent, it didn't sound all that Italian. But it evidently didn't matter because Angelo pulled me harder against him, my breasts mashed against his pecs, and kissed me until I forgot my own name.

When he finally broke the kiss, I was breathless and grinning. "Back to the hotel?" I asked, thinking of the king-sized bed in our room.

His hands swept down my back and closed on my ass. I felt his cock harden against my thigh. Then he whispered in my ear, that deep, musical growl resonating right through my body. "Not *just* yet."

The End

Thank you for reading!

The story of how Arianna, a young CIA agent, is sent to Moscow to seduce and spy on Luka, only to fall for him, is told in *Lying and Kissing*.

The Malakovs also appear in *Kissing My Killer,* in which a Russian hit man is sent to assassinate a female hacker...but finds he can't pull the trigger and is forced to go on the run with her instead.

A female FBI agent is given plastic surgery so that she can impersonate the evil girlfriend of Russian mob boss Konstantin Gulyev in *The Double*. But once in his life, she begins to find her feelings for him becoming all too real.

There's also a whole trilogy set at Fenbrook Academy. *Dance For Me* is about a troubled ballet student who falls for the billionaire who hires her as his muse. *In Harmony* is about a good-girl cellist forced to team up with a bad boy rock guitarist. *Acting Brave* is about an actress running from her dark past who's determined that her feelings for her sexy new co-star are just part of the show.